W.A. NOBLE

# BEASTSPEAKER

## DRAGON HOME

*Beast-Speaker 3: Dragon Home*
By W.A. Noble

This edition published in 2025 in South Australia
by Staurolite Books

Originally published by Morning Star Publishing in 2019
Reprinted by Wipf & Stock Publishers, Oregon USA

ISBN
Print: 978-0-6451215-9-9
eBook: 978-1-7641335-0-0

Cover design and illustration by DM Cornish
Claw image by Sofia Morgado on Pixabay

A catalogue record for this
book is available from the
National Library of Australia

staurolitebooks.com.au

The Beast-Speaker Series by W.A. Noble:
*Beast-Speaker 1: Dragon Flight*
*Beast-Speaker 2: Dragon Friend*
*Beast-Speaker 3: Dragon Home*
*Beast-Speaker 4: Dead Man's Fingers*

Wendy can be contacted at
wendynoble.com

Dedicated to
Frank and Margaret Greig; Lionel and Lorace Noble;
Hollis and Verdine Davis.
Gone but not forgotten.

# Acknowledgements

D. M. Cornish for the amazing book covers for the series. Dr Rosanne Hawke for being my mentor, example and friend. Thomas East: Battle-master extraordinaire, who knows something about lots of things. My cheer squad: Dr Mark Worthing, Jeanette Cooper, Sue Jeffries, Judi Carpenter, Liz & Bryan Paice, Mark & Cal Petrusma, Heather & Kim Thoday, Ali Chapman, Kayla Daking, Kathy Lindsey, Sue Hoy and everyone who read books 1 & 2 and asked for more. Thank you to the inspirational people—including World Vision, UNICEF and War Child Australia—who rescue and rehabilitate child soldiers. Finally, thanks to my husband, Jeff, who finds stray letters and abhors excess commas; who's not afraid to say, 'You need to rewrite this', but who also encourages me to keep going when I'm tempted to give up.

# Contents

One ........................................................................................ 1

Two ..................................................................................... 12

Three .................................................................................. 20

Four .................................................................................... 32

Five ..................................................................................... 41

Six ...................................................................................... 53

Seven .................................................................................. 66

Eight ................................................................................... 76

Nine .................................................................................... 88

Ten ...................................................................................... 97

Eleven ............................................................................... 102

Twelve ............................................................................... 114

Thirteen ............................................................................ 124

Fourteen ............................................................................ 136

Fifteen ............................................................................... 142

Sixteen .............................................................................. 153

Seventeen .......................................................................... 164

Eighteen ............................................................................ 172

Nineteen ............................................................................ 178

Twenty ............................................................................... 187

Twenty-One ....................................................................... 201

Twenty-Two ....................................................................... 214

Twenty-Three .................................................................... 228

Twenty-Four ...................................................................... 241

Twenty-Five ....................................................................... 251

Twenty-Six ........................................................................ 261

Twenty-Seven .................................................................... 270

Twenty-Eight ..................................................................... 278

Beast-Speaker 4: Dead Man's Fingers ................................ 294

A Postscript on the Tragedy of Child Soldiers ..................... 297

# One

## Seeger Speaks

'Boyd!' I called. I heard a rustling in the hay above Shirra's stall. 'I know you're up there.'

Ever since Boyd got back from Midrash, he's been nothing but trouble. He and some of the other returned child soldiers have been roaming Seddon getting into mischief. Some in our town say that they wish the children had been left in Midrash.

'Get down now,' I said.

His head popped up near the railing. 'I suppose your nosy camel told you I was here.'

I threw the blanket over Shirra's back and put the saddle on. She stood up so that I could tighten the girth straps.

'That's what happens if you hide in her stable.'

'Is anyone else around?' he said.

I shook my head. 'What have you done now?'

He climbed down the ladder. Bits of straw stuck in his hair and on the back of his tunic. 'What's got into you this morning?' he said.

'What were you doing up there?'

'Just a little misunderstanding with a few revellers at the Noisy Duck last night,' he said. 'Things got a bit awkward so I slipped in here.'

I knew it! He'd got into a fight again. 'You haven't been home all night?'

He shook his head and brushed some straw off his shoulders.

'Your parents must be sick with worry.'

He shrugged, bent over and ran his hands through his hair. 'I doubt it. I'll use your privy and then I'll be off.' He gave his head one more shake and then walked towards the stable door.

'What's got into you, Boyd?'

He turned to stare at me. 'I don't know what you mean.'

'Ever since we got back, you've been acting like a spoilt brat.'

He sneered. 'I won't keep you. You obviously have important things to do.' He walked off, slamming the stable door behind him.

I sighed as I went to open the door again. Shirra and I left the stable and headed out onto the road.

*You're upset,* Shirra said.

*Nothing's right,* I said. Mind-speaking is so much easier than talking. *Riff's a misery guts. Riva spends all her time playing nursemaid. Mother's still not happy about us going back to Midrash. Boyd's acting like an idiot. Everything's a mess.*

I'd thought that once the stolen children had been rescued, and the evil regime in Midrash had been dealt a crushing defeat, things would go back to normal. I expected a happy ending.

*Don't worry,* Shirra said. *The sun is shining, our bellies are full and today is a new day.*

Shirra happily plodded along to the stables. I carried the cloud of misery on my shoulders all the way there. It didn't help that Father shouted at me for being late. He stood in the doorway of his office and beckoned me over.

'I'm sorry, Father,' I said as I walked towards him. 'Is something wrong?'

'Come in here,' he said.

He sat down behind his desk and waved at the chair in front of it. 'Sit you down,' he said. 'I've had Bevan in here this morning, looking for his son. He thought I might be hiding Boyd in the stables. He carried on like a madman: blaming me, blaming you. He said that if we were keeping Boyd from them, Lorna's decline in health would be on us. Do you know anything about this?'

I shook my head. 'I hardly see anything of Boyd these days. Last night he slept in our stable at home—'

Father looked as though he was going to say something but I kept talking.

'I didn't know he was there until I fetched the camels this morning. I say true, Father. He'd got into a fight at the Noisy Duck and then hid in our loft.'

Father placed his elbows on his desk and leant forward towards me. 'His parents are worried sick about him.'

'I told him that but he didn't seem to believe me.' Father frowned. 'I tell you, Father, I don't know what's got into him since he came home but they can't blame me. He rarely talks to me and, when he does, he always seems annoyed with me. Frankly, I'm getting sick of it.'

Father nodded. 'Where is he now?'

I shrugged. 'Don't know.'

He fiddled with the pens on his desk, lining them up in a neat row and then realigning them. I thought they'd looked perfectly tidy the first time.

'Seeger?' he said, still staring at the pens instead of looking at me. 'How are you now? Have you settled back into life here in Seddon? Are you happy?'

I squirmed in my seat; suddenly I couldn't get comfortable. These were things I had chosen not to think about. My left leg started to jig but I put my hand on my knee and that calmed it down.

'I suppose you're missing the dragons,' Father continued. I nodded. 'I've noticed that things aren't the same between you and Riva.' My leg began to jig again. 'And, you haven't shown any interest in going back to Foundation, even though you haven't finished your education.'

He stared at me, waiting for a reply. I swallowed … hard. Where should I begin? How could I begin?

'Will you please go back to Foundation?' he said.

I shook my head. 'I can't, Father. Please don't make me?'

He closed his eyes for a few seconds. 'We can't have you aimlessly wandering around, Seeger, getting into mischief.'

'That's not fair! I'm not like Boyd and the others. I'm here at the stables every day.'

He rubbed his forehead. 'It won't be many lunar cycles before you will have sixteen years and you are still so … You have a lot of catching up to do.'

I hung my head and studied my hands. My fingernails were dirty.

'Luckily, I have a solution and Bevan's agreed to it. Starting tomorrow morning, you will go to Asher's house to be tutored,' Father said. 'You will have lessons in the mornings and then you will work here in the afternoons. Boyd will also study with our Record Keeper.'

I opened my mouth to argue but he held up his hand to stop me.

'This is very gracious of Asher. He's a busy man. So, I expect you to pay attention, mind your manners and work hard. Understood?'

I nodded.

He picked up one of his pens. 'That is all.'

The only good thing about that morning was that Juniper had delivered her litter. Seven squirming little pink piglets nuzzled at her side. They were perfect, even though one was on the small side.

The next morning Asher was his usual enthusiastic self. 'Come in, come in, Seeger! Into the front room, that's the way. Where's your camel? Out the front? Very good. Sit down! Sit down! Boyd isn't here yet but that's all right. He'll be along soon.' He clapped his hands together. 'I'm going to enjoy this so much. We'll explore all sorts of wonderful things.'

Kieran wandered in and sat next to me. He nodded at me. 'Morning.'

'Kieran will be joining in as well,' Asher said. 'He's here to learn, so he might as well do it with friends. Right?'

I nodded my agreement and smiled at Kieran. He winked.

'While we're waiting for Boyd to arrive,' Asher continued, 'I was wondering if you've heard from the dragons at all.'

I shook my head. 'Not since they flew north from Midrash.'

Asher patted my shoulder. 'I didn't think so. Well, I have some news that might interest you.'

I sat up straighter and looked at him hopefully.

He chuckled and sat down opposite me. 'I've been corresponding with your friend, Jarl. He's been very concerned for dear old Myrmee. When he couldn't fly home with the rest of the Flight, he sank into a bit of a depression. Poor old chap.'

I'd been afraid that might happen. 'Is he going to be all right?'

'Jarl and I have been discussing that and we've come up with a brilliant plan. Jarl is going to teach Myrmee to read and write! Isn't that wonderful?' He positively glowed with delight.

Kieran shook his head. 'An animal? Writing? Ridiculous!'

'How is it possible?' I said.

'Dragons are extremely intelligent. If they can converse, then why not teach them other ways to communicate? Not everyone can talk with them like you, dear boy. The most difficult thing for the dragon has been mastering the use of a pen but Jarl says he's got the hang of it now. They tried using charcoal pencils but Myrmee kept snapping them in two, so he's using a pen and ink. It's just brilliant!'

I was stunned.

'Jarl says they work at it every day,' Asher continued. 'I think they're both in need of some company. Myrmee doesn't leave the stables very often. Tatum is doing a good job organising the new ruling body and running the city, but he doesn't know what to do with the old dragon. He doesn't want to ride it around the place, to intimidate the Midrashi like the previous Commander did.' He shrugged. 'Although, it would be very effective. After the way the Flight devastated the city with their fire, most Midrashi are very nervous around Myrmee. He keeps out of the way, spending most of his time in the stables with Jarl.'

Poor old Myrmee. I wish we'd found a way to help him go home with the rest of the Flight. I'll never forget the sight of Shadreer and the others weeping as they set off on the long flight back to the Land of the Dragons without the old fellow.

'Jarl says Myrmee has already learned the alphabet and can write his name and other simple words,' Asher said. 'It's been astonishing how quickly the old dragon has picked things up.'

He got up and began pacing around the room. 'Where's Boyd? I want to get started.'

Kieran stood up. 'I'll go make us all a hot drink.'

'Put a pinch of cinnamon in mine, please,' Asher called after him.

He began to pace back and forth, every now and then stopping to stare out the front window. After a while, irritated by Asher's nervous energy, I went into the kitchen to help Kieran. I say "help" but I just watched him heat up the goat's milk. He took four beakers out of the cupboard and set them out on a tray.

He looked at me. 'It wouldn't surprise me if he doesn't turn up.'

I shrugged. 'There's no telling what he'll do.'

'He hasn't settled since he's got home, has he?' Kieran said, lifting the jar of cinnamon down from the top shelf.

'Doesn't seem like it,' I said.

Kieran unscrewed the lid of the jar and scooped out a little spoonful of the sweet spice. He sprinkled it across the top of one of the beakers of hot milk.

Just as he picked up the tray, we heard a knocking at the front door followed by Asher's cry of, 'Welcome! Welcome!'

'I guess that's him,' I said. 'Let's get this circus on the road.'

I followed Kieran back into the front room and, sure enough, Boyd was standing there with his arms folded across his chest. There was an enormous bruise that circled his left eye and trailed down over his cheek bone.

'What happened to you?' I said. 'Been in a fight again?'

Boyd slumped into a chair and crossed his legs at the ankles. 'Not everyone is as delighted as you to see me back home.'

Kieran handed him a beaker of hot milk and gave him a quick pat on the shoulder, before picking up the drink with cinnamon and handing it to Asher. Then he sat down, reached forward and got himself one.

'Help yourself, Seeger,' he said.

I picked up the last beaker and sat down next to Boyd. 'Does it hurt?' I said.

He stared at me, his fingers gently stroking his cheek bone. 'What do you think?'

'Do you want to talk about it?' Asher said. Boyd shook his head. 'Very well. I'm going to give you a few short tests this morning. Now, now, don't panic. I just want to see what we'll be working with. Drink up while I fetch some paper and writing utensils.'

We three lads sipped our drinks gloomily. No one was thrilled at the thought of tests.

'What's Riva doing?' Kieran said.

'You mean, apart from mooning over Riff? She's having lessons with Jonathan at the Temple. Mother organised it. She's never been taught to read or write, so she'd have trouble fitting in at Foundation.'

'Another misfit, like me,' Boyd said, staring moodily into his beaker.

'Indeed,' I said. 'She'd be miles behind us and that'd just upset her more. There's no point bringing her here.'

'She wouldn't want to be with us anyway,' Boyd said. 'Or at least, not with me.'

I said, 'I don't think she'd—'

'Yes, Asher?' Kieran said. Then he turned and glared at me.

# One

Asher stood in the doorway. 'Could someone help me?'

'Would you go, please Boyd?' Kieran said.

Boyd heaved himself up out of the chair and went to help Asher.

'What's the death stare for?' I whispered to Kieran.

He leant forward. 'Can't you tell Boyd's upset?' I shrugged. 'For a bright fella, Seeger,' he said, 'sometimes you can be a bit thick.'

Asher bustled into the room, carrying a stack of slates. Boyd followed behind with a large bag slung over his shoulder.

'I wasn't sure how much to bring,' Asher said, 'so I brought the lot. I hope you don't mind using slates. I didn't want to waste good paper on something we're not going to keep.'

Kieran moved the beakers' tray and Asher plonked the stack down in the middle of the table. Then he took the bag from Boyd and tipped out an assortment of chalks. Most were white—or more specifically a dirty off-white—but there were a few reds, yellows and light blues scattered among them.

'Get yourselves a slate and some chalk,' he said, 'and make yourselves comfortable.'

We spent the rest of the morning being tested on spelling, mathematics and some general knowledge questions. Thankfully, there was nothing about algebra in any of it, so I think I did all right. By lunch time I could eat my own arm, I was so hungry.

Asher was delighted with our efforts. 'You're all very smart young men. It's going to be a pleasure to teach you.' His smile was so bright, it was almost blinding. 'I'm proud of you.'

He started stacking up the slate boards. Kieran helped him. I scooped up a few chalks and handed them over. Boyd just sat and studied us from under the shade of his furrowed eyebrows.

'For the next several days,' Asher said, 'I'm going to teach you everything I know about maps. It's going to be such fun.'

Now that was more like it. Even Boyd looked interested.

'Not only are maps intriguing, they're extremely useful,' he said. 'I think every well-educated person should know how to use them and how to make them.'

Remembering how helpful a few old maps had been when we laid siege to Midrash, I thought Asher was probably right.

'In fact,' he said, turning to look directly at me, 'I think you should bring Riff with you tomorrow, as well.'

'Riff?' As if he'd want to go back to Foundation.

'With his arm so badly damaged, he's feeling useless. In his condition, I doubt he'll be allowed to remain a well-keeper. But if he could be a map-reader then the Master Well-Keeper might consider keeping him. What's more, I think he'd be very good at it.'

I shrugged. 'I'll ask him but I can't promise anything. These days it takes all his energy just to get out of bed.'

'Have a word to your father,' Asher said. 'I'm sure he'll back me up. I'll expect Riff to be here with you first thing tomorrow. Now, run along lads. I don't know about you but my stomach thinks I've had my throat cut.'

Kieran picked up the tray of empty beakers, said, 'See you tomorrow', and left the room. Boyd and I took it in turn to shake Asher's hand and then left together. My camel, Bruce, was waiting patiently in the front yard.

'Where's your ride?' I said.

Boyd didn't even look at me. 'I walked.'

I frowned. That would explain why he was late. 'Would

you like a ride back? Bruce is wearing a double saddle.'

*It's all the fashion these days,* Bruce said.

Again, Boyd didn't look at me. He stared off into the distance as if there was something fascinating floating above the Citadel's wall. 'Don't want you going to any bother.'

I nearly said, 'Suit yourself' but Bruce said, *That boy is very sad, Seeger. Be kind.*

I held his arm. 'Boyd, we're mates. Let me give you a ride.'

He turned to look at me and his eyes were full of pain. 'Are we, Seeger?'

'Always.' I gently squeezed his arm. 'Mother's made soup and there's plenty for you to share. Come eat with us before I go to the stables to work.'

For a moment I thought he was going to refuse. He stared at his boots, frowning. Then he shook himself, as if he'd suddenly felt a cold breeze. 'Very well. Let's go.'

*Well done, mate,* Bruce said.

We climbed into the saddle, Bruce lurched up and off we went. As we ambled down the hill towards the gates, I said, 'Who hit you, Boyd?'

The silence from the saddle behind me was deafening.

# Two

## Boyd Speaks

On the slow journey back from Midrash, I'd wake up in the middle of the night with my heart racing like a runaway carriage. Dad kept saying things like, 'When you're back in Foundation' and, 'You'll soon put all this behind you'. The more he talked, the more I felt he was reassuring himself more than comforting me.

The closer we got to Seddon, the more anxious I became. I can't tell you why. I'd jump at any sudden noise, no matter how innocent it was. I'd watch the people around me, waiting for them to turn on me. My heart would lurch in my chest with such a sudden jolt that I thought I was having a heart attack. It took me ages to fall asleep at night, even though the long march through the dessert was exhausting. As a result, I was so tired all the time that I continually felt sick. However, I was terrified someone would know what was going on, so I snapped at people and pushed away even my closest friends. Seeger, of course, wouldn't give up on me so he bore the brunt of most of my bad humour.

The strange thing was, I never felt like this while I was in Midrash. Of course, I was afraid when we were pushed into battle and the arrows were raining down but it was a different sort of fear. Back then there was an obvious cause: the possibility of injury or death. When we got back to the barracks, my nerves would settle down again. Now, I was anxious all the time.

The only ones who seemed to understand were the other rescued children. We spent as much time together as possible. They called me, "Patrol Leader". My dad didn't approve. He said that I should forget all that. He said those days were in the past and I should just be a boy again.

My parents weren't sure what to make of me. Of course, they were glad I was home. My mother didn't stop weeping tears of joy for three whole days. But, as time passed, I could tell that they didn't know what to do with the new Boyd.

One evening, I overheard them talking in the gathering room when they thought I was asleep.

'He's not himself,' I heard Ma say.

'He'll get over it,' Dad said. 'He just needs to knuckle down and get back to Foundation. Once he's back in a good routine, he'll settle down.'

'I don't think so,' Ma said. 'He's too damaged. I don't think he'll ever be the same.' She began to weep softly.

'Don't be silly. He just needs to pull himself together.'

Ma mumbled something that I didn't quite hear.

'I'm not letting him droop about here for the rest of his life, feeling sorry for himself,' Dad said. 'Don't you worry. I'll soon knock some sense into him.'

I refused to go back to Foundation. I tried it for two days. The other kids, with fear in their eyes, kept their distance.

You'd think the Midrashi had turned me into a monster. Had I grown horns overnight? Miss Ashton did her best but even she treated me differently. I was no longer just one of the boys in her class. I was now, "dear Boyd, who's come back to us after suffering as a captive of the Midrashi". I was, "be kind to Boyd, who's been through so much".

I couldn't bear it and I told my dad I wasn't going back. That was the first time he hit me. I stood staring at him in shock, rubbing my cheek, with the salt water welling in my eyes.

Ma screamed. She grabbed Dad's arm as he raised it to hit me again. 'Bevan, don't! How could you?'

I backed away slowly, still rubbing my cheek. Dad pointed at me. 'You're going back tomorrow, Boyd, and that's that!'

I turned and ran out of the house and down the street. I ended up at the docks. I sat on the fishing jetty until late in the evening, long after the sun had sunk into the sea. By the light of the moon, I watched the ocean washing in and splashing against the jetty's pylons. There were some boats tied up at the wharf. I thought about asking if one would take me on as a deckhand. I even got up and walked over to the largest boat but, as I got close, all I could smell was fish and men's sweat and my stomach heaved. It was only as I neared home that I thought of what it would have done to my mother had I gone through with the plan.

She was waiting in the kitchen. She'd kept a plate of food warm for me, even though dinner time was long gone. When she said that Dad had already gone to bed, I felt my shoulders drop and the knot in my stomach began to unravel.

'Tell me, dear, why won't you go back to Foundation?' Ma said.

# Two

So, I told her about the other children and the teacher and how it all seemed so futile. What's the point of all that learning when death is waiting just around the corner? I'm a returned soldier now, not a scholar.

When I'd finished she said, 'But surely, eventually the other children will relax and you'll be fine. It'll just take a little time.'

She didn't understand. I shook my head. 'I've changed, Ma.'

'I don't—'

I smiled. 'Come on, Ma. You know it. We all know it. I don't belong there anymore. I'm not the only one. The others are finding it just as hard to fit back in. Even Seeger doesn't go to Foundation now.'

She wiped her eyes with the dishcloth that she'd used to carry the hot plate from the oven to the table. 'At least Seeger works in the stables,' she said. 'You don't do anything.'

I felt a rush of heat in my cheeks. 'It helps if your father's the Beast-Master. It's not so easy for me to find a place. Dad won't have me at his work.'

She sighed, crumpling the dishcloth in her hands. 'It's not his place to say whether you can or can't work there. He's not the owner of the business. Besides, he's always wanted better for you, like Randi. You need to finish Foundation if you want a good job.'

'Maybe, but I'm not going back.'

For a few days I would leave home in the morning pretending to go to Foundation and then, when I was out of sight of the house, I'd go to the beach or down to the archery grounds, or anywhere except where they thought I was. I'd go home in the afternoon, when I saw the other kids out in the street. They were a few peaceful days.

One night as we ate the evening meal Dad said, 'How was Foundation today, Boyd?'

'Fine,' I said.

He put his fork down and leant back in his chair, a strange look in his eyes. 'Anything interesting happen?' he said.

I shrugged. 'Nup.'

'Are you sure?'

I nodded.

'Fair enough,' he said. 'I guess a visit from your old man isn't that far out of the ordinary.'

The mouthful of food I'd just swallowed hit the bottom of my stomach with a thump and then began to climb its way back up my gullet. I closed my eyes and god-spoke, 'Oh Sed, oh Sed, oh Sed.'

I heard the scrape of his chair as Dad stood up and then there was a swishing sound. I opened my eyes and saw that he'd removed his leather belt. At that time, he'd never used it against me, so I couldn't think why he'd taken it off.

'Now, Bevan,' Ma said.

'Stay out of it, Lorna.' Dad pushed his chair away, strode around the table to me and then he grabbed the neck of my tunic. He yanked me out of my chair, spun me around and began to flog me with his belt.

It wasn't the first time I'd endured a beating—I'd been whipped in Midrash—but it was the first time I'd ever been beaten in my own home. I heard the spirit of Idris say, 'Stiff upper lip, Boyd.' I bit my lip and tried not to make a sound but I could hear the whimpers sliding out despite my best efforts. *This can't be happening,* I thought. *This is my dad!*

I wrapped my arms around my head and sunk to the floor. Dad kept belting my arms, back and legs. The whole time he beat me, he screamed at me, 'Ungrateful brat!

Where's the hero now? You lazy piece of selfish misery! You WILL obey me!' and on and on.

Ma tried to pull him off me but he didn't stop until the red rage had left him. He then put his belt back on, returned to his chair and resumed eating his meal. Ma was sobbing.

'That's enough, Lorna,' Dad said.

Ma hiccuped and took a few deep shaky breaths. She bent to help me up but Dad said, 'Don't! He doesn't need your help.'

She let go of my arm and backed away. I slowly got to my feet. My body throbbed as though the beating was still happening.

'Lorna, Boyd's had enough to eat,' Dad said. 'You can clear his plate away.'

I waited until my legs weren't shaking as much and then I slowly, carefully, made my way to my bedroom. I drew the blanket back and got into bed, fully clothed. I pulled the blanket up to my chin and lay there shaking. I couldn't believe what had just happened. *So, this is why I've been afraid,* I thought. *This is what I've been waiting for.*

And that was the pattern from then on. I would refuse to go to Foundation and, in the evening, I would be beaten by my Dad. Welcome home, Boyd.

On one of my visits to the archery ground, I found Rimini already there, peeking over the fence, watching the soldiers practising. She nodded at me as I walked up but didn't say anything. I didn't bother to ask her why she wasn't at Foundation. In companionable silence, we watched the bowmen practice.

As the soldiers were packing up their equipment, their training session over for the day, she said to me, 'Sometimes I wish I was back there. You know?'

'I know,' I said. 'We don't fit anymore.'

She frowned. 'What's it like at your house?'

I took her arm as we walked away from the fence but she winced, so I let it drop. 'My dad beats me every night. What about you?'

She didn't answer straight away. I flicked a quick glance at her face, saw the saltwater threatening to spill down her cheeks, and looked away again.

Eventually she said, 'While I was in Midrash my mother stopped eating. My father says it was her grief that made her like that.'

I nodded. 'Mine was the same. She replaced food with weeping.'

We headed down to the beach.

'She'd always had poor health,' Rimini continued. 'So, when she didn't eat and then she didn't drink … Well … She died two lunar cycles before I came home. My father says her death is my fault.'

I stopped still. 'It's *not* your fault!'

She shrugged. 'Father doesn't know what to do with me. He looks at me and sees my mother. Lately, he's begun to hit me. It happens at random times. I guess it's when he's tired or feeling frustrated or if he's missing Ma. He says he's heard what we girls "got up to" while we were in Midrash. So now I'm a slut and no decent man will ever want to marry me.'

I felt the heat rise within me. I was definitely my father's son. I wanted to punch Rimini's father until he saw stars.

'You listen to me,' I said. 'I'm sorry to say it but your father is a fool! You're one of the bravest, most decent, most loyal people I've ever met. Any man would be proud to call you his wife.'

That did it. The saltwater tumbled over her eyelids and lashes and streamed down her face. Her shoulders shook.

# Two

She put her hands over her face. I don't know if it was to stem the tide of the water or to simply hide from the world. Perhaps it was both. I put my hand on her shoulder and she flinched. I pulled my hand away.

'I'm sorry,' I said.

She wiped her cheeks and sniffed. 'These days I can't stand to feel a man's touch. It seems all you men want to do is beat me ... or do the other thing.'

'Not all of us, Rimini,' I said. 'You'll see.'

We spent the day walking along the sand, picking up shells and then throwing them back into the sea. We said no more about our lives or our homes. We just let the sun pour its warmth into our bodies and let the water whisper its mysteries to us. Before we parted, I promised Rimini I wouldn't tell anyone about her situation. It was her story to tell if she so chose. I told her I was there for her and would always be her friend.

She shook her head. 'You'll always be my patrol leader.'

When someone asked Dad about my bruises, he told them I'd been in a fight. It didn't take long for the rumours to spread. I couldn't do anything about it. If I denied it, who'd believe me? After all, it was my father who said it and everyone knew what a fine upstanding citizen he was. I was even more alone and anxious than when I first came home. I wanted to tell Seeger, so many times, but his life couldn't be more perfect. He wouldn't understand.

# Three

## Seeger Speaks

We settled Bruce into the stable and walked in through the back door. Mother was in her element: stirring things in pans, slicing bread, shouting orders to Riva ... As soon as she saw who was with me she dropped everything, ran to Boyd and threw her arms around him.

At first he stiffened but, when she hung on, he slowly sagged into her embrace.

'Boyd, my dear boy!' she said. 'It's so very good to see you. Sit you down. You're eating with us, of course. Riva, fetch Boyd a beaker of tapanj juice.'

'I'd like one, too,' I said.

Mother frowned at me. 'You're quite capable of getting your own, son.'

I sighed and went to pour myself a drink, while Mother and Riva fussed over Boyd. 'What happened to your lovely face, dear?' Mother said.

# Three

Boyd's hand stroked his cheek. 'It's nothing.'

She nodded and patted his hand. 'Of course. Of course.' She smiled at him. 'Are you doing well? It must seem strange to be home again, after all that time away. I know it took Seeger a long time to adjust.'

Riva sat next to me but she didn't look at me, so I guessed we still weren't talking.

Boyd mumbled something.

'What was that, dear?' Mother said.

He looked up at Mother and then swung his head wildly, looking around the kitchen. He stood up. 'I'm sorry,' he said. 'I can't do this. Thanks for the drink.' He rushed out the door.

Mother sat staring at the back door with her mouth hanging open.

Riva said, 'That was rude.'

I sipped my juice, silently agreeing with Riva, but then I remembered the pain I'd seen in his eyes. I was going to say something but Father walked in. He pointed back over his shoulder.

'I was just coming in the gate, when Boyd shot past me running as though his pants were on fire. He didn't even stop to greet me. What did you do to him?'

Mother shook her head. Riva sniffed.

'Mother asked him how he was doing,' I said. 'He didn't want to talk about it.'

Father raised his eyebrows at Mother and she nodded.

'The poor lad,' she said. 'His face is badly bruised. I suppose he was fighting again and didn't want to admit it.'

I drained the last of the tapanj juice, slapped the beaker down on the table and grabbed Boyd's abandoned drink.

Father pursed his lips as he thought about Boyd. He slowly nodded. 'He's certainly changed since he's been home. You'd think he'd had enough of fighting. It just doesn't make sense.'

'People are weird,' Riff said. He was standing in the doorway.

'Nice to see you out of bed,' I said.

'Shut your face!' He walked into the kitchen and sat at the table. Riva got up and fetched him some juice.

'Now boys,' Mother said.

Father sat down. 'Fee, let's eat. I've got a lot to do this afternoon.'

'Yes, dear,' she said. She hurried over to the counter, picked up a ladle and began spooning soup into bowls.

'Riva?' she said.

Riva carried the first bowl of soup to Father. He bowed his head, said thanks to Sed, then scooped up a spoonful. He blew on it to cool it down and then closed his eyes as he took the first sip.

'It's really good, Fee,' he said.

Mother smiled as she filled another bowl. 'It was worth getting up early. The clams were fresh off the boat.'

I tore a chunk of bread off the loaf in the middle of the table, while I waited for Riva to bring my bowl. Of course, she served Riff next.

'By the way,' I said. 'Asher is going to teach us all about maps.'

Father broke some bread for himself and dipped it into his soup. 'That'll be good. Maps are his specialty.'

Riva plonked my bowl down in front of me. 'Thanks,' I said. She'd put it down so hard there were a few splodges of soup on the table. I mopped them up with my bread. 'He says he wants Riff to come with me tomorrow.'

Riff dropped his spoon into his bowl. 'Don't be ridiculous!' he said. 'I finished Foundation years ago!'

# Three

Father put his hand on Riff's shoulder. 'Now, son. Calm down. I think it's a wonderful opportunity to learn an important skill. No one knows more about reading, studying and making maps than Asher does. I often wish I had his ability.'

'Asher says Talia might keep you on if you could map-read,' I said.

Riff thought about that for a moment and then his ruffled feathers settled back down. He picked up his spoon and finished off his soup.

'For some reason, Riff,' I continued, 'Asher thinks you'd be good at it. Don't ask me why. Anyway, he says he expects you to be there with the rest of us tomorrow morning.' He glared at me, not saying anything. 'I told him you hardly get out of bed to change your mind, so he shouldn't expect you.'

'Right!' Riff said, standing up. 'I'll be there. But don't expect me to help you when you get things wrong.' He stalked out of the room.

I turned to Riva. 'How did you get on at the Temple this morning?'

She rolled her eyes. 'As if you care.' She stood up and followed Riff out of the room.

I looked at Mother. 'What did I do this time?'

'Oh, Seeger,' she said, shaking her head.

I turned to Father. 'I can't win.'

He stood up, too. 'The soup was wonderful, Fee,' he said. 'Come on, son, let's get back to the stables. We're going to name Juniper's piglets this afternoon. You can help.'

That was more like it. Women are a mystery to me. Give me pigs any day.

The next morning Riff was dressed and ready to go before I'd even had breakfast. We both rode Bruce up to Asher's house but, being the oldest and the bossiest, Riff rode in front. Bruce thought it was a great joke. I don't know what it is about maps, why they're so alluring, but Boyd was waiting at the front door when we arrived. What a change from yesterday.

'Morning, Boyd,' I said. 'You're early. How's your face?'

He reached up and stroked his cheek bone. 'Fine. Hello, Riff.'

Riff grunted as he climbed down from Bruce's saddle. I'd held out my hand to assist him but he'd brushed it away.

Asher flung the door open. He must have been watching for us through the window. 'Gentlemen!' he cried. 'Come in! Come in! Hello, Seeger. Lovely to see you, Riff. How's the arm? Never mind, you can tell me when you're ready to talk about it. Boyd? Your bruise is quite a striking purply-green now, isn't it! Fascinating. Come in!'

He walked behind us, shooing us in like a small flock of hens. Kieran was already waiting for us, seated at the small table which was covered in a stack of rolled up parchment.

Once again, we all picked up a slate board and some chalk and Asher gave us our first task. We were told to draw the room we were in, including the things we thought were important features. As the rest of us began scrawling on our slates, Riff sat stiffly with his lip curled up in a sneer. It was obvious to anyone who looked at him that he thought the class was beneath him.

Suddenly he flung his chalk down onto the table and shoved his slate away from him. 'This is baby stuff,' he said. 'I'm too old for this. I'm going home.'

He stood up, glaring a challenge to the rest of us to try to stop him.

Asher smiled and gently pushed Riff back into his seat. 'I began my journey with maps in the same way, dear boy. I had all of thirty years under my belt at the time. This is not

24

beneath you. I don't mean to insult you. When you first became a well-keeper, did you know everything there was to know about the job?'

Riff shook his head and stared at the edge of the table in front of him.

'Exactly!' Asher continued. 'Please be patient and forgive this old man for not being a good teacher. It's not my regular profession, you know.'

Riff didn't say anything. He kept staring in front of him as if no one else was in the room. Boyd folded his arms across his chest and studied Riff. Kieran looked at me and shrugged.

'Perhaps you could explain why we're drawing this room, Asher,' I said.

'Of course, dear boy. Of course. Maps are drawings that represent areas of space and land, with the important features marked on it. They're little drawings, or representations, of different sections of the known world. So that you can understand how they work, I wanted to start with what you know and build on that. I chose this room because we can all see it. It will be easy to compare each other's efforts and see if we've all marked the same important features. This will give you a basic understanding of how maps and mapping works. It's a foundational exercise but not a childish one.'

Kieran and I nodded. Boyd shrugged, and then went back to work, drawing on his slate. Riff didn't move. While we all sketched our version of Asher's front room on our slates, Riff sat staring at the table. He barely twitched an eyebrow. Asher didn't force him to participate so Riff did nothing.

Just as I was finishing my drawing, the light suddenly switched on in my head. Kieran was right. I *am* a bit thick! It was Riff's left arm that'd been crushed. He was left-handed. I should have realised straight away what the real problem was. Now I had to think of a way to help Riff save face and be part of the class.

When Asher examined our drawings of the room, we discovered that we'd all made it too detailed. We'd all made a proper drawing.

'I don't want a piece of art to hang on my wall!' Asher said. 'A map is meant to be simple. Here's what I'm looking for.'

He held up his slate. On it he'd drawn lines to represent the walls, with a slash across those lines wherever there were doors or windows. He'd put a rectangular box to represent the large cupboard against the wall and a smaller square that was the table we were sitting around.

'Keep it simple,' Asher said.

Riff nodded and then turned to look at me, a slight sneer curling his lip. I nearly left him to stew all morning but I couldn't do it. He's my brother after all.

My chance to get Riff involved came with the next assignment that Asher gave us. 'Now I want you to draw a line from your house to mine,' he said. 'Remember, keep it simple, with just the major turns in the road, or any major intersection that you have to cross. Include some easily recognised landmarks.'

I immediately turned to my brother. 'I'm going to need your help, Riff. How about we work on this together? Is that all right with you, Asher?'

He smiled. 'Of course, lads. Kieran, you team up with Boyd. Find a quiet spot in which to work together. Off you go! I'll give a shout when your time is up.'

Riff and I moved our chairs to the far corner of the room and settled down to work. I balanced the slate on my lap and sorted out the chalks I'd brought with me.

# Three

'I thought I'd use white for the road and blue for the landmarks. What do you think?' I said.

He leant in close to my face and whispered, 'I know what you're up to.'

'What do you mean?'

'I don't need your pity, Seeger,' he hissed.

I whispered back, 'This isn't about you. It's about me! You know how easily I get confused when it's anything to do with direction. I need your help. All right?'

He leant back and stared at me for a while. I stared back, looking him straight in the eye. Eventually he shrugged, ran his good hand through his hair and said, 'Let's get started then.'

Within a couple of days, Riff was choosing to stay behind after the lessons and do more work with Asher, including learning to write with his right hand. It turned out he was pretty good at understanding maps. As a result, he stood straighter, walked lighter and had the spark back in his eyes.

One day Kieran brought out the map of the western region. He pointed to Forabad. 'Do you remember? This is the town that fella mentioned when he was talking to Brianna before we rescued her,' Kieran said.

Asher nodded. 'That's right. He said something about the slave markets of Forabad. I'd forgotten about that.'

Kieran tapped the map. 'Well, I haven't. This is where we should start the search for my sister, Maraed.'

Boyd shifted forward in his chair. 'What's this all about?'

Kieran told Boyd about his town's crooked mayor, and the way he'd hoodwinked the people of his island for years. How he'd pretended that there was a dragon that demanded a chest of gold and the sacrifice of a maiden, every winter solstice. How he would take a large portion of the gold and the foreigners, who were part of the scheme, took the rest and sold the girls in the slave markets of Forabad.

'All this happened when you were still in Midrash,' Kieran said. 'We went to the island, while the army was preparing for the journey to rescue you and the others. We saved the latest victim, Brianna Tooley, and caught the mayor red-handed.'

Kieran blushed when he said Brianna's name. I nudged his shoulder and grinned at him.

Asher said, 'That's when we met the wonderful Fitzee, the red dragon. You must remember him? He took part in the battle with Midrash.'

Boyd nodded. 'I remember. And your sister?'

'She was taken the year before,' Kieran said. 'I want to find her and bring her home. Riff says he'll come with me.'

Asher stood up and began to pace back and forth. 'It would be a marvellous adventure. It's been a long time since I've been to the western region. What if they won't let her go? What if they attack us? How would we get there? It's a long way to walk. We'd need help and it'd take some planning ...'

I studied our little group. Kieran, of course, was deadly serious. Riff seemed excited. There was a definite twinkle in his eye. Asher had obviously already begun making plans. Boyd was the most animated and focused I'd seen him since we came home.

'I could ask some of my friends if they'd like to come with us,' Boyd said. 'We all know how to fight.'

I shook my head. 'What about your family? We've only just brought you and your friends home. Your parents have been grieving for you for almost a full turn of the sun! They thought they'd lost you for good. Now you want to leave them again? They won't let it happen.'

28

# Three

Boyd glared at me.

'He's right,' Riff said. 'It nearly killed our mother when Seeger left her again to go back to Midrash. I can't imagine what it would do to your parents if you went away so soon after coming home.'

Boyd leaped up and shouted. 'What would you know about it? You have no idea what it's like for me coming back here. I can't go back to Foundation and no one will give me a job. I don't fit in anywhere. I'm damaged goods! Kieran's expedition is the first thing I've heard of where I know I could fit in. I know how to fight. I could help. I could finally *do* something!'

He stared at us all, sitting there with our mouths open and our eyes wide. He snorted. 'Oh, what's the use? You just don't get it.'

He strode towards the door, with a stricken Asher hurrying after him.

'My dear boy—' Asher said.

'Don't worry. I'll be back tomorrow,' Boyd said, wrenching the door open and leaving the house.

Kieran rolled up the map. Riff coughed. I tugged down the sleeves of my tunic. That was quite an outburst by Boyd. I knew he'd struggled since he'd got back and I could sympathise—I remember how difficult it was for me—but I had no idea just how bad it had been. I should have been more supportive.

Asher slumped into his chair, shaking his head. 'He's right. I had no idea. That poor child. I suppose it's the same for many of the other children, too.'

Kieran shrugged. 'I suppose that means I can forget about any help to rescue Maraed.'

'Of course, not,' Riff said. 'It'll just need some careful planning.'

29

'What about his parents?' I said.

Riff turned to look at me, smiling wryly. 'Boyd isn't the only one to have issues with his parents. It'll be no easier for us. Let's leave that to Sed to sort out and just get on with making our plans. You'll be in it, won't you, Asher?'

Asher nodded vigorously. 'Of course! Are you sure you don't want to keep it to just your own townsfolk, Kieran?'

He shook his head. 'They sent off a small search party not long after we'd rescued Brianna, with no luck. The Town Council won't send any more men out. It's just a small town and the men are needed at home. Besides, they don't have the resources and skills that are here in Seddon. For a start, they don't have anyone like you, Asher, who knows lots of things about almost everything. I'd rather go with all of you.'

Asher combed his beard with his fingers, looking rather pleased with himself. 'Lots of things about everything, hey? Why thank you, young fellow.'

Kieran snorted. 'Don't go thinking you're everything and a biscuit. I didn't say you're a genius.'

That took the wind out of Asher's sails. He pursed his lips and frowned. 'Yes, well … I just wish we could go with the blessing and help of the Commander and I don't want there to be bad blood between myself and your parents, Riff. Kane is one of my oldest and dearest friends.'

We all sat staring moodily at the map on the table in front of us.

'It's early days,' Riff said. 'Something will turn up. I'm with Boyd. This is finally something I can get my teeth into. Talia has already said there's no room for one-armed men in the well-keepers. I'm not trained for anything else. But this … I could do this.'

'Let's just keep it between ourselves for now,' I suggested. 'No point stirring up trouble before we need to.'

# Three

Not long after, while we were eating the evening meal Riff, the big mouth, announced that Kieran wanted to search for his sister and bring her home again.

Father said, 'I expect there'd be a number of the Islanders who'd want to join him in that endeavour.'

Riff said, 'I told him that I'd go with him, as soon as he's ready.'

Mother's head snapped up. Her eyebrows swooped down into the V formation.

'You can't do that,' Riva said. 'You're not well.'

Mother nodded. 'Quite right! I think you've done enough damage to yourself, going off on these ridiculous adventures.'

'Now, Fee,' Father said, laying his hand on her arm.

Riff leapt up. 'Just stop it, you two!' He pointed at Mother. 'I'm not a baby.' Then he pointed at Riva, 'I'm not an invalid. You two are driving me mad with your constant fretting and fussing. Leave me alone!'

He got up and strode towards the back door. Riva hurried after him and held on to his good arm.

'Riff?' she said.

He wheeled around, yanking his arm free. 'For Sed's sake, Riva, just leave me be!'

He stormed out of the room, slamming the back door as he went. Mother and Riva both burst into tears. I didn't know where to look, so I studied my plate. Then Riva punched me on my shoulder.

'Hey! What's that for?'

'This is your fault!' she said. She thumped me once more and then ran towards the stairs. I guessed she was going to her room to cry some more.

I sat rubbing my sore shoulder, trying not to look as happy as I felt.

# Four

Boyd brought Rimini with him to Asher's house. She looked thinner and sadder than when I last saw her at the siege of Midrash. Boyd introduced her to the group. She nodded but didn't speak when we greeted her.

Riff smiled and offered her his chair. Asher said, 'Sit down, young lady. It's a pleasure to have you in my home.'

She sat down but she didn't seem happy to be there. She looked as though she was ready to fight each one of us, if we so much as breathed in her direction.

Boyd said, 'Rimini wants to come with us when we go to the west.'

'Tell me, dear,' Asher said, 'what about your parents? Won't they be distressed if you leave them again?'

She shook her head so vigorously, her black curls snapping and slapping her face, that I half expected her hair to crack in the air like the ends of a whip.

'My mother died while I was in Midrash,' she said. 'I think my father would be relieved if I went away.'

# Four

For a moment or two, there was an awkward, shocked silence. Kieran reached out his hand to pat her shoulder but she cringed and leant away from him. He quickly pulled his hand back.

'I'm sorry,' he said. 'I was just trying to comfort you.'

She rubbed the side of her cheek and shrugged. 'I know. I don't like being touched.'

Asher blinked rapidly. 'But dear,' he said, his hands spread out, 'Boyd held your hand to lead you into my house.'

She shrugged. 'He's my patrol leader.'

'Give her time to get to know you,' Boyd said. 'Kieran, perhaps something to drink?'

Kieran leaped up. 'Juice, everyone? Very good.' He hurried off towards the kitchen.

I said, 'I'll help' and followed him out.

I set up the beakers on a tray, while Kieran squeezed the tapanji. I scooped up the pips and peel, and spread them out on a tray to dry, while Kieran poured the juice. Some of the seeds would be planted, in the hope of growing another tapanj tree and others, with the peel, would be ground down for their oil. Tapanj oil is used for all sorts of things: medicine, perfume, and even for cleaning the home. Every household collects the seeds and peels and takes them, once they've dried, to their local healer-house. We try not to waste anything.

'What do you think about Rimini?' Kieran said.

'She's been damaged, like Boyd. I can't imagine some of the things she's seen and been through.'

He nodded, picking up the last tapanj to squeeze. 'She hasn't told us everything.' He sliced the fruit in half and then ground each half, one at a time, against the spike in the middle of the juice-maker.

'Do you blame her? She doesn't know us.' I scooped up the pips and peel and added them to the drying tray. 'We'll probably learn more, when she's learned to trust us.'

He grunted. 'I suppose you say true. Will she be useful on the mission?'

I spread out the seeds and peel so that they were more evenly spaced and put the tray on the window ledge.

'If Boyd says she's a good soldier, then she is,' I said.

'Yes, perhaps ...' He picked up the tray. 'Time will tell.'

We walked back into the front room and gave everyone their drink. Kieran served Asher first, who took three sips from his beaker and then leaped up.

'I'll get the maps,' he said.

'While we're waiting,' Riff said, 'tell us about your sister, Kieran. What's she like?'

Kieran settled more comfortably into his chair.

'She's got flaming red hair, lots of freckles and green eyes, like me. For a younger sister, she's quite bossy. She sings like an angel, but she can spit like a camel when she's in a mood. She used to irritate me to the edge of madness but now she's gone I miss her. I can't bear to think of her being ill-treated, or locked up somewhere, or being worked to death down a mine.'

He put his beaker down on the table and sat with his head in his hands. 'I just want to get her back.'

Riff patted his back. Rimini studied Kieran, her brows swooping down to the bridge of her nose.

'Has she been taken to be a soldier?' she said.

Kieran, his head still in his hands, said, 'I don't know.' He sat up and looked at Rimini. 'If she has, she'll be a fierce one.'

Rimini nodded and then turned her head away.

Asher bustled in with an armload of maps and the moment passed. Boyd and I collected the slates and chalk, which Asher had stored in the large cupboard near the table, and handed them out. He set us to work memorising the special marks that mapmakers use to identify significant landmarks: rivers, roads, mountain ranges, swamps, deserts, towns and so on. For example, three wavy lines, one above the other, meant water.

When we were all busy, testing each other to see how much we'd remembered, and checking the lists or one of the maps to make sure we were right, there was a loud thumping on Asher's front door.

'Carry on class,' he said, as he got up to answer the knock.

He'd barely got the door open when Bevan pushed his way into the room. 'Is my son here?'

Boyd put his slate down and stood up. His arms hung loose at his side and he seemed relaxed, but I noticed that his hands were clenched.

'Come in! Come in!' Asher said. 'Kieran, fetch the gentleman a chair from the kitchen.'

'Don't bother,' Bevan said, waving at Kieran to sit down again. 'I won't stay. Just checking that Boyd is here and there's really a class going on.'

Asher frowned and folded his arms across his chest. 'What else would we be doing, sir?'

Bevan scanned the room, taking in the tray of empty beakers, the slates and chalk, the maps—some open, some still rolled up—and seemed to relax.

'Just checking,' he said. 'Had to make sure you weren't up to any funny business. Making sure Boyd was staying out of trouble.'

Asher's chest puffed out like a rooster ready to fight. 'You forget yourself, sir! I am the Record-Keeper of Seddon. I *never* get up to funny business.'

I flicked my gaze towards Kieran and saw that he'd smothered a laugh. I guess he'd just had the same picture in his head that I had in mine: Asher dancing a jig in a cave, by the light of dragon-fire. However, Asher was an important member of the ruling council and Bevan, in his rudeness, had gone too far.

Boyd didn't look at his father. He stood still in front of his chair, with his head down. Bevan studied all of us, his eyes wild with passion. Riff glared back at him. Rimini worked on her slate as if Bevan wasn't there. Kieran and I tried to keep our faces neutral, but I could tell the Outer Islander was feeling protective towards his mentor. He sat on the edge of his chair, ready to leap into action.

'I suggest, sir,' Asher said, 'that you go home, or to your place of work, and trust that I am teaching your son as I agreed to do. Next time, if you have any doubts or concerns about Boyd's education, I suggest you see me privately, rather than during class time.'

Bevan made a curt nod at Asher, hitched up his trousers and said, 'I'll see you later, son.' Boyd just nodded. 'Sorry to waste your time, sir,' he said to Asher.

Asher walked him to the door and closed it firmly behind him. Boyd slid back down into his chair. Riff picked up the nearest map and began to compare the list on his slate board to the drawing in front of him. Rimini kept studying her slate as if nothing had happened. I caught Kieran's eye and he shrugged.

'Are you all right, Boyd?' I said. He nodded.

'Are you in trouble?' He shrugged.

Asher patted him on the shoulder before sitting down. 'Let's get back to work, class.'

'I wonder what he thought we were doing?' I said. 'Does he know about our plans to go to the west, Boyd?'

He shook his head. Finally, he looked up at me. 'He's suspicious of everything lately. Don't worry about it.' He turned to Asher. 'I apologise, sir. If you'd prefer it, I'll stop coming here.'

That made Rimini pay attention. She put her slate down and put her hand on Boyd's arm.

'Don't be silly,' Asher said. 'I insist that you keep coming. You're a bright young man and I enjoy your company.'

If they shot up any higher, Boyd's eyebrows would disappear altogether.

'Here's what I think,' Asher continued. 'We need to let off some steam. Let's clear the table and chairs to the sides of the room, so we can dance.'

Boyd spun around to me and mouthed the word, 'Dance?' I nodded, grinning. I realised that Boyd and Rimini had never seen Asher in action.

'Come along, Kieran,' he said. 'Let's show them how it's done.'

After Asher and Kieran had begun jigging and tapping their way around the room, Boyd leant towards me and whispered in my ear, 'Never any funny business, hey?'

I laughed. Riff stood stiffly to one side, watching the two dancers. I thought he might disapprove but, suddenly, he leaped into the middle of the room and began to stomp back and forth.

'Is this how you do it, Asher?' he said.

'Not quite, lad,' Asher said, between puffs, 'but it's a good start. For now, just have some fun with it.'

Boyd and I looked at each other, shrugged and then, giggling, joined Riff in the centre. We just shuffled about, spending more time laughing than dancing. Rimini watched from the safety of the doorway.

'Come on, Rimini,' Boyd said. 'It'll do you good.'

She shook her head. I couldn't tell what she was thinking or feeling, as her face was a blank page. She probably wasn't impressed. Kieran was the only genuine dancer in the room. Asher was enthusiastic but he was no match for Kieran's skills. The rest of us were hopeless. Still, it felt good to stomp and leap about. I could see why Asher was addicted to it.

When all of us, except Kieran, were standing bent over, hands on our knees, gasping for air, Asher called a halt to the dancing. He was bright red in the face. 'Time to get … some work done … before the morning … is over.'

We all helped put the furniture back in place and then settled back into the business of learning the language of maps.

'It's just as well my dad didn't come back while that was going on,' Boyd said, picking up his slate board.

We all laughed at the thought and I even saw a grin flash momentarily across Rimini's face.

I spent most of the afternoon in the pigs' stall, talking with Juniper about her piglets while taking it in turns to give each one a cuddle. We'd named them all after flowers: Sweet William and Aster were the two boys, and Lily, Violet, Ivy, Hyacinth and Daisy were the girls. I was worried about Daisy, the littlest piglet. Being small and weak, she often got pushed aside by her bigger siblings when she tried to latch on to a teat.

*She's just too little,* Juniper said. *If she gets the wheezes and sneezes, that could be the end of her.*

*Have you talked to Father about it?*

*No. She must find a way to get what she needs or she'll die.* She nuzzled Violet with her snout, as the youngster leant against her shoulder. *Not that I want to lose any of my babies! I love them all but it's the way of the world.*

# Four

*I'll talk to Father,* I said. *We'll keep an eye on her for you.*
*Thank you,* she said.

I watched as Daisy squirmed her way into the scrum at her mother's side. She'd just latched on and had begun to suckle when Sweet William, in a manner not reflective of his name, pushed her off and grabbed the teat for himself.

'Hey!' I said. 'Don't be a bully.' I found another teat that was free and pushed Daisy towards it. 'Come on guys, look after your sister.'

They all ignored me. I could see that if we didn't do something soon, it was possible that poor little Daisy would starve to death. I gave Juniper a final scratch behind her ears before leaving her and her brood to go brush the camels' hides.

As I climbed over the low wall of Juniper's stall, there was a break in the constant rumble of contented piglet grunting and I heard a couple of quick, delicate sneezes.

I sat perched on top of the wall and studied the babies to see which one it was. Juniper sniffed and nuzzled each piglet in turn. Then she got to Daisy. Within seconds of touching the little one's face with her snout, Juniper's head whipped around towards me. *She's got a fever, Seeger.* I jumped down and ran straight to Father's office.

That evening, Father rode home on Karmal, cradling the sick piglet in his arms. When we got home, he handed Daisy to Mother and said, 'This little girl needs help, Fee. Daisy's weak, she's hungry and she's got a fever.'

'Give her to me,' Mother said, tucking the sick piglet in the crook of her arm and holding it up against her chest, like she would a human baby. 'I know just what to do.'

The little pig looked up at Mother, wrinkled its snout and sneezed.

'Bless you!' Mother said, 'Come along, precious, I'll take care of you.'

Carrying Daisy, Mother begun poking around in the kitchen cupboards, finally coming up with an old baby bottle. She handed it to Riva. 'Here, fill this with warm milk, please. Bring it to me when it's ready. I'm going to make up a cosy bed for this little girl. Aren't I, sweetie? Yes, I am.'

She walked away, cooing to the piglet and rocking it in her arms.

Father nodded, smiling, as he watched her carry Daisy away. 'Couldn't be in safer hands.'

That night, as I lay in bed, I heard Shadreer calling my name.

# Five

I was sound asleep and dreaming of Shadreer. We were flying over the desert, watching the wild camels walking along the dunes, their shadows stretched out like giants on the sand. Then Shadreer turned his head and said, *Seeger, wake up.*

I thought, *That's an odd thing to say when we're flying over the dunes. I* am *awake.*

*No, you are not. You are dreaming,* Shadreer said. *I need you to wake up now. WAKE UP!*

I opened my eyes but no one was there. *I really miss him,* I thought. The room was dark, with just the moonlight to give some shape to the shadows, so I knew it was still night.

*Good. You are awake. I need to talk with you and your father. Please get him and meet me on the roof.*

'What?' I pinched myself. 'Ow!' I was awake.

*Get moving, hatchling, before the night is over.*

*Shadreer? Is that really you?*

I heard the dragon sigh. *Please do not waste time, hatchling.*

41

I ran to Father's room and shook him awake. It took some doing. Father could sleep through a riot. Eventually he opened his eyes.

'Wha'? Seeger?' He sat up, rubbing his temples. 'What's going on?'

Just then I heard a delicate little sneeze. 'Is that Daisy?' I said.

'Yes,' Father said. 'She sleeps in a nest of blankets near your mother's side of the bed. Did you wake me just to ask that?'

'No. Sorry. Shadreer is on our roof. He says he needs to speak with both of us.'

Father ran his hand across his forehead. 'Oh, Seeger. It was just a dream, son. Go back to bed.'

*Tell him I have a request to make to the Commander. I need your help.*

'He says he needs our help. He wants to ask the Commander for something.'

I could see Father still thought it was wishful thinking on my part.

*Shadreer, could you drop your tail down past my father's bedroom window?*

*Of course, hatchling, if that will help.*

'Humour me, please Father? Come to your window.'

He sighed heavily but he climbed out of bed. 'If it will help you go back to sleep,' he said.

We walked past Daisy, tucked into a pile of blankets. She sneezed again. *Hello, Seeger,* she said. *I'm sick.*

*I know, Daisy, but Mother will make you better.*

*Did you know there's a big animal up on the roof?*

*Yes. He's a friend of mine.*

*Oh, good,* she said. *I tried to tell the Beast-Master but he wouldn't wake up.*

# Five

*It's all right. I'm here now. Go back to sleep.*

She snuffled and grunted, got up, turned around three times and then snuggled back as best she could under the covers. *Would you please pull up the top blanket?*

I stooped down and pulled it up to her chin. She smiled and said, *Thank you.* She really was a cute little thing.

Father said, 'Is she all right?'

I nodded and we moved up next to the window. *We're ready, Shadreer.*

The dragon's thick, scaly tail—it looked like a giant snake—dropped past the window. Father leapt back. 'Flipping heck!' he said. 'That scared the begonias out of me! Is that ...?'

'It's his tail.'

*Thanks, Shadreer,* I said. *We'll be right up.*

'Come on,' I said. 'He's up on the roof.'

Father pulled on a robe over his nightwear and followed me out to the staircase that led to the roof. We hurried up the steps and there he was, Shadreer the Leader of the Flight, waiting for us in the moonlight.

I ran to him and threw my arms around his chest. 'I've missed you so much!'

*I have missed you, too, hatchling. We all have. Please extend my greetings to your father.*

'Father, Shadreer says hello.'

Father walked up to the dragon and stretched out his hand. Shadreer gently placed his right claw onto Father's palm.

'Greetings, Shadreer,' Father said. 'It's delightful to see you again.'

Father gave the dragon's front foot a gentle shake, as he would if he were greeting a friend, and then let it go.

*Tell your father I apologise for the inconvenient timing of my visit but I need your help.*

'Shadreer's sorry it's so late at night but he needs our help.'

'Tell me what I can do,' Father said.

Shadreer explained that there aren't many dragons left in Draageer. The remaining few hide out in the upper reaches of the highest mountains. The survivors have told the Flight about the slaughter of their people. He didn't wish to tell that story twice, so he would wait until he was with the Commander. Captain Blunt and his troop have joined forces with the Xanthi. The dragons need our help. The Flight have been gone too long and there are too few of them. Will Father speak on their behalf?

Father said, 'Of course I will. Are you here alone?'

*I have Azree, Fitzee and Hizaree with me,* Shadreer said. *They are waiting in the sea caves. Jondalee has remained in the mountains to defend the survivors. We thought we would need to bring most of the Flight, to transport you back to Draageer.*

I repeated this to Father who said, 'I will go to the Commander in the morning and request that he and General Mika meet with you. Knowing how these things work, I expect it won't happen until the day after.'

Shadreer said that he and the rest of the Flight would keep watch for our arrival. He then flew off into the night. We watched him leave and for a few moments his silhouette was like a large bird framed against the shining ball of the moon.

I stood staring after Shadreer, a silly grin on my face. It was so good to have the dragons back in my life. Ever since they returned to the north and I came south to Seddon, I had felt as though a part of me was missing. It felt as though I was the one who had lost the use of his arm, not Riff.

Father nudged me. 'Come on, back to bed.'

# Five

As we walked back down the stairs, Father said, 'Say nothing of this to your mother. Give her another day's peace, at least.'

The next morning at Asher's house, I shared the news with the rest of the group. Asher, of course, was delirious with delight.

'That's just lovely, lovely, lovely!' he said, clapping his hands. 'I can't wait to see them all again.'

Riff shook his head. 'I'm not sure I want to face another fight so soon,' he said. 'I'm not sure what use I'd be with only one good arm.' He shivered. 'Dear Sed, what will Mother do?'

Boyd and Rimini looked at each other. There was the trace of a slight smile on Rimini's mouth.

Boyd said, 'I'm not worried about the fight, nor of seeing Blunt again, but I'm not sure about the dragons. Shouldn't we help the humans, our own kind, against those creatures?'

Asher leaped up, knocking his chair over, his hands up in the air in horror. 'What? Turn our backs on those noble beasts, when they've asked for our help? The same noble beasts who fought for your freedom? I can't believe what I've just heard! Shame on you, young man.'

Boyd shrugged. 'It doesn't seem natural to me to side with giant, fire-breathing lizards. Besides, they were the ones who took us to Midrash in the first place.'

*Ah*, I thought, *so that's the real problem.*

'They only did that because they were honouring the bond they'd made with the Midrashi,' I said. 'Once they'd realised their mistake, they were quick to help us. They've done more than enough to clear their debt. They are noble creatures and their word is solid. I trust them far more than I'd trust most men.'

'Exactly!' Asher said. 'You haven't had the chance to get to know them as well as we have. Give them a chance, Boyd.'

I'd noticed that so far Kieran had kept his head down and his mouth closed. 'What say you, Kieran?' I said.

He shrugged. 'Oh, don't mind me. You go ahead and enjoy your reunion. I'll just clear away the beakers.' He began placing our empty beakers on the tray.

I reached out and held his arm. 'We're not going to give up on Maraed,' I said.

He shrugged once more. 'No, of course not. We'll just have a little war with the Xanthi that'll go on for who knows how long and then, after that, when we've got a few spare lunar cycles, we'll pop across to the west.'

He lifted my hand off his arm, picked up the tray and carried it out to the kitchen.

I looked to Asher for help.

'No, no, Kieran!' he yelled. 'Not so. Come back in here. I have a plan.'

Kieran slid back into the room and dropped down into his chair. He wouldn't look at any of us.

'Now listen, boy,' Asher said, leaning forward, 'stop sulking and pay attention. It'll take Mika some time— perhaps only a short time but nevertheless—to sort out how many soldiers she'll send, who will lead them and so on. Then, they will have to gather their supplies together, while she and the appointed leader make some strategic plans. It will take some time, just as it did when we went to Midrash. Then there is the long trek to the north. I think there will be plenty of time for us to take the dragons to the west, rescue your sister and so forth. The army will have to stop at Midrash to refresh their water and food supplies. We can meet them there and then travel northwards together. After all, the dragons can fly vast distances much faster than a fighting force can march them.'

Kieran sat up a bit straighter in his chair, his brows still furrowed in thought. 'I suppose so,' he said. 'Of course, you assume that it will be a simple thing to find Maraed and to take her from whoever has her. I won't be able to refund her owner the money he paid to the slave market, so we'll have to steal her away. Still, assuming all goes smoothly, I suppose it's a plan.'

Riff agreed with Asher. 'If we could fly to the west with the dragons, that would make a huge difference to our travelling time there and back. Also, dragons come in very handy when one is trying to make a point to anyone who is being difficult.'

Asher smiled his thanks at Riff and then studied Kieran again. What he saw seemed to reassure him. 'That settles it. I shall accompany Seeger and Kane when they take the Commander to meet with the dragons. I'll put forward my plan then and see what they say. I'm sure it will be fine. We're not giving up on Maraed. Not while there is any chance of finding her.'

I said to Riff, 'You can tell Riva that the dragons are back but do it out of Mother's earshot. Father says we shouldn't worry her until it is absolutely necessary for her to know.'

He nodded. 'You say true. Don't worry, we'll keep it secret but Riva will be keen to see them, too. She's known them a lot longer than you, remember.'

'Thanks for pointing that out,' I said. 'I had no idea.'

He smirked. 'No need to be sarcastic, Seeger. It doesn't hurt to be reminded of how others are feeling, now and then.'

'I don't need you to tell me about Riva,' I said. I wanted to smack that smirk right off his face. 'After all, I've known her a lot longer than you have, remember?'

He glared at me and I glared back.

'I'm going with Father and the Commander, to meet with the dragons,' I said, 'so I will be sure to tell them Riva sends her love.'

Riff flicked his hair off his brow with his good hand. 'Why should you go and not the rest of us? What makes you so special?'

'Really?' I said. 'Are you serious?'

'He's the only one who can talk with them, Riff,' Kieran said. 'Remember?'

Riff huffed and pouted. 'I don't see why we can't all go.'

'Now boys,' Asher said, 'settle down. I think that's an excellent suggestion, Riff. I shall tell Kane that I am taking you all on a field trip. Riva is welcome to come along as well. Kieran, get out the map of the Western Region please. I want you all to work out the best route to take to Forabad. Meanwhile, I'll just jot down a short note to Kane, which Seeger can take back with him.'

He studied our little group. Kieran was still sulking, Rimini and Boyd were whispering together, and Riff and I were shooting daggers at each other with our eyes.

He clapped his hands. 'Come along! Get to work.'

Kieran stood up slowly, as though it pained him to move, and went to find the map. Boyd and Rimini handed out the slates and chalk. Riff continued to glare at me.

I said, 'You've got Riva, Riff. At least let me have the dragons.'

He frowned. 'What?'

'You heard. I've got the message loud and clear. She's no longer my girlfriend. She's yours. I'm not happy about it but there's nothing I can do. Just don't rub my face in it, all right?'

He shook his head, his forehead a mess of wrinkles. 'I had no idea, Seeger. I say true.'

Flipping Nora! He really didn't know. 'It's about time you paid attention, brother,' I said. 'You must be the only person in Seddon who doesn't know.'

Boyd butted in. 'He speaks true, Riff. We all know it.'

Riff looked around the group, his bewilderment written all over his face. 'Really?'

'Really,' everyone said together.

'Even you, Asher?' Riff said.

'Indeed, dear boy,' Asher said. 'I don't know how you missed it. Perhaps it was because the delectable Riva blinded you with her beauty.'

Riff shook his head again and turned to me. 'Why didn't you say something?'

Kieran laughed. 'Because he's as thick as you! It's taken him all this time to figure out what the rest of us saw at the siege of Midrash. You two twigs are cut from the same branch.'

'I'm sorry, Seeger. Why would I think you two were together?' Riff said. 'She hardly ever speaks to you. She's always short-tempered with you. I thought she didn't like you.'

'Yes, well ... For some strange reason, she seems to blame me for the loss of your arm.'

From the corner of the room, Rimini said, 'She probably feels guilty about the change in her feelings from you to Riff, so she hides it in anger.'

We all turned to stare at her. My mouth dropped open; partly from the shock of hearing Rimini join in the conversation and partly from the shock of what she said.

'What?' I said.

She shrugged. 'You should talk to her.'

Huh! That will be easier said than done.

'I'm truly sorry, Seeger,' Riff said. 'Will you be all right?'

'Let's not talk about it anymore,' I said. 'Things to do. Plans to make.'

He nodded.

'Thank Sed for that,' Asher said. 'Now get to work.'

I delivered Asher's letter to Father when we met at home for the midday meal. He read it, shaking his head.

'What is wrong with that man?' Father said. 'He can't just invite himself and his class along to an official meeting!'

'What's that, dear,' Mother said, putting a platter of cheese, figs, nuts, sliced tapanji and buttered bread in the middle of the table. 'What meeting? Help yourselves, everyone.'

Riff and I grabbed some cheese and fruit, while Riva waited politely until we had filled our plates. I don't know why she waited. I often wondered whether she still didn't feel completely at home with us.

Father rubbed his forehead. 'Nothing important. Just a little trip to the eastern shore with the Commander and a few others. Seeger is coming along in case we meet with any wild beasts.' She gasped and clutched her chest. 'Don't panic, Fee. It's just a formality. We don't expect any trouble.'

Mother relaxed and nudged Riva. 'Eat up, dear.'

'Now that fool of a man has invited himself and his class and you too, Riva, along for the journey. He claims it will be educational!'

Mother nodded. 'I expect it will be. I don't see why you're making such a fuss if it's nothing important. After all, Asher is a member of the Ruling Council. He knows how to behave himself around the Commander. I'm sure he'll keep his class in check. It'll do Riva good to get out in the fresh air for a day. You go ahead, dear, and I'll make your excuse to Jonathan.'

# Five

It was as easy as that.

Father sent a return message to Asher, telling him to bring himself, Kieran, Boyd and Rimini to the eastern gate, first thing the next morning. We would meet him there.

That afternoon at the stables, while we were cleaning out the camels' stalls, I decided to take Rimini's advice.

'Err, Riva,' I said.

'What?' She kept raking up the trampled straw and didn't look at me.

'We need to talk.'

She leant the rake against the wall and grabbed the shovel. She scooped up a mound of straw and dung and heaved it into the wheelbarrow. 'We need to work,' she said.

I walked around and placed myself between her and the wheelbarrow. 'We need to clear the air,' I said. 'I don't want this ... whatever it is ... to go on. You're always angry with me. I don't know what I've done, or not done, but I'm sorry.'

She sighed and leant on the shovel's handle. For a few minutes, she didn't say anything. Then she straightened her back and looked at me.

'You're right,' she said. 'It can't go on. If nothing else, it's exhausting staying angry all the time.'

'I've noticed that things aren't the same between us,' I said. She grimaced. 'I've also noticed that you're attracted to Riff.'

She opened her mouth to speak but I kept talking. 'It's hurt and confused me. I thought we were together. I still like you, very much.'

She put her hand on my arm and her eyes were pools of sadness.

'It's all right, Riva,' I continued. 'I know that Riff is the handsome one in the family. I get it.'

She shook her head. 'No, Seeger, you're just as handsome.'

'I don't need your pity,' I said.

'Don't be ridiculous!' She punched me on the shoulder.

I winced and rubbed the spot where her fist had landed. I wish she wouldn't do that.

'I didn't mean for it to happen,' she said. 'It just did. Slowly, over time, I found myself thinking of him more and you less. He's so kind and caring.'

'What, and I'm not?' I can be just as kind and caring as Riff, the stork!

She gave me a gentle shove. 'You daft thing. Of course you care. The thing is … Well, the thing is … Look, I *like* you, Seeger, I'll be your friend for life, but I don't love you.'

Her words fell into the space between us, with edges so sharp they pierced my heart. I reeled under the pain. Finally, I understood there was nothing I could do.

'Will you be all right?' she said.

Everyone wants to know if I'll be all right! 'Sure,' I said.

She smiled at me and I stared at her lips. *I'll never kiss them again*, I thought. I swallowed the lump that had formed in my throat.

'Right,' I said. 'Let's get back to work. No more snapping at me for nothing though, all right?'

'You say true,' she said. She smiled again as she grabbed hold of the shovel and scooped up some more muck.

I left her to it and went to clean out Bruce's stall. I told myself that as I hadn't died then and there, I would most probably live. Still, there was an ache in my chest where my heart lay bleeding from a thousand cuts.

*Well done, young feller-me-lad*, Bruce said.

*Shut up, Bruce.*

# Six

The next morning Father, Riff, Riva and I rode out to the eastern gate. I wondered if the same men who were guarding it the night I came home would be on duty. Sure enough, long before I could make out the features on his face, I could see the red hair blazing in the morning light. What was his name? Garry? Davin? Gavin, that's it!

I greeted him as we drew close to the gate. 'Good morning, Gavin.'

He frowned. 'Do I know you?'

I smiled. 'You were on duty the night my friend and I asked for your help. I'm the Beast-Master's son.'

He studied my face for a while. Then he did the same with Riva. Then he turned back to me, again. 'Well, I never! I didn't recognise you two. You're both looking much better than the last time I saw you.'

I laughed. 'My mother's cooking has made sure of that.'

He reached up and shook my hand. 'I'm glad to hear it, son.' He turned to Father. 'Please excuse my bad manners, sir. Good morning and may Sed be with you.'

'And also with you, Gavin,' Father said. 'Don't let us keep you from your work.'

Gavin saluted and went back to his post at the open gate. Shortly afterwards, Asher, Kieran, Boyd and Rimini turned up. Asher and Kieran shared one camel and Boyd and Rimini another. After greeting each other and exchanging the usual pleasantries—lovely morning, going to be a glorious day, and so forth—we waited for the official party to arrive.

I noticed that Riva and Rimini seemed to be sizing each other up. They'd not met before, which surprised me a little. Then again, there were a lot of people at the siege of Midrash and, once Riff was hurt, Riva had spent most of her time at his side. A light flashed in my brain. *Oh Seeger, you really are as thick as a stack of bricks!*

Eventually the official party turned up: General Mika and the Commander, accompanied by a contingent of archers led by our old friend, Felix, who winked at me as they drew close. If the Commander was surprised to see Asher and the other hangers-on, he didn't show it. We saluted the Commander and the General and then set out through the eastern gate towards the Great Sea Caves.

Our party was subdued. There was very little chatter. Asher tried to engage General Mika in some banter but she wasn't interested. He then attempted to have a conversation with Father but he said, 'Not now, Ash.' So, eventually, he gave up and we rode in silence. Even the camels were quiet. I suppose they could sense the atmosphere and didn't want to disturb it.

At one point, Shirra said, *Are you two-legs all right? What is going on? Why are you breathing like that, Seeger?*

*This meeting with the dragons is important. It could mean that we will go to war again. I suppose people are thinking about that.*

# Six

*Perhaps you should stop for a while and let Asher do some dancing? That would cheer everyone up. It makes me smile.*

My stomach was jittery and I had to keep taking deep breaths to get my breathing under control. I knew—from the emotion underneath Shadreer's words the previous night—that he was the bearer of tragic news. For once, I wished it was Father who could dragon-speak and not me.

Once again, it was Hizaree who spotted us first and who bugled the warning to the others. The Flight swooped out of the caves and flew in formation towards us. They were a striking sight to behold, their scales flashing green, blue and red in the morning sunlight. I heard some of our group gasp at the sight. Everyone smiled to see the dragons again. Well, I say everyone but that's not quite true: Boyd and Rimini didn't show any emotion at all.

When the Flight had landed and we had all got down from our camels—all except the bowmen, who never relaxed—we sat together on the sand in front of the dragons. They were lying close together, their legs touching and their heads lowered to the ground, so that they were as near to us as they could get.

Before we could begin the formalities, Riva and I ran to the dragons and hugged each scaly, gnarled head, one after the other. They murmured their love to us. Inspired by our example, Asher then proceeded to do the same. He spent the longest time with Azree. I'd forgotten that those two had a special bond. I told him that the Flight gave him their love, too. I also passed on their greetings to the official party and their appreciation of the Commander and the General for making the time and effort to meet with them.

Once the welcome was over and everyone was settled back in their places on the sand, it was time to get down to business. Shadreer was the spokes-dragon. I stood next to his head, facing the group who had travelled out with me. I saw Father and Asher smile their encouragement to me. Riff gave me a brief nod, as if to say, 'You've got this.' I took a deep breath and we began.

*Dear Commander, dear General,* Shadreer said, *we dragons from the Land of Draageer need your assistance. We do not know to whom we can turn if you, our friends from Seddon, refuse us help.*

I repeated his words.

'Of course,' the Commander said. 'Tell us what you need.'

*We only have a few adult females left. Those who were hatchlings when we males went to Midrash, will soon be mature and in their full powers. However, it might not be in time and there are so few of them.*

I repeated his words. Father asked, 'Why is that Shadreer?'

*The Midrashi did not keep their promise to protect our nesting places, or our females, or our hatchlings. They broke their covenant with us as soon as we, the Flight, had left Draageer. Within the space of a seven night, all the Midrashi soldiers had left our land. Then the Xanthi came.*

As I was translating, I saw the General and the Commander both sadly shake their heads. Asher exclaimed, 'The filthy swine!' He then turned to Father and said, 'Sorry, Kane. I mean no disrespect to the piggies in your care.'

The left corner of Father's mouth curved upwards for a second. 'Don't worry, Ash. I understand.'

Shadreer continued. *The females tell us that the Xanthi laughed as they trod upon the unhatched eggs. They smashed in the heads of the new hatchlings with the butts of their spears. They sliced open the bellies of the ones that were old enough to leave the nest but not yet able to fly. They surrounded the females, as they tried to defend their young, attacking them from all sides at once, with spears and swords and stones flung from leather straps. The mothers fought bravely and fiercely, but many died.*

Rimini and Riva covered their mouths with their hands as I told the terrible tale. I felt as though I was choking on every word and the saltwater streamed down my cheeks. It was hard but I had to keep going.

By the end of the second sentence, Mika's lips were pinched tight and her forehead was puckered. Asher sat with his mouth open and with salt-water leaking out of the corners of his eyes. Riff and Kieran stared at me as if I was suddenly speaking a foreign language. Father's face had lost its colour. The Commander, Boyd and Rimini showed no emotion on their faces, but their arms were folded tight and their backs were ramrod straight.

'I don't understand,' Father said. 'Why didn't the females simply flame their attackers?'

Shadreer tilted his head to the right and said, *Do you not know? Only male dragons have fire.*

I repeated his words and everyone groaned. I turned to look at the Flight and saw that all four were weeping.

*It was a slaughter,* Shadreer said.

I threw my arms around his neck. 'I'm so sorry!' I could hardly breathe.

Asher leaped up and ran to Azree. He embraced him, just as I had done with Shadreer. 'Oh Azree, to think that your families and your friends were destroyed in such a monstrous fashion!' he said. 'My heart breaks for you.'

Riva ran to Hizaree and Kieran did the same to Fitzee. This was the same Kieran who used to hate dragons!

Suddenly the camels were rumbling and groaning. The females were bellowing. The sound swept over all of us like a tidal wave of noise.

'What are they doing?' Boyd yelled, putting his hands over his ears.

'They're angry and they're grieving for the lost,' I said. *Shirra, I understand how you feel but, please, we need to hear the rest of Shadreer's tale.*

*They killed their babies!* Shirra said.

*I know. I know.*

After a while, the camels calmed down and the noise was reduced to the occasional deep rumble. Shadreer recovered his composure and once more I stood next to his head ready to be his mouthpiece.

'If everyone could settle down,' I said, 'Shadreer would like to finish his story.'

*Some, only some, of the little ones escaped. They hid in cracks in the rocks, or under piles of leaves, or even in the burrows of other creatures. When the Xanthi left, they crawled out and began calling for their mothers. Some of the females had also survived. They had been forced to retreat when they saw that they could not rescue their young. Imagine their surprise when they heard the little ones calling.*

When I said this, Riva gasped. 'Thank, Sed!'

*They gathered them up and carried them into the mountain tops, away from the green fields. Away from the streams and lakes. Away from the enemy. Some younger females left Draageer, flying away in search of another place to call home. We do not know what happened to them. The others stayed up among the rocks, cared for the hatchlings and waited for us to come home. They had no idea it would take so long and that there would be so few of us who would return.*

I'm not ashamed that I wept as I said these things and I wasn't the only one.

*Since we have been gone, the Xanthi have built their shelters in the fields where the adult dragons used to perform the courting dance. It was a safe place to build for there has not been an adult male dragon in Draageer for over a hundred years, thanks to the Midrashi's lies. The only good thing was that they chose to leave the dragons alone, up on the high mountains.*

*Now, Captain Blunt and his men have joined the Xanthi. He is making an army for himself. He is teaching them new ways to fight. They call him, 'General'. He is training them in warfare. When he thinks they are ready, they will come up into the mountains and finish the job they started all those years ago. They plan to wipe us all out. Then, they will turn to the south. Blunt has grand plans of conquest. I do not think he intends to stop at Midrash. He has cause to hate Seddon. We need your help to save our people and, in the end, to save yours as well.*

When I had finished repeating everything, I sat down next to Shadreer's head and leant against his cheek. We waited for the Commander's response.

He and General Mika walked a short distance away from the rest of us and whispered together. Mika's hands flapped and pointed in various directions. In comparison, the Commander was as still as a post but I could see the tension in his shoulders.

I looked across at Felix and the archers. Although they were still poised, ready to defend the Commander, several of them were studying the dragons with sadness in their eyes. Felix's face was pinched tight with anger. I caught his eye and he dipped his head in a brief nod to me.

The Commander and the General re-joined the group and the General sat down. The Commander remained standing as he addressed the Flight.

'There is no doubt that you have suffered a grievous wrong from the Midrashi and Xanthi people,' he said. 'We are deeply saddened by the news of the slaughter of your young. In a civilised world, the young are sacrosanct. Still, when we consider how the Midrashi used our children in warfare, we should not be surprised that they allowed such cruelty to other creatures.'

'It was Blunt who executed little Tam,' Boyd said. 'He's a cold-hearted monster.'

The Commander suddenly looked tired. He ran his hands over his face, as if he could wipe it all away.

'We want to help you,' he continued, 'but we are unsure what would be the best response. We are a long way from your homeland and waging a war from such a distance, and for a potentially long time, would be difficult for our small city. Even if we request support from the Boroni and Rigoni, we couldn't raise a large enough army to fight an entire nation. Also, we were—'

'Sorry to interrupt, sir,' I said, 'but please wait. Shadreer wants to speak.'

The Commander nodded and waited until I could repeat what the dragon-leader said.

*We do not expect you to wage a full-scale war with the Xanthi. They have been settled in our fields for over a hundred years. However, Captain Blunt must be stopped.*

The Commander nodded when I told him this. 'How do you know what Blunt is planning to do?'

*We have excellent hearing,* Shadreer said. *They see us flying high overhead but they do not realise that we can hear them. Two-legs always underestimate creatures that are not the same as them.*

I repeated his words.

'I see,' the Commander said. 'What do you want us to do?'

Shadreer continued. *We wish you to send a fighting force*

*to help us deal with Captain Blunt and his army. He is a dangerous man.*

As I repeated Shadreer's words, I saw that General Mika was nodding in agreement. That boded well for the Flight.

The Commander said to Shadreer, 'That is a reasonable request. General Mika?' He looked at her.

'I should never have let Blunt leave Midrash,' she said. 'This is my fault.' She nodded. 'It will take a while to select a special squad of elite forces and equip them. And then there's the long trip north. I'm afraid this won't happen overnight.'

Shadreer inclined his head and I told the Commander that he understood.

Asher stood up. 'This seems the ideal moment to share my plans with you.'

Father tugged Asher's trouser leg. 'Sit down, Ash.'

Asher's chin went up and he folded his arms across his chest. 'I am a member of the Ruling Council, Kane, not some naughty child. I ask you to treat me with respect.'

Father's mouth dropped open and his eyebrows disappeared into his hairline. 'Why ... err ... of course, Ash.'

'Thank you,' Asher said. 'The sister of my assistant, Kieran, was stolen from her people just over a full turn of the sun ago and sold in the slave markets of Forabad. I ask that the dragons fly me and my small band of helpers to the west to rescue her. Instead of weeks of travel, the dragons could get us there in a matter of days. We could find the girl, bring her home, and meet up with the Seddonese armed forces in Midrash. What say you?'

I could tell that Shadreer was interested but before he could reply my father spoke. 'I have several problems with your proposal, Asher. How can you be sure that you will find this girl quickly and easily? Who are the "helpers" of whom you speak? Will there be anyone capable of defending you, if you come to grief?'

Asher flapped his hand as if shooing away a fly. 'Pish posh, Kane. Those are petty details.'

The Commander said, 'Nevertheless, Asher, they are reasonable questions. What say you?'

Asher closed his eyes in thought for a moment, then he drew his skinny frame up and stood tall. 'I have friends in the western region. My good friend, Luka, has just retired from the department of record-keeping and he has already agreed to aid us in our quest. With his help, I will easily access the slave market records and find out where Maraed has gone. The band of helpers are the young people who are here today.'

Father leaped up.

'Now, Kane,' Asher said, 'I know what you are going to say but I want you to think before you speak. First of all, one old man and a group of young people won't raise suspicion or ill-will like an armed band of soldiers would. Also, since his injury, Riff has no longer been acceptable to Talia as a well-keeper. This expedition will prove his worth and give him his self-esteem back. Boyd and Rimini are trained in weaponry and have had battle experience. They are capable young people who also need to be useful. Both are experiencing difficulty in their home life, so it would be good to get them away for a while. You do know that Bevan is regularly beating young Boyd?'

Boyd's head whipped around. He stared up at Asher, his mouth open in shock. I could tell from Boyd's face that Asher was speaking true. I also stared; first at Asher and then at Boyd. I'd thought his bruised face was the result of a fight! I had no idea that he was being beaten on a regular basis. Trust old Ash to know the truth! With his odd manner

# Six

and his funny ways, it was easy to forget just how wise the old man was.

Father took a deep breath but before he could speak Asher interrupted him. 'As for Seeger and Riva ... We will need Seeger because of his extraordinary gift of beast-speaking. You, Beast-Master, will not be able to leave the stables again so soon after the trip to Midrash. What is more, you can't speak dragon. And, Riva? It will be good to have another female to accompany Rimini, and Maraed once we've found her. Also, I've heard she's a good cook.'

The Commander and General smiled at each other. Asher had obviously given this a lot of thought.

Father said, 'I understand how Kieran must feel because of the loss of his sister. I was very sad to hear it and I sympathise. However, Asher, is it worth placing the lives of these young people in danger, in the hope of finding one young woman?'

Asher took a step back, clearly shocked at what Father had just said. 'Kane! An army went to find your son. Surely you don't begrudge a small band of volunteers to rescue Kevin and Gwennie's daughter?'

Father pushed his hands through his hair. 'It's not the same thing! There were a lot more children than just Seeger who had been stolen.'

'Yes,' Asher said, 'but what if it *were* just Seeger? Would you have begrudged him a rescue mission?'

Father's cheeks blazed red. He closed his eyes for a moment. Then, he made another attempt to keep Riff and me home.

'What of Fee?' he said. 'Seeger's disappearance nearly killed her. You remember what she was like. When we all left her to go to Midrash, she nearly broke down again. Then,

Riff returned injured. Do you seriously think I can let the boys leave again, so soon?'

Asher tilted his head and smiled at Father. 'Kane, my old friend,' he said, 'dear Fee must learn to let the lads grow and become men. She can't keep them tied to her apron forever. She is a strong woman and she will survive. Find her a waif that needs her loving care and her heart will mend sooner.'

'Daisy!' I said. Everyone turned to stare at me. 'Perhaps, Father, Sed's hand is in this. Mother is already consumed with loving and nurturing that little one.'

Most of the group looked at each other, confused by this information.

'Daisy is a piglet,' Riva said. 'She's the runt of the litter and is quite ill. Fee is nursing her at home.'

Rimini looked at Boyd, who shrugged. Kieran and Asher smiled.

A new voice joined in the conversation. 'If it please the General I would be happy, indeed honoured, to accompany Asher on his rescue mission.'

It was Felix! We all turned to stare at him, even the other archers.

'What say you, General?' Asher said. He grinned at Felix and mouthed, 'Thank you' at him.

General Mika slowly nodded. 'I don't see why not,' she said. 'You will then re-join the force in Midrash. I had, in any case, already intended to send you north as the leader of a company of archers.'

'Wonderful!' Asher said, clapping his hands. 'Lovely, lovely, lovely.'

Father shook his head. 'Wait! Wait! This is all happening far too fast!'

'You're right,' Asher said. 'We haven't heard from the dragons yet. Seeger?'

# Six

*We would be happy to go on another adventure with you,* Shadreer said. *It will fill in the time while we wait for the army to get organised.*

*After all,* Azree said, *it was just such an adventure that found us Fitzee. Who knows what we will find this time?*

I told the group that the dragons were happy to take us on the rescue mission.

'But ... But ...' Father said.

The Commander slapped Father on the back. 'It is decided, Beast-Master. General Mika and I will get to work on this as soon as we are back in Seddon. I'll send messenger birds to Tatum in Midrash. Asher, when do you intend to leave?'

Asher beamed. 'The day after tomorrow, Sed willing,' he said. 'I just need to gather some supplies.' He turned to the dragons. 'Will you meet us, not tomorrow morning but the following morning? There is a low range of hills, a short distance from the western gate. We could meet you there.'

I didn't need to interpret. All four dragons nodded their agreement. Then they leaped into the air and, calling their goodbyes to me, they flew back to the Sea Caves.

Father shook his head. 'What am I going to tell Fee?'

*Hey,* Ajax shouted. *No one asked us camels. We want to go, too!*

The camels grumbled all the way back to Seddon. Father kept shooting angry glances at Asher. I hoped this hadn't damaged their friendship. Asher was cock-a-hoop now that he had got his way. He and Kieran chatted about maps and supplies. Riff and Riva rode side by side making moon eyes at each other and, with dread building in my gut, I thought of Mother.

# Seven

'You what?' Mother yelled. 'Our babies, Kane. Our babies!' She dropped into the nearest chair and began to wail.

Daisy, asleep in her nest of blankets near the stove, woke up and began to squeal in sympathy. Riva ran to the piglet, scooped her up and cuddled her. Father stood in the middle of the kitchen, his shoulders slumped and his arms dangling uselessly by his side. Riff and I stood back near the door keeping out of the way.

'Look what you've done,' Mother said, pointing a shaking finger at Riva and Daisy. 'You've even upset the piggie.'

'I think that was more likely you, than me,' Father muttered. I couldn't decide if he was being brave or foolish.

Perhaps Mother didn't hear him or perhaps she chose to ignore it, having more important things to focus on. 'We've only just got them back barely alive. Poor Riff's arm is crippled and Seeger faints whenever things get too emotional.'

I bristled at that. I do *not* faint.

Mother continued. 'Our sons are already damaged enough. Now you want to send them back into harm's way. They could die!'

She threw her apron over her head and cried even louder. I was surprised our neighbours hadn't come running to see who was being murdered. The combination of Mother's wailing and Daisy's squeals sounded as though we were being slaughtered by a pack of sand devils.

Father said the only thing that had any chance of saving him. 'It was the Commander's decision. Not mine. I had nothing to do with it.'

Mother lifted her apron back off her face. 'Well then, we will just refuse to let them go.'

Father shook his head. 'We have no choice, Fee. I'm the Beast-Master of Seddon, answerable to the Ruling Council. I must obey the commands given to me, whether I like them or not. We all have our responsibilities. I will do my job. Riff, Riva and Seeger will go with Asher and Felix to rescue Kieran's sister. You will continue to nurture Daisy and help her grow into a strong young sow. She needs you more than the boys do, right now.'

Mother sniffed. Her eyes flashed. Although her weeping had slowed down, her anger was still a raging fire. 'Why do Riff and Riva need to go?' she said stiffly.

Father sighed and sat down facing her, speaking to her more gently now that she was somewhat calmer. 'Asher needs an older, reliable person to help him on the mission.'

'Older?' Mother said.

'He has nearly twenty years, Fee, so yes, older. Talia has dismissed Riff from the well-keepers but that doesn't mean he's forgotten his training. He's still fit and strong, apart from that one arm. Riva will be a help with any animals they come across. Also, she'll be company for the other female in the party, as well as for the rescued girl. Riva is a capable young woman and she will be a strong asset to Asher's team. What's more, they'll have Felix with them.'

Mother nodded slowly. 'I see. And Seeger?'

'He's the only one who can dragon-speak. It is essential that he goes with them.'

She didn't seem impressed. 'Who is this Felix person?'

Father held her hand. 'He's the best archer in all of Seddon. He will keep our loved ones safe.'

'You should see him in action, Mother,' I said. 'He can shoot down a fly at a hundred paces.'

She glared at me. 'Well, when you are attacked by a swarm of flies you will have nothing to worry about.' Her head whipped around to Riva and Daisy. 'Daisy! That's enough. Riva, take her into the gathering room, please. I can't hear myself think.'

Realising she was being banished, Daisy squealed all the louder. Riva grabbed some bread—I assume to bribe the piglet into silence—and took her away. For such a little thing, Daisy could make an enormous racket. I guess it was a sign that her lungs were clearing up.

'A simple rescue mission, you say,' Mother said. 'So, it shouldn't take too long?'

Father patted the hand he was holding. 'Asher is convinced it will be easily done.'

She nodded. 'I see. And then, they'll come straight home.'

I could tell that Father hadn't much practice in lying to her. He should have agreed right away but he made the mistake of hesitating. She was on to it, like a seagull on a lazy crab.

She yanked her hand away. 'Tell me they'll come straight home, Kane.'

He tried to grab her hand again but she pulled it away. 'They'll come home as soon as they can,' he said.

'What aren't you telling me?' she demanded.

He did his best to recover. 'I promise, they *will* come home once the mission is over. I just can't say when that will be. They've got a few errands to do for the Commander, as well as rescuing Kieran's sister.'

A few errands? Like: deal with Captain Blunt and his growing army; fight the Xanthi and negotiate a peace treaty. I guess "errands" was one way of putting it.

'You know how it goes,' Father said. 'Sometimes these things get a little more complicated than expected. But, you don't need to worry, Fee. They'll also have four dragons with them, all of whom are devoted to Seeger. They won't let any harm come his way.'

She sniffed again and stood up. 'There's something you're not saying. I can tell. But, I can also tell you have no intention of coming clean. I warn you, I *will* find out. In the meantime, I'd best get some clothing sorted for the three of them. They'll need something warmer if they're going into the western region. It can be a lot cooler there.'

She left the room. Father sagged in his chair and rubbed his forehead. Riff and I quickly looked at each other and then went to his side.

Riff said. 'Are you all right, Father?'

He glared at us both and then he jabbed his finger at Riff's chest. 'Don't you think for one moment that I'm happy about this! I blame you, Riff. You've encouraged Asher in this hair-brained scheme and you've dragged your brother into it with you. I am so angry I think you'd both best leave the house for a while in case I do something I'll later regret.'

I didn't need to be told twice. I swiftly headed for the back door. From behind me I heard Riff say, 'But, Father—'

'GET OUT!' Father roared.

We both ran out into the yard, where we stood looking at each other.

'I don't know about you but I'm not going back in there for a while,' I said. 'Will Mother be all right?'

'I have no idea,' Riff said. 'I've never seen them this angry with each other, or with us.'

'So, what do we do now?' I said. Riff shrugged. 'I think I'll go to the stables,' I said. 'Want to come with me?'

He shook his head. 'I'll take a stroll down to the docks. See you tonight.' He left through the side gate. I saddled Shirra and asked her to take me to the stables.

Shirra didn't speak to me all the way there. I could tell she was upset with me, too. I couldn't miss it; not with all the rumbling and puffing she was doing. When I led her into her stall I said, 'I'll go get Suri.'

She didn't answer. Instead, she turned her head away from me and rudely blew air out of her cheeks, her lips extended and flapping.

'Don't be like that,' I said. 'Please. It's bad enough that Mother and Father are both on the warpath. I don't need you being angry with me as well.'

*We've just got you home and you want to leave us again,* she said. *If you must go, then why can't I take you there? What if I never see you again?*

I rubbed her cheeks. 'I'm sorry, Shirra. If the General says she needs some camels, I'll ask Father to include you and then I can meet you in Midrash. It'll only be a few seven nights at the most before we're reunited. All right?'

She grumbled but eventually agreed. *Very well, but if anything happens to you and you die, I'm warning you now I'll never speak to you again.*

The atmosphere during the evening meal was chilly. No

one said anything apart from yes, no and pass the bread. Mother had burned the chicken but no one dared complain.

*A bit of charcoal won't bother me,* Daisy said.

*You're obviously feeling better,* I said. *Perhaps you should go back to the sty with your siblings.*

She sneezed and made a little wheezing sound. Mother immediately got up and hurried over to the piglet's bed, to fuss over her.

*You sly minx!* I said. *You've certainly landed on your trotters in this house.*

*I'm just a little piggie that's not well. Don't be mean to me.*

'Seeger? Seeger!' Father said. 'Who are you talking to?'

I shook my head. I'd forgotten he could read my face. 'Just Daisy, Father. She's telling me that she's improved a lot but she's still not well.'

'You don't need to beast-speak to know that.' Riff said. 'You can tell from just looking at her. Even I can see it.'

Riva held out the bread plate to him and Riff took another chunk. That was his third for the meal!

Riva said, 'I expect that Seeger's just giving us a summary of the conversation, rather than a word for word report. Am I right?'

She looked at me with one eyebrow raised. I don't know how she does it. I've tried to do it but every single time both brows go up together.

'That's right,' I said. 'We were just chatting.'

Mother said, 'Hmph!' and came back to the table. She took the bread from Riva and carried it over to the counter top. Then she broke off a couple of pieces, dipped them in the leftover chicken fat, and gave them to Daisy.

'Tomorrow morning,' Father said, 'I'll take the three of you to the cobbler. You'll need some sturdy boots for your trip. The western region around Forabad is too cold for sandals.'

71

Mother sniffed and hmphed again, but she didn't say anything.

'Thank you, Kane,' Riva said.

'Yes, thanks,' I said.

Riff added his thanks to mine. Father nodded, drained his beaker of ale and stood up. 'I have some accounts to work through. I'll be in my office. Thank you for the delightful meal, Fee.'

She mumbled something about "burned" but didn't turn to look at him. He stared at her back for a moment before sighing and leaving the room.

The next day we went with Father to the markets and, as well as a new pair of boots, he bought us each a warm jacket. Mother had given Riva a list of food supplies to buy. She said she didn't trust Asher to feed us properly. She refused to come with us, saying that Daisy needed her at home. I wouldn't be surprised if, by the time we return to Seddon, that piglet will have moved into my room and made it her own.

Early the following morning, we sat at the table eating porridge with honey and toasted bread with cheese. Mother still wasn't speaking to us. She plonked the dishes down in front of us, with a great deal of sighing and groaning but without saying one word.

Finally, it was time to leave. Father said he'd walk with us to the western gate. Mother stood in the kitchen cradling Daisy as if she were a baby. Mother's eyes were dark with grief. Still she said nothing.

I ran to her and threw my arms around her and the piglet. 'I love you, Mother. I promise that I'll come back. Please god-speak for us every day, as I will for you.'

She jerked her head in a brief nod and pinched her lips together.

Riva also gave her a hug goodbye and then kissed her on the cheek. 'I won't forget the things you've taught me. You're the mother I've always wanted. Don't worry. We'll be back before you know it.'

With one arm, the other still cradling Daisy, Mother returned Riva's hug. Her chin wobbled.

Riff then said his farewell. 'I'll make sure we all return safe and sound, Mother. I promise that we will make you proud.'

Mother patted him on his back and then the salt water spilled out of her eyes.

'I love you all,' she said. 'Stay safe and may Sed bring you all home again. Keep an eye on Asher. Sometimes his enthusiasm can cause him to make rash decisions.'

We promised, hugged her again and then we picked up our swags and followed Father out of the house and down the road that headed to the docks. My new leather boots squeaked as I walked. Father said they would soon soften with wear and the squeaking would cease. I was grateful that he had decided to walk with us because I had no idea how to get to the western gate, never having been there before. Father also led Shirra, so that he could ride her back to the stables once we had left. I had begged her to behave herself with no emotional outbursts and, so far, she had kept her word.

We found the others already waiting at the gate. Bevan was there, pacing up and down and looking agitated. When he saw us, he rushed up and grabbed Father by the arm.

'What's going on, Kane?' he said. 'Do you want to break his mother's heart?'

'You should be proud of Boyd,' Father said. 'He is on a noble mission, commissioned by the Commander himself.'

Bevan let go of Father's arm and resumed pacing up and down in front of us, his arms waving in the air as he spoke.

'He's off on a fool's errand. He should stay here, go to Foundation and get his life back in order!'

Father stared at Bevan for a moment and then he said, 'No amount of beating will force the lad to become the sort of man you wish him to be, Bevan. He has sixteen years. He needs to make his own way in the world.'

Boyd's dad stood still, staring at Father with his eyes opened wide. He took a breath but before he could say anything, Father spoke again.

'Don't deny it, Bevan. We know he hasn't been fighting. We know you beat him. While he's gone, perhaps you can use the time wisely. Talk with Jonathan about controlling your frustration and anger, before you totally destroy your family.'

Bevan stood still, staring at Father. I could see his chest heaving. His fists were clenched at his side and there were high spots of red on his cheeks.

'How dare you,' he said. 'I don't need you to tell me how to care for my family.'

Father didn't reply, he just looked at his old friend with pity shining out of his eyes. Felix walked over and stood shoulder to shoulder with Father, staring at Bevan while holding his bow. Finally, Bevan sagged, as though all the air had been sucked out of him.

'Very well,' he said. He turned to Boyd. 'Make sure you come home again. Good luck.'

'Thanks, Dad,' Boyd said.

His father was already walking away. As a farewell gesture, he briefly held his hand up in the air but he didn't look back. Then he turned the corner and was gone.

Father thanked Felix, who dipped his head in reply.

I patted Boyd on the back and he smiled ruefully at me. I

saw Rimini watching us both, so I said, 'Your father's not here, Rimini?'

She shook her head but didn't answer.

I then saw her shiny new footwear. 'At least he bought you some boots for the journey.'

She shook her head again. Boyd said, 'Asher bought us both a pair. He said that sandals wouldn't be good enough.'

We gathered up our swags and the kitbags stuffed full of supplies and, after saying a final farewell to Father and Shirra, we walked out of the western gate taking the road that headed towards the low hills in the distance. It didn't take long for my back to ache from carrying one of the heavy bags. Thank Sed, it would only be for a short distance and then the dragons would take up the burden. Even though it was still early in the morning, the sun already beat down on our shoulders. I questioned the need for fur-lined jackets and leather boots.

# Eight

It turned out the hills weren't as close as they seemed. Distances can be deceptive when the land is flat and the air is shimmering with the heat. For quite some time, no matter how long we walked we didn't seem to draw any closer.

Felix, Boyd and Rimini looked as though they could keep walking all day but the rest of us struggled, mainly due to the heavy baggage we carried. A couple of times Asher called for a short halt and we would all gratefully sink down onto the ground. All that is except Felix, Rimini and Boyd. They remained alert, constantly scanning the horizon.

In too short a time Felix would say, 'Come on. Time's a-wasting.'

We'd then heave ourselves back up, hoist up our bags and start walking again. I couldn't get over how unfit I was compared to Boyd and Rimini. I remembered the trek through the wastelands to Midrash and how weak Riva, Kieran and I were, compared to the soldiers and well-keepers. I hoped that, just like then, we would toughen up as the journey continued.

I looked at Riff, who was red in the face and breathing roughly. 'Are you all right, Riff?' He nodded. 'You're still recovering from your injury. Would you like me to carry your swag for a while?'

He fiercely shook his head. 'I'm just a little out of practice.' He took some deep breaths. 'I'll get there. You just worry about yourself.'

Only one traveller passed us along the way. It was a cloth merchant from Boron; his goods piled up in the back of his cart. He tipped his hat in greeting but didn't stop. Asher said that the western gate wasn't used as often as the ones on the east and in the north. So, the lack of traffic wasn't that surprising.

My new boots were rubbing the tops of my toes. I expected that there'd be blisters by the end of the day. I could tell by the way Riva was placing her feet that she was having a similar problem. She didn't complain. She walked steadily onwards, keeping up with Riff's long strides even though they were nearly double the length of her own.

Finally, we seemed to have made some headway. The hills in the distance appeared bigger than they were when we set out. Instead of the blurred shapes that they were first thing in the morning, I could now make out some distinguishing features: large boulders, clumps of saltbush and even some small crevices. I could see where the road wound its way into and through the ranges. I stood still for a moment and studied the sky and the peaks in front of me, hoping to spot the dragons, but I couldn't see anything. Not that that meant much. Those beasts had an uncanny knack of hiding in plain sight.

Finally, as the road began to curve towards the gap in the hills I heard a familiar voice.

*There you are! We have been waiting for ages.*

*Greetings, Hizaree. I can't tell you how glad I am to hear you. My feet are killing me.*

*How strange,* the young dragon said. *Why would your feet want to do that?*

*They're not used to walking so far.*

*Do not fret. Soon, you will be sitting astride Shadreer's strong back and then you can make friends with your feet once more.*

'Asher,' I said. 'The dragons are nearby. I can hear them.'

'Thank Sed for that,' he said, lifting his hat up to wipe his sweaty forehead. 'My feet are killing me! Where do they want us to meet them?'

*Hizaree, where shall we meet you?*

*Stay where you are and we will come to you. There is no one on the road, in either direction, so there is no need to hide.*

'They say we can stay here,' I said. 'There's no one coming so it should be safe.'

Asher dropped his bundle and sank down on top of it. 'Brilliant,' he said.

Once we were astride the dragons and according to Asher flying south-west, the journey was suddenly easier. Asher was with me on Shadreer, so he could give directions to the Leader of the Flight. Felix and Kieran rode Azree; Riff and Riva rode Hizaree, and Boyd and Rimini rode Fitzee. I watched Boyd as we took off and noticed that he kept his head down. It was just as I remembered from the first time we flew on a dragon. He was like Asher: heights made him uneasy.

It was fascinating to see how the landscape changed below us, the further we flew. At first, it was the same terrain in which Seddon lies: red sandy soil, interrupted by occasional clumps of yellow, brown and white boulders and the grey haze of salt bush. But gradually, the earth turned from red to brown. The boulders remained but they were now shaded by spindly, stumpy trees with a scattering of leaves on the ends of their branches. Grasses and shrubs took over from the salt bush.

We stopped at midday, at the base of a low hill that was covered with high grasses and low trees. While the dragons guarded our gear, we all took off in different directions to relieve ourselves. The boys headed towards the trees and the girls ran into the long grasses, where they soon dropped from view. The dragons thought that was hilarious and I could hear the rumble of their laughter as I searched for the right bush to water.

Shadreer said, *I suppose this is something to do with privacy?*

*That's right.*

*All creatures relieve themselves, hatchling. I do not understand why you try to keep it a secret.*

*It's not a secret! We just don't want to see or to be seen while we're doing it.*

*How odd,* the dragon said.

Once we were flying again, I asked Asher about the changes I could see happening on the ground below. I described them in detail because he had his eyes firmly shut.

'Surely you didn't think that all the world was desert, Seeger?' he said.

'I used to when I was younger,' I said. 'What causes these changes?'

'There isn't a simple answer,' he said. 'It depends on where the land is in relation to the great ice shelves in the south. It depends on the type of soil and what nutrients are in it. Then there's the distribution of seeds by birds and other creatures. The further south we go, the closer we are to the land of ice, and the cooler the temperature and the higher the rainfall. It's a complicated matter, Seeger.'

'Will it be like this at Forabad?'

He shook his head, which caused his hat to flap. He slapped a hand on top of it and pushed it down tighter. 'No, no,' he said. 'There are more changes to come yet. You'll see.'

Of course, he was right. By the time we were looking for a place to spend the night, the spindly trees had been replaced by taller, sturdier ones with thicker foliage. We camped that night with a rocky cliff at our backs and a thick copse of trees in front of us. Shadreer and Fitzee slept up on the hill behind us, while Hizaree and Azree stayed below. There wasn't room for all four of them in the clearing. It was a bit of a squeeze but sleeping up against the dragon's sides gave us some extra warmth during the long cold night. In the morning, a few of the less sturdy trees on the edge of our campsite leant at an interesting angle, although they had been upright the night before.

In the morning, the dragons went hunting while Riff and Riva prepared breakfast and Felix and Asher studied the map that the Record-Keeper had brought with him. Both men were doing a lot of pointing at or tapping on the map, and then waving their arms about. I don't think they agreed on the best route to take.

Kieran and I took the water flasks to refill them at a nearby spring. The dragons had smelled the water the previous evening, which is why they had brought us to that spot.

We crouched down next to the trickling stream that tumbled over the rocks and held out the flasks to fill them.

# Eight

'How long do you think it will take us to get there?' I asked Kieran.

'Hopefully only one more night but maybe two.'

'How long would it have taken us to walk it?' I said. I lifted the flask out of the water, screwed the cap tight and reached for another one.

He shrugged. 'Before we left Seddon, I would have said about two seven nights but after seeing how Asher coped before the dragons met us, I now think it might have been a full lunar cycle. Or even longer. Thank Sed, we have the Flight.'

I laughed.

'What's so funny?'

I screwed the cap back on the flask and put it down next to the first one. Then I patted him on the back. 'I never thought the day would come when I would hear you say such a thing.'

He smiled back at me. 'You say true.' His smile faded. 'How are you managing, Seeger?'

'What do you mean?'

'The situation with Riff and Riva.'

I didn't answer straight away. I held another flask in the stream and watched the water trickling over the pebbles and weeds while I thought about it. The breeze wafting through the nearby trees made it sound as though the wood was sighing with me.

'I don't like it but there's nothing I can do,' I said. 'I must get used to the notion that I will never kiss her again, or hold her close, or share secrets like we used to do. I won't be that special person in her life. Riff will.'

He put his hand on my shoulder. 'I think you're giving the impression of holding up very well.'

'Thanks.'

By the time we got back to camp Felix and Asher had reached an agreement, the map was back in Asher's kit and breakfast was ready. I helped Riva serve it out. Rimini watched us as we handed out the porridge. When I brought a bowl to her she mumbled her thanks but, instead of tucking in, she continued to study me as I served the others.

When we went back to Riff, who was in charge of the pot, I leant in and whispered, 'What's going on with Rimini? She keeps staring at me.'

Riff whispered back, 'Well, it can't be your good looks.'

'Very funny. Ha. Ha,' I said.

'She watches all of us,' Riva said. 'Give her time. She'll soon get to know us.'

We cleaned the pot and bowls down at the spring and then packed up the camp. We didn't have long to wait for the dragons to return. Hizaree said they'd found a flock of wild goats but I told him I didn't want to hear the details. With full bellies, we set off on the next leg of the journey.

The morning's flight was uneventful. Once again, I watched the changing landscape below. The hills became higher. Some had rounded slopes, like an old man's shoulders, covered in green grasses. I'd never seen so much green before! Other hills were bare and jagged, with rocky fingers poking up into the sky. As the morning wore on, we saw more trees and less open plains. A herd of griven, that were grazing in a clearing, scattered in a mad rush for the shelter of the trees when the dragons' shadows slid over them.

At midday the dragons let us dismount and then took off straight away. They wanted to see if they could find those griven. Once again, we found a private spot to relieve ourselves. Afterwards, Riva handed out some dried figs that she had stashed in her kitbag and Kieran cut us some slices of cheese. Apart from Asher, who chose to eat sitting in the shade of an old paperbark tree, the rest of us took the opportunity to walk around for a change. It was a peaceful spot, apart from the cawing of a crow somewhere.

From the shelter of his tree Asher said, 'I wish that bird would shut up.'

I stood still and listened. The bird did seem to have a lot to say: Aaah! Aaah! Aaaaaaah! Then there was a jolt in my head and I could understand what it was saying: *Help! Help!*

'Can you see where it is, Asher?' I said.

Asher stood up, brushing the dust off his backside. He joined me out in the centre of the clearing and we both searched the tops of the trees that surrounded us.

'What are you doing?' Rimini said.

'There's a crow out there,' I said, waving my hand above my head. 'It needs our help. We're trying to find it.'

'I like birds,' she said as she helped us search the trees.

*Over here! Over here!* the bird called. *Get a move on. I'm going to faint. I just know it.*

Boyd put away the knife he'd been sharpening against a rock and joined us. Suddenly Rimini flung her arm out, pointing to a tree diagonally across from us. 'Over there. Look. It's hanging upside down.'

For a moment I couldn't see it but then the shadows shifted and there it was, its wings flapping and its head hanging down. It was looking straight at us.

*Hurry up!*

We ran to the tree. I said, 'Its foot is caught in something.' I turned to Rimini, 'Give me a leg up. Don't worry, little crow, we'll soon have you down.'

*Oh please,* it said, sarcasm dripping off each word. *I'm not a crow, I'm a raven. Any dummy could tell you that.*

I said to Asher, 'It says it's a raven, not a crow. I can't see any difference.'

*Look at my neck. See those fine feathers? I'll raise them up. See? That's my hackles. I've got hackles, pal. Crows don't have hackles. Honestly! The ignorance of the great unwashed!*

'Cheeky beggar!' I said.

Asher called up to me. 'What did he say?'

I pointed to the long feathers ruffled at the front of his neck. 'He says ravens have hackles like these and crows don't.'

'That's not cheeky,' Asher said.

'He called me the great unwashed!' Asher pinched his lips together and made a spluttery sound. 'It's not funny, Asher!'

He burst out laughing. 'Yes, it is!'

I glared at him. Felix, Kieran, Riff and Riva heard his laughter and wandered over to see what was happening.

Asher pointed towards the bird's head. 'Its eyes are still brown, so it's a youngster. They turn white when they're adults.'

*Not completely ignorant then,* it said.

'How do you know that?' I said.

Asher preened. 'As Kieran said, I know lots about all sorts of things.'

Kieran sighed. 'I wish I'd never said that.'

'And,' Asher continued, 'I also know ravens and crows belong to the same family and there's really no difference.' The bird screeched. 'Apart from the hackles, of course,' Asher said, 'and that most ravens are bigger than crows and that they hate each other. They're feuding cousins.'

I was finally sitting astride the branch from which the raven dangled. By now the whole crew had gathered below the tree and were watching intently.

# Eight

'The dragons will be back soon,' Felix said. 'We haven't got time for this. It's just a bird.'

Boyd turned to him. 'Every life is precious! We don't leave anyone or anything in captivity. Not one! Get it?'

Felix shrugged. The bird stared at him. I think Felix made an enemy then.

'You be careful up there,' Riva called.

'Yes, Mother!' I called back. I inched my way along the branch. 'Hey, there are bits of what looks like netting wrapped around the tree.'

'Probably a fowler's net,' Felix said. 'Someone's been catching birds to fill their cooking pot. I saw a small village towards the east as we flew over the wood. Mind you, I wouldn't have thought that ravens would make for fine dining.'

'It has somehow snagged its foot in the mesh,' I said.

'I'm coming up so you can use my knife to cut it free,' Boyd said, grabbing hold of the lowest branch and pulling himself up.

*I'm sorry Mr Raven,* I said. *Was the rest of your flock caught in the nets, too?*

*I don't want to talk about it.*

Once Boyd had reached me, I edged a bit closer to the bird. *Please excuse me, friend, but I am going to hold you steady. Don't peck me. All right?*

*Fair enough, squire, but if you hurt me all bets are off.*

*I'll be very careful.* I reached out my right hand and gently held the bird's body, tucking its wings against its sides. With my other hand I pulled up the net so that Boyd could slide the knife under the mesh and cut the trapped claws free.

*Easy! Easy! Don't stab me, human!*

'Not long now,' I said. 'There, it's done.' A cheer went up from the audience below us. 'Will you be all right if I let you go?'

*Pfft!* it said. *Of course I'll be all right. I'm a raven, I am. Get a grip, pal.*

I let go and the bird fluttered down, landing on the ground in front of everyone, where it promptly fell over.

'You might have to stay off that foot for a while,' I called, as Boyd and I began to edge our way back along the branch. 'Riff, would you please hold it until I get there?'

I heard Boyd suck in his breath but I didn't think much of it until I saw Riff try to pick up the bird. The creature fluttered and squawked and Riff couldn't get a good grip. I'm such an idiot! I'd forgotten about his ruined arm. Riva's glare shot daggers at me and Riff went red in the face.

Rimini said, 'Can I hold him? Please?'

Riff nodded. 'Feel free.'

'Thanks. I love birds.' She carefully scooped the raven up and held it firmly with both hands. Once I'd reached the ground, I apologised to Riff which seemed to annoy him even more. Riva sniffed and, linking her arm through Riff's good one, she led him away. I sighed, thanked Rimini and while she still held the bird, I looked at its foot. It didn't seem broken but it was rubbed raw from its struggle against the netting and it might have been sprained.

'Looks like you'll need some help for a while, fella,' I said. 'We should wrap it up.'

Felix walked back towards our bags. 'Time to go,' he called. 'Everyone put on your jackets. We'll be heading further south, so it's going to get colder.'

'There's some bandages in my kit,' Kieran said. 'We'll fix it up at the next stop.'

The others took their cue from Felix and began to get ready to leave. I could hear the flap of the dragons' wings as they circled, preparing to land.

*Warning! Warning! Monsters coming back,* the bird called.

# Eight

'It's all right,' I said. 'They're our monsters. Rimini, would you take care of the bird for now?'

She nodded shyly and very carefully tucked him down the front of her tunic, holding him in place with her left hand.

'You should be safe in there,' I said. 'Thanks, Rimini.'

Boyd ran up, holding Rimini's coat. 'Here. You'll need this.' He helped her put it on.

*I don't suppose you have any spare seed or nuts handy?* the bird said.

'No,' I said. 'We'll find you some food next time we stop.'

*Fair enough. Wake me up when it's time to eat.* His head drooped forward and he promptly fell asleep. Within seconds he was making a funny wheezing sound.

Rimini grinned at me. 'He's snoring!' She ran over to Fitzee, still cradling the bird inside her tunic, and Boyd helped her mount the dragon.

# Nine

Felix was right. It grew colder and colder as we flew on. The air was snapping against my cheeks, running icy fingers down the back of my coat.

Late in the afternoon Shadreer said, *We must find shelter. There is a storm approaching from the south.*

I shouted this news in Asher's ear. He nodded and bellowed back, 'According to my maps, there should be a low mountain range in this area. I suggest we try to find something there.'

Shadreer passed on Asher's advice to the other dragons and all four banked slightly towards the left. Soon I could see the hills up ahead. I could also see the sky turning grey and the clouds churning. We were racing straight towards the storm. The dragons flapped their enormous wings and picked up speed. We reached the range just as the first drops of rain began to fall.

The dragons skimmed over the tops of the peaks, as we all studied the land below us looking for a possible site to land.

# Nine

'There! There!' Kieran shouted, pointing towards one of the smaller hills. 'I'm sure I saw a cave.'

The dragons swerved in the direction of his outstretched arm. We all peered ahead, trying to see what Kieran could see. The wind was now howling in our ears, while snatching at our clothes. Asher kept one hand firmly planted on his hat. I was pleased to see that his knees tightly squeezed Shadreer's side. I hoped that the others were doing the same. The last thing we needed was for someone to fall off.

*I see it!* Hizaree said. *Follow me!*

He peeled off, racing away in front of the Flight. Shadreer muttered something about reckless youngsters. Then, above the howling of the wind I could hear Riff and Riva cheering. I squinted. At first I couldn't see anything but then, there it was: the dark yawning mouth of a cave near the base of the hill. It was partially concealed by a protruding rock shelf. We would have missed it if we had approached the mountain range at a slightly different angle.

The dragons took turns off-loading their human cargo, as there was only room for one of them in front of the entrance. From what I could see, the cave wasn't large enough to hold four dragons as well as eight people.

*What will you do?* I asked Shadreer. *I don't like the thought of you fellows being out in this weather.*

*Do not fear, hatchling. It will take more than a bit of wind and rain to bother us. We will find somewhere to roost, nearby. Stay here for the night. The storm will be gone by the morning.*

*As long as you'll be all right.*

*Of course. Sleep well.*

The Flight took off, flying into the storm, almost as if it were an act of defiance. I hurried into the cave. Felix had already gathered rocks to build a fire pit. He looked up at me and said, 'See if you can find something to burn, Seeger. Just don't wander too far away.'

'I'll help,' Boyd said.

We stood in the cave's entrance and studied the scene in front of us. We were in a wide ravine, with some straggly trees growing along its length. It looked as though it had been a river, sometime in its ancient past. There was a small stand of five trees just a short distance away to our left. We ran over to it.

Boyd said, 'I'll collect smaller pieces for kindling and you look for some bigger pieces.'

I nodded and began to scour the ground for fallen branches or, hopefully, a log or two.

'Thanks for what you did,' Boyd said.

'What? It's hard to hear you over this wind.'

He shouted, 'I said, thanks for what you did!'

I straightened up and frowned at him. 'What did I do?'

He juggled the few pieces he'd already collected in the crook of his arm. 'Trusting Rimini with the bird.'

I flapped my hand. 'Oh, no problem. I'm sure she'll do a good job looking after it.'

Boyd smiled. 'Of course, but you could have just as easily kept it for yourself. After all, you're the one who can beast-speak.'

I shook my head. 'You don't have to do that to look after a creature. The more time she spends with it, the better she'll get to know it. The raven will help her. It's a very clever bird.'

I saw a decent sized branch lying braced against one of the tree trunks and hurried over to pick it up. I had to give it a good tug, as the bottom was wedged into the dirt at the base of the tree but eventually it came free. I pulled it into the small space in the middle of the trees and then searched for more.

# Nine

The rain had moved past the droplets stage and was now falling steadily, pushed sideways by the wind.

'We'd better get a move on,' I shouted. 'The weather's getting worse.'

Boyd nodded. We scurried about, working as fast as we could to collect enough fuel for the fire to last through the night. When I had a reasonable pile of branches, I gathered up several of them and staggered back to the cave. I had to make several trips to get it all inside.

It didn't take Felix long to get a decent fire going and we huddled around it, trying to get warm. Asher had placed the cooking pot just outside the cave's entrance, past the rocky overhang, to collect some rainwater. Once it held a reasonable amount, he and Kieran brought it back in and placed it in the fire to heat the water. Riva and I chopped some tubers and threw them in the pot. Kieran added some dried herbs and Asher put in some dried strips of goat's meat.

While we waited for the soup to cook, I studied the rest of the group. Riff was in charge of stirring the pot. Riva had taken out our dishes and spoons and sat next to Riff, holding the eating utensils ready. Rimini was bent over the bird, stroking its head. I remembered that we needed to strap up his damaged foot so I reminded Kieran of his offer. He rummaged in his kitbag and found the first aid packet. He tore a strip off a larger piece of cloth and gave it to me. I took it to Rimini and she held the raven, while I bandaged its foot. She fed it the last of the dried figs and promised it some of her share of the goat's meat. I noticed she'd begun calling it, "Joffre" and it was happy about that. It seemed content to stay cradled in her lap.

*How are you?* I asked him.

*Just fine, squire,* he said. *I've never had a name before, apart from raven. Please tell this young human that I am grateful.*

'Rimini, Joffre thanks you for his name. He says he's never had a name before.'

She smiled and ran her fingers down his back. Boyd sat down next to Rimini and the raven.

'Remember when we were taken, Boyd?' I said. 'Sitting in the cavern, watching the fire?'

He nodded. 'It was the first time you'd ever eaten griven,' he said. 'You asked the Midrashi if he had anything you could eat instead.'

'I wonder what happened to old poo-breath?'

'I hope he's rotting in hell.'

Asher and Felix pored over the maps, again. Asher was muttering to himself; something about "slightly off-line" and "shouldn't be that far".

Felix put his finger on a row of inverted V shapes. 'I think this is the mountain range we're in. We're down here at the eastern end, where the hills are lower. See? Here's the ravine.'

Asher scratched his head, pushing his hat back off his forehead as he did so. 'Yes. Yes. I see,' he said. 'Then I should be looking over here …' He pointed at the left-hand corner. '… instead of over here. Hmm.' He tapped his long forefinger against his lips.

'Oh yes. Here we are!' he said. 'That's it, there!'

Felix frowned. 'I didn't think your friend lived so far out from Forabad.'

'Yes. Yes,' Asher said. 'He's retired and bought himself a little farm. Don't worry.' Felix was still frowning. 'It was only a short time ago, so he's still up with the latest information. The good thing about being out there is we won't have to worry too much about hiding the dragons. I gather hardly anyone bothers going out that way. It was one of the reasons he bought the property.'

# Nine

He rubbed his hands together. 'This is lovely, lovely. We should be there mid-morning tomorrow. Not long now, Kieran!'

Kieran smiled. Riva patted his back.

Riff said that the meal was ready so I got up to help hand it out, but Boyd told me to sit. 'You did most of the work gathering the fuel. I'll serve tonight.'

I didn't need telling twice! I plonked myself down next to Rimini and grinned my thanks to Boyd.

Felix said, 'Just a quick word, while we're all listening. Ladies use the back of the cave if you need to pass water. Men go outside. Understood?' We all nodded. 'Good.'

Joffre, the raven, muttered, *What am I supposed to do?*

*As long as you don't do it on any of us, or our gear, you can do what you like.*

He ruffled his feathers and hunched his head down. *You seem determined to spoil my fun.*

Shadreer was right. In the morning the storm was over, the sun was shining and it was a beautiful day. Several of us had dark shadows under our eyes and I, for one, couldn't stop yawning. Boyd must have had bad dreams during the night, as several times his shouting and screaming had woken us up. No one mentioned it and Boyd said nothing. I figured he'd talk about it if he wanted to.

Asher, of course, had slept like the dead and was now awake and full of energy. He was keen to get moving, knowing that his friend's home was only a short flight away. He kept hopping about, as if starting to dance and then changing his mind just as he was about to launch into a jig.

Our kit was packed, we'd finished breakfast and we'd all passed water. We were ready to go, but the dragons had not yet returned. We sat in the mouth of the cave and waited. I checked Joffre's foot and changed the bandage. It was still sore but he could put his weight on it while it was strapped up, so I knew it wasn't seriously damaged. He even had a quick fly around the area near the cave, to stretch his wings. When he returned, he swooped over us, dropping a white splotch on Felix's arm, and then perched on Rimini's shoulder.

Felix leapt up, glaring at Joffre. 'You miserable little ...! Why I ought to ...!' He rummaged through his kit, muttering to himself.

Joffre squawked. *I can't help it. After all, I'm just a bird.*

*You did that on purpose,* I said.

*He should have more respect.*

*He'll have even less now,* I said. *Behave yourself.*

Felix found a kerchief and rubbed the mess off his sleeve, all the while glaring at the offending bird. I noticed that Rimini sat with her hand over her mouth. Her eyes were sparkling. I'm sure she was trying not to laugh.

I said to Riva, 'I hope the dragons are all right. They don't usually keep us waiting.'

'It was a rough night,' she said, 'but I'm sure they're fine. They're strong beasts.'

*We are here, hatchling,* Shadreer said. *I apologise for keeping you waiting.*

I said, *Are you all well?*

*Of course. We found suitable shelter but it was a little farther away than we had hoped. We will land one at a time, so tell Azree's riders to be ready to mount up. Then it will be Fitzee, followed by Hizaree, and I will land last.*

'Felix and Kieran, Azree is about to land. You're up first.'

They ran to get their kit and within moments the dragon had landed. While they were climbing up onto Azree, I told Boyd and Rimini to get ready. Joffre squawked when she tucked him into her tunic again but he soon settled down when I told him it was the only way he'd be joining us. He couldn't possibly keep up with the speed of the dragons.

Riff took only a little bit longer to collect his gear. He's becoming more adept at doing things one-handed. I noticed that Felix took some of the cooking utensils with him this time. He didn't ask Riff, he just did it. Riff didn't react the way he usually did when I tried to help so I decided that from then on I'd do the same: I'd just do it without asking. I figured Riff was grateful for help if no one pointed out the reason why he needed it.

I held on to Asher as we flew. He kept jiggling, which worried me. I guess he was excited about seeing his friend. Finally, I shouted at him, 'Keep still, Ash! You'll have us both off if you keep squirming!'

'Sorry! Sorry!' he shouted back. After that, he settled down.

By mid-morning, I could see ahead of us a large city sprawled out on the plain. It wasn't surrounded by a wall, like Seddon or Midrash, and so there didn't seem to be any order to it. It was as if a giant had thrown a collection of buildings and roads down from a great height. It was splattered on the ground, the edges shooting out in all sorts of directions. I figured out it was Forabad, just before Asher shouted its name.

However, we didn't aim for the city. We headed instead towards a small collection of buildings situated some distance from Forabad. As we drew closer, we could see that it was a farmstead and, judging by the fencing, it was surrounded by a large stretch of land which seemed to contain mainly plots of trees—possibly fruit trees—and vegetable beds. There was plenty of room for the dragons to and and they headed towards an empty field behind a large shed at the back of the house.

As the Flight circled, a figure ran out of the house, waving both arms and yelling something. At first, I thought the man was warning us to leave. I figured that somehow the authorities in Forabad knew what we were up to and were lying in ambush. But then, as we drew closer, I could see he was grinning like a kid on Sed's birthday. His tall, skinny figure, with its wisps of floating white hair sprouting out below his hat, looked familiar.

*Well, well,* Shadreer said. *If Asher was not perched on my back, I would swear it were he down below.*

We landed close to the shed and began to climb down off our dragons. Asher slid off in a rush and ran, yelling, to the stranger, 'Luka! Luka, my dear fellow!'

The man was screaming even louder, 'Asher! Ash, my dear chap!'

They threw themselves into an embrace and then, in tandem, began to bounce up and down on the spot, laughing and thumping each other's backs.

Shadreer was right. The two men could be twins.

# Ten

## Boyd Speaks

When I told Dad about the trip to the West, he said, 'I forbid it!'

Ma didn't say anything but she wilted in her chair, like a wildflower out in the midday heat. The colour drained from her face and saltwater pooled in her eyes.

'We won't be gone long,' I said. 'Asher will be leading us and we will have one of the General's marksmen with us.'

Dad shook his head. 'I don't care. You're not going and that's that.' He pointed at Ma. 'Look what you've done. Don't you care for your mother?'

He was red in the face and his chest began to heave with his heavy breathing. I closed my eyes and braced myself for the punch I knew was coming.

'Bevan, please,' Ma said. 'I can't take this violence anymore. Leave the boy alone!'

I opened my eyes. Dad was standing close to me, his arm raised. He stood frozen like that for a moment or two, or twenty—it was hard to tell—and then he slowly lowered his arm. He backed away.

'Very well, Lorna,' he said, 'but don't you worry. He's not going. I won't let him.' He nodded as though his neck was stiff and sore. 'I'm off to the Noisy Duck.' He stormed out of the room.

'I'm sorry, Ma,' I whispered.

She shook her head and whispered back, 'I don't want to lose you again but I understand why you want to leave.' She pushed her hair back off her forehead but it immediately flopped back into place. 'He doesn't mean to be cruel. He's just out of his depth, at a loss to find the right way to go about things.'

'I know,' I said, 'but I can't wait until he's found it. He's killing me.'

Nothing more was said about it. When Asher bought the boots and tunics for Rimini and me, we left them at his house until the day of our departure to keep them secret.

The night before we left, I kissed my mother goodbye while Dad was out drinking. In the morning, I woke up while it was still dark and crept out of the house. I thought I'd got away with it. However, not long after I'd greeted the others at the gate, Dad turned up.

He grabbed me and shook me so hard that my teeth rattled in my skull. Asher threw his hands in the air, saying, 'No, no! This is not acceptable!'

Then Felix arrived. He ran to us and dragged Dad away from me. He put his hand on Dad's chest and said, 'You stay right there, sir. That's enough.'

Dad sucked in air, his chest still heaving and his face glowing red in the early morning light. He raised his fists up

# Ten

in front of him. 'Come on then,' he said. 'Take your best shot.'

Asher said, 'Now, now, sir. There's no need for that. Calm down.'

'Calm down?' Dad said. 'You're kidnapping my son and I'm supposed to calm down!' He took a step forward but Felix wouldn't let him pass.

'No one's kidnapping anyone,' Asher said. 'Boyd is one of our brave volunteers for a very important mission.'

I thought he took a bit of liberty with the truth there but I wasn't going to argue.

'I forbid him to go!' Dad said.

Felix put a hand on Dad's chest again, which was promptly slapped away. 'The lad has sixteen years, sir. He's old enough to make his own choices.'

Dad began pacing up and down, his hands still clenched. He said he'd get us thrown in the Watch-house. He said he'd rally a group of his friends and they'd ride out after us and teach us a lesson we'd never forget. He called Asher a "child-snatcher" and Felix a "jumped up thug". He was just getting into his stride when Seeger, Riff, Riva and Kane turned up. He immediately ran up to Seeger's father and grabbed his arm.

I'm not sure what Kane said to Dad. I stood back out of the way. However, something Kane said stopped Dad dead in his tracks. I could see he was shocked. Felix walked over and stood shoulder to shoulder with Kane. Then, it was as if all the air was sucked out of him. Dad's shoulders drooped, his head fell forward and his hands unclenched. He turned around, wished me luck and told me to make sure I came home again. Then, that was that. He walked away, not once looking back.

I couldn't believe it! I thanked Kane. He put his hand, briefly, on my shoulder and said, 'Your father loves you, Boyd.' I nodded and no more was said.

I was proud of the way Rimini and I kept pace with Felix. I could hear the others puffing and wheezing as they walked. Rimini was on full alert, even though we weren't marching into battle. Old habits die hard.

I felt sick when I had to climb up onto the dragon's back. I could see how little the others worried about it. In fact, they all seemed to enjoy it. I couldn't get the image out of my mind of that perilous flight in the middle of the night, my hands tied to the pommel of my saddle, being carried away from home. I tried opening my eyes but the world lurched and the ground was so far away. I shut my eyes again and kept my head down. Apart from my allergy to heights, the first day and night was uneventful. The further we flew away from Seddon, the lighter the weight on my shoulders. I even began to enjoy myself.

Then we found the bird hanging from a tree and I was consumed with rage. The world is a cold, hard, cruel place. When Felix said we shouldn't worry about it as it was only a bird, I couldn't keep quiet. Only a bird? I know Rimini and Seeger got it, but the others obviously didn't understand. Why is it always the weak, the small, the innocent and the vulnerable that are made to suffer? How can anyone with an ounce of humanity in their bones stand by and watch another living thing suffering and do nothing about it. If I had a sword I'd have run Felix through, so it was just as well that I wasn't armed.

Later, as we flew on from there, Rimini said, 'It's not Felix's fault. He hasn't lived with the Midrashi.'

She was right, of course. Gradually the red tide of anger ebbed and I could breathe evenly once more. However, that night as the storm raged outside the cave, every time I tried to sleep ghosts would haunt me. I'd see that little lad in the sorting arena, losing his head. I'd see Drebbin lying on the

# Ten

ground, blood streaming from where his feet used to be, saying, 'Please, Boyd. Please?' I'd see Idris smiling at me as Derk thrust the blade into his side. I'd see the children who died while on patrol, shot with arrows or caught in traps. I'd see the homes of the Rigoni burning and hear the families screaming. I'd plead for their forgiveness. I'd beg them to go away. For a short while they'd leave me in peace and then it'd start all over again.

In the morning, I noticed that several of our group had dark smudges under their eyes. Seeger kept yawning and then apologising for his rudeness. He'd flick a glance at me and then act as if nothing was wrong. I couldn't look at them, so I went to sit in the mouth of the cave. Soon after, the rest of the group joined me as we waited for the dragons. I was about to say I was sorry for keeping them awake but, just then, the little raven pooped on Felix's sleeve. It took all my energy not to giggle. If it had been Seeger, or Asher, I would have laughed, but Felix is another story; he didn't see the funny side. Still, I was grateful for the bird as its antic released some of the tension that was fizzing in the air around us.

We finally drew near to Forabad—a strange looking city—and headed towards the homestead of Asher's friend. I'd wondered what the fellow was going to look like but I never could have imagined the reality. He was the mirror image of Asher!

# Eleven

## Seeger Speaks

I thanked Shadreer for the safe flight before climbing down and standing next to him, all the while watching Asher and his friend, hugging each other and jumping up and down together.

*I did not realise there was room in this world for two Ashers,* Shadreer said.

*I know! It's uncanny how much they are alike.*

*It is a good thing for friends to reunite. One day I will greet Myrmee again and we will also celebrate.*

*I bet it won't be quite like that!* I said. *I'm trying to picture the two of you hugging each other and dancing around but it doesn't seem likely.*

*Of course not,* he said. *We dragons have dignity. Nevertheless, it is a grand thing to be reunited with those you love.*

Felix walked up to the two cavorting men and said, 'Asher. ASHER! Time is a-wasting. Shall we get on?'

The two men calmed down and, still grinning like children at a birthday feast, turned to face the rest of us.

'This is my cousin, Luka,' Asher said.

'I thought you said we were meeting your friend,' Kieran said.

'Yes, yes. He's my cousin and my dear, dear friend. We've always been close. When we were little, people mistook us for brothers.'

'Welcome to my home,' Luka said, as he stared at the dragons. 'They're lovely, fearsome beasties. I never thought I'd see the day when dragons would come to Firestone. Oh my, Ash ...' he thumped Asher on the back, 'how can I ever repay you for such a treat? Err ... will they be staying?'

'No,' Asher said. 'They're about to leave.'

Luka sighed. 'You'd best come inside.'

I thanked the Flight and suggested they find somewhere safe to roost and rest, but near enough to hear my call. We began to file into the house but when Luka saw that Joffre was on Rimini's shoulder and was coming in as well, he put his hand up and said, 'I'm sorry, young lady, but I can't have that bird inside. It's unlucky to have a black bird in the house.'

Felix muttered, 'Hear. Hear.'

Joffre was not pleased. *I'll give him unlucky! The nerve of the fellow.*

*Behave yourself! It's his house and we're his guests. Surely you can manage on your own out here for a while?*

He ruffled his feathers. *I suppose so. I'll go chat with the chickens.*

I wasn't sure if he could be trusted around the hens, so I said, *Don't you dare hurt them!*

*Oh please. Have you seen the size of those things? I wouldn't dare try. No, I'll just pass the time of day with them and see if I can scrounge a feed.*

'What's wrong with the boy?' Luka said.

I shook my head and smiled at him. 'Nothing's wrong. Don't worry, Rimini, Joffre says he'll wait out here with the chickens.'

Luka spun around and grabbed Asher's arm. 'He's a beast-speaker?'

Asher nodded. 'Even better. He's a dragon-speaker. He's still discovering what he's capable of.'

Luka stared at me with a strange expression on his face. 'Extraordinary! Oh my. Just imagine the power—'

Asher interrupted, 'Now's not the time. Shall we go in?'

Unlike the houses in Seddon, there wasn't a separate kitchen and gathering room. There was just one central room, with a table at one end near the fire and cooking utensils, and some comfortable chairs arranged in a semi-circle at the other. The stairs leading up to the second floor, divided the two areas.

We piled our kitbags and swags together at the back of the room behind the chairs and settled down in the sitting area. Felix stood at the side of the window that faced the path, which led into the homestead from the main road. He regularly looked outside, forever on alert. Asher and Riff took a chair each, Rimini and Riva shared one and Kieran, Boyd and I sat on the floor, leaving one chair spare for Luka. He bustled around in the kitchen area, preparing some drinks.

Asher said, 'Come sit down, Felix. No one knows we're here.'

Felix ignored him. Asher sat perched on the edge of his seat, his hat in his lap. He'd been wearing it for too long and most of his locks were smeared onto his scalp, sodden with sweat. Only the bottom edges were dry and loose. He was too excited to relax and sit still. I watched him, fully expecting that at any moment he would leap up and begin jigging around the room. His feet were already tapping the beat.

'How long since you retired, Luka?' he said.

Luka arranged some mugs on a tray, while he waited for the milk to heat up. 'Oh, just over a seven night. Not long at all.' He reached up to a shelf above the counter top and took down a jar of spice. 'I'm sure that some of them haven't yet realised I've gone!'

Asher nodded. 'Luka was a record-keeper, same as me,' he said. 'If anyone will know how to find the information we need, it'll be him.'

Luka poured the milk into the mugs. Kieran got up and ran over to help him. 'I'll carry the tray for you,' he said.

'Thank you, young man,' Luka said, following him into the sitting area.

Kieran held the tray, while Luka handed out the mugs. We all murmured our thanks as he gave us our drink. Then Kieran put the tray down on the small table in front of the semi-circle of chairs and took his own drink before settling back down on the floor next to me. The mug was warm in my hands and smelled of cinnamon.

'Drink up, while I tell you the plan,' Luka said. 'Asher will masquerade as me. He will then be able to walk straight into the slave market and ask to check the records. He can simply announce that he's doing a surprise audit. They're used to that sort of thing. If they have heard about my retirement and challenge him, he can simply say that he's been given one last task as Vern is off sick.'

'Vern?' Asher asked.

'He's a co-worker in the Records Department. He's the regular auditor of the Slave Market.'

Riff said, 'Couldn't you just ask Vern to get the information?'

'He's ill with the lurgy and is home in bed,' Luka said. 'So, you will have a good excuse for being his replacement.'

Felix raised his hand. 'Why don't you go get us the information? Surely that would be simpler and less risky?'

Luka nodded. He put his mug down on the tray and scooted forward in his chair, his hands clasped in front of him. 'Of course! That would be quite sensible if not for one thing: my handicap.'

I studied Luka. I couldn't see anything wrong with him, apart from his skinniness and his age. I could see the others scrutinising him and, going by their frowns, they reached the same conclusion as me.

'I'm sorry,' Felix said. 'What handicap is that?'

Luka shrugged. 'I'm prone to attacks of extreme anxiety, to the point where I can't breathe. I vomit, or faint and I think I'm going to die. I'm afraid that … well … I'd simply go to water. Do you see?'

I remembered the times I lay curled up on the floor of Shirra's stall, or on my bed, unable to move except for the uncontrollable trembling. Oh yes, I saw. I wondered what had happened to Luka to make him like that.

We all nodded, except for Felix. He stared at Luka, with his eyes narrowed in suspicion.

Luka continued. 'Most of the time this has no impact on my life, provided I avoid stressful situations. It's one of the reasons I moved to this place. It's peaceful out here in the countryside.'

Felix looked out the window once more then turned to speak to Luka. 'So, you're a coward?'

Asher leaped out of his chair. 'How dare you, sir!'

Luka cringed as if he'd been struck, his eyes filling with saltwater. 'Asher?'

Riva rushed to the old man, squashed in beside him,

threw her arms around his chest and began to gently rock him.

'You're safe, sir,' she said. 'You're safe.' She glared at Felix. 'Just breathe, Luka. That's the way.'

Asher said, 'Don't judge what you don't understand!'

I was going to say something as well but Riff surprised me by speaking up. 'I've seen Seeger curled up into a whimpering, shaking ball, but he's one of the bravest people I know. I've learned not to be so hasty to judge another because of something I don't understand.'

Riva glowed with pride. Luka smiled at Riff. Asher patted his back. I stared at him with my mouth agape. Then I noticed Boyd looking at me, so I pressed my lips together. I could hear my father speaking in my head, 'Stop catching flies, Seeger.'

Felix shrugged. 'So, Asher, you will have to masquerade as your cousin.'

Asher beamed. 'It'll be easy! Unlike my dear cousin, I blossom in challenging situations.'

I remembered when he was challenged by a Midrashi guard outside the walls of Midrash. He handled that situation with ease. I think most people tend to underestimate Asher.

He smiled gently at Luka. 'Tell me what I need to know and do. Hopefully we can get it done this afternoon.'

'So soon? I thought you'd rest up today and go in tomorrow.' Luka took a few deep shaky breaths. 'Well ... the first thing is you need to have a bath, Ash. You smell, and your hair looks peculiar.'

Poor Asher. It didn't assuage his hurt feelings when we all burst into laughter.

When our noise had died down, Luka continued, 'In fact, you all smell. I'll run a bath shortly. We'll dress you, Ash, in my clothes. You will need a servant with you, to carry your bag with the scrolls, pens and ink, and wax and seal. You'll need to make it look like an official audit and that'll include my seal on the page. You know the sort of thing.'

Asher nodded. Kieran sat up straight and said, 'I'll go with him.'

'No,' Luka said. 'You can't go.'

Kieran frowned. 'Why not? It's my sister we're rescuing! I've been Asher's apprentice for well over one turn of the sun.'

Asher smiled sympathetically at Kieran. 'You couldn't look more like an Outer Islander if you tried, son. Look at your red hair, your freckles and your green eyes. They'd spot you as a fake within a moment.'

Kieran scowled and slumped back down.

'I'll do it,' Riva said.

Luka shook his head. 'I'm sorry but girls can't be record-keepers.'

Riva and Rimini both bristled at that.

'Why not?' Riva said.

'It's not how things work here,' Luka said. 'You're not in Seddon now.'

She frowned. 'I think that's a load of old griven dung.'

Rimini nodded in agreement.

I stood up. 'I guess it'll be me, then.'

I felt someone grab my leg. 'Not so fast,' Boyd said. 'Why can't it be me?'

I hadn't thought of Boyd. Of course, he was just as capable as me. I shrugged and scratched my head.

Luka stood up. 'Let's get you all clean and then we'll decide who does what. Ladies, while the men are bathing, would you please gather the eggs for me? There's a basket over there, by the door. Thank you for the kindness.'

A look passed between the two girls that I didn't understand but which didn't look good for the rest of us.

'I bet Joffre will be glad to see you,' I said.

Rimini brightened up at that and the two went outside, Riva picking up the egg basket on her way out.

Once they'd gone, Luka said, 'Those girls mustn't go into Forabad. It isn't a safe place for unmarried females who are travelling with a group of unrelated males. There are many who would think that they are women of loose morals and would want to take advantage of them.'

'What?' I said.

I could see that Riff, Boyd and Kieran were just as bemused by this as I was. Felix's expression didn't change but Asher nodded.

'Indeed,' Luka said. 'It's a strange city, with strange customs. The women of Forabad mustn't leave their houses unless accompanied by a male relative, or by several old women to chaperone them. Their main purpose in life is to run the household, have children and keep their menfolk happy.'

'Oh dear,' Riff said. 'I hope Riva never gets to hear that.'

'How do you feel about it, Luka?' I said.

He grimaced. 'It was a great culture shock to me when I first came here. My parents apprenticed me to Leng Dow, a senior in the Records Department of Forabad. He's been dead these past twenty years, may he rest in peace. It took me some time to learn how to behave here in an acceptable manner. It's another reason why I'm happier living in the countryside.'

For a moment, I felt that there was something else he wanted to say but the feeling was fleeting. Perhaps he was remembering his arrival in Forabad. If I were Asher, I'd be thanking Sed that my family didn't apprentice me to someone in a strange city. Even though I was male, I couldn't imagine living in such a place.

From his position by the window, Felix said, 'This will make our search more difficult. If Maraed has been taken into a household it could be very tricky to retrieve her.'

He turned to Luka. 'Tell me, does the servant have to be a young person?'

A smile briefly flickered on Luka's mouth. I could swear he seemed pleased with the question. 'No, no. In fact, you would fit the bill nicely. Or, this young chap with the damaged arm.'

Felix said, 'I'll think on it. The rest of you, get yourselves cleaned up.'

As we followed Luka to the bathing room, Boyd nudged my arm and whispered, 'Who died and made him Commander?'

Once everyone had finished bathing, we sat down to eat the vegetable stew that Luka had made. Asher was dressed in his cousin's clothing, including a cape embroidered with scrolls and quills. With his hair and bread trimmed, it was difficult to tell the two men apart.

'Are you sure you're not twins, separated at birth?' Kieran said.

Luka grinned. 'Our mothers were sisters and our fathers were twin brothers, so it isn't surprising that we are similar in appearance.'

Felix shifted his chair in closer to the table. I could tell he was impatient with the friendly chatter. 'Time is wasting. We have an army to meet.'

Luka blinked rapidly, his hand fluttering up to his throat. 'Oh my! No one said anything about an army.' His hand shook as he fiddled with the neck of his tunic.

# Eleven

'Don't worry about it,' Asher said. 'Just focus on the task at hand.'

As Luka talked with Asher and Felix—telling them how they should greet the keeper of the books at the slave market; describing the expected procedures; giving them directions on how to get to the market, and where they should go once they were inside the building—Kieran and I cleared the table and cleaned the plates and mugs. Riff sat next to Felix and listened intently to Luka's information. Anyone would think he would be going, too. Rimini and Riva went for a walk around the farm. I'm sure Joffre joined them as soon as they went outside.

Then, when Luka had finished, Felix asked, 'How will we get into the city, sir? Will we walk or do you have some sort of cart? I haven't seen a camel since we got here.'

'I have a donkey,' Luka said. 'He's in the large barn. He pulls a small cart that I use when I need to go into Forabad.'

A donkey? In Seddon, everyone relied on camels for transport. I couldn't wait to see what manner of creature a donkey was. Of course, I'd heard of them but I'd never seen one.

'I'm glad I thought to keep him in there today with the goats,' Luka continued. 'I had no idea you'd be bringing dragons with you. The poor things would have died of fright.'

Asher asked Felix, 'Are you familiar with donkeys?'

He nodded. 'I remember them from my childhood. Don't worry, we'll manage.'

'The donkey is very placid,' Luka said. 'Riff could easily manage him if you want him to be your driver. It might be wise to have another adult with you, just in case. The young ones will be fine here with me.'

Felix and Asher both nodded.

111

'Are you happy to come along, Riff?' Asher said,

'Of course!' Riff said.

'The sooner we leave, the sooner we can get back,' Felix said. 'We'll need the bag of equipment. The scrolls and ink and stuff?'

Once again Luka's hand shook as he straightened the sleeves on his tunic. 'Yes, of course. I'll go get it.' He hurried over to the stairs. 'Don't go near the donkey until I get back. It'd be better if I hitched him up and led him outside. He's not used to strangers. Wait here. I won't be long.'

'I'll come with you,' Asher called.

Luka shook his head. 'No need. No need. I won't be long.' He climbed the stairs and disappeared down a passageway.

'Something's worrying him,' Riff said.

'Oh, it's just his nervous nature,' Asher said.

'Well, you know him better than the rest of us,' Riff said, 'but I can't help thinking there's something he hasn't told us.'

I sat down at the table next to Riff and said, 'I agree. Something's going on.'

Felix shrugged. 'I'm not worried about handling the donkey. I'll go get things started. It'll save time.'

He walked to the door but as soon as he opened it, Joffre flew in.

*The girls went into the barn. Rimini squawked. They didn't come out again. I looked in where the wall is clear, like water. There are men with long sharp sticks and they put the girls in a net!*

I told Felix what the raven said. He swore under his breath and hurried over to the window where he'd left his bow and quiver. Boyd pulled a knife out from his boot and his face hardened. In the blink of an eye, he became the stern, world-weary soldier I'd seen in Midrash.

# Eleven

Asher whispered to me, 'Seeger, summon the dragons.'

Just as I began calling, *SHADREER!* Luka's voice came from the top of the stairs. 'What's happening, gentlemen?' He had the record-keeper's bag slung over his shoulder.

*SHADREER! SHADREER!*

I felt a stirring in my mind and then there was a faint reply. *We are on our way, hatchling.*

# Twelve

Luka stayed at the top of the stairs. 'You shouldn't take your bow with you, Felix, if you're going to be Asher's servant.'

Felix strode over to the stairs. 'Get down here, now.'

Luka frowned but he did as he was told. 'I don't understand.'

Asher walked over to his cousin. 'There are men in your barn and they've taken the girls.'

Luka dropped the bag. 'Oh dear.' Then he saw Joffre and shrieked, 'Get that bird out of here!'

The raven landed on my shoulder. *I'm not going anywhere. There's something wrong with that man.*

'Forget the bird,' Felix said. 'What do you know about the men in the barn?'

He didn't answer. He looked at Asher and then the rest of us, and then back to Asher.

'Luka?' Asher said. 'Tell me.'

He crumpled, flopping down onto the bottom step and, putting his head in his hands, he began to gasp quick, shallow breaths. His legs began to tremble.

# Twelve

Felix pulled him back up and dragged him over to a chair. He threw Luka into it and then stood over him, an arrow notched and ready to fire. 'Talk, old man.'

Luka cringed, his hands up in front of his face. 'Don't hurt me!'

The rest of us stood in a semi-circle behind Felix. As I stared at Luka, squirming and whining in his chair, I realised he was in it up to his earlobes.

I pointed at him. 'You're part of this.'

Luka shook his head but Asher nodded. 'Oh yes,' he said. 'You never were very good at lying. Speak up, cousin. Felix means business.'

Then Boyd moved around behind the old man and placed his knife up against Luka's throat. 'So do I,' he said.

Luka gasped. 'Asher, please?'

*Let me peck him.*

*Not now, Joffre, but maybe later.*

Suddenly, Luka stopped shaking and dropped his hands into his lap. As I'd thought, it had all been an act.

'Very well,' he said. 'I knew that bird was bad luck.' He glared at Joffre, still perched on my shoulder. His gaze was pure venom. 'I told the men to wait until Asher and his party had left for the city but they're stupid, greedy and impatient. Idiots!'

'Luka!' Asher said. His face drained of colour and he swayed on the spot. I put my arm around him to hold him steady.

'How many?' Felix said.

'Six,' Luka said. 'They're all armed, too.'

Asher stood with his hand over his mouth and his eyes welling up with salt water, staring down at his cousin, the man he called "friend".

'What was the plan?' Felix continued.

'Once the adults had gone to Forabad, the men would take the young ones and sell them to the slave traders. We'd share the spoils. We'd get a pretty sum, especially for the two girls and the green-eyed lad.'

Asher groaned.

'I was keeping you safe, Ash! When you got back from the city, I was going to tell you that bandits had raided my farm. Everything would have been fine.' He glared at me and Joffre, again. 'This is all that bird's fault.'

Joffre squawked at him. Asher stepped forward and slapped Luka across the face. 'This is *your* fault. Shame on you!'

Luka shrugged and rubbed his cheek. 'It doesn't matter. There are six of them and only one of you that's worth a damn when it comes to fighting.' Boyd gritted his teeth, fire sparking in his eyes. 'I'll ask them for mercy for you, cousin, but I can't promise anything.'

Felix smiled. 'Really? You think that's all we've got. You've forgotten something.'

Luka smiled back. 'I don't think so. One archer, an old man, a one-armed man and five children. I don't think I've missed anything. Oh, unless you count that feather duster on Seeger's shoulder.'

Joffre's hackles rose. *Can I peck him now? I could put his eye out in a flash.*

*I'm sure you could but wait.*

Felix slowly shook his head. 'We also have dragons.'

Luka laughed. 'Not here, you don't.'

'Seeger?' Felix said.

'They're on their way.'

Luka sat up straighter in his chair. So much for his panic attacks. He looked as though he was completely in control.

'So you say. I expect they're bringing that so-called army with them,' he said. 'I suggest you pop out to the barn and warn the men. I'm sure they'll quake in their boots.'

Asher shook his head. 'You always were a silly child, Luka, but I'd hoped you'd grown out of it. Just tell me, why?'

Luka stared up at his cousin and smirked. They were no longer mirror images of themselves; they were like dark and light, night and day. Asher had warmth and goodness glowing in his eyes but Luka was brittle, hard and cold.

'How do you think I could afford this property?' he said. 'A simple record-keeper working for the department isn't exactly rolling in money. Not like the great Record-Keeper of Seddon.'

'I just assumed your parents had left you a legacy,' Asher said, 'and you'd been careful with your money.'

Luka laughed. 'Shows how much you know.'

'I've loved you like a brother, Luka. How could I be so wrong?'

Luka shrugged. 'It's just business.'

'Enough chit-chat,' Felix said. 'We have to do something about the men in the barn. How long now, Seeger?'

I listened. *Shadreer?*

*Nearly there, hatchling. What is the problem?*

*There are six men, who are hiding in the large barn. They have Riva and Rimini.*

*Very well. Please warn the old man that we may have to do some damage to his building.*

*It won't matter, Shadreer. He's part of the problem.*

'What's wrong with that child?' Luka said. 'Every now and then, he goes a bit doolally.'

'They're almost here,' I said. 'They know the situation.'

While Felix and Boyd guarded Luka, the rest of us searched the house for something to bind him. Asher suggested we use the belts that Kieran had found in Luka's bedroom. We put one around his arms, one around his knees and one around his ankles. Then Felix could relax but Boyd stayed put, standing behind Luka's chair, his blade still close to the old man's throat.

Riff came out of the kitchen, clutching a knife he'd taken from the cutlery drawer. 'Just in case,' he said.

'If they hurt one hair on Rimini's head, so help me you'll be sorry,' Boyd said to Luka. 'I've killed for less than this.'

Luka smirked again but Felix said, 'Listen to the lad. He's been trained by the Midrashi.' The smile slid off Luka's face.

Then I heard a familiar sound: the beating of very large wings. 'They're here.'

Felix told Boyd to stay with Luka. The others ran outside to watch the landing of the Flight. I hesitated at the door for a moment, looking back at Luka and Boyd. My friend had a grim, chilling smile on his face and Luka looked very uncomfortable. Whenever I saw this side of Boyd, I realised how much his time in Midrash had changed him.

Shortly after I had joined the others out in the yard, Fitzee landed on the roof of the barn. Shadreer positioned himself in front of the door and Azree and Hizaree stood in the cleared space behind the back wall.

Felix then called out, 'Hello, the barn. Release the girls and come outside with your hands in the air.'

A voice answered him. 'You put *your* hands up or we kill the girls.'

From the sounds issuing from the barn, it seemed the animals inside had sensed the dragons. The goats were bleating, there was a strange honking noise that I guessed came from the donkey and we could also hear thudding that sounded like one of the animals was kicking his stall.

# Twelve

*Shadreer, would you please tell the animals you're not going to eat them?*

*I told them, Seeger, but they do not believe me. I suggest you talk to them.*

I concentrated but it was difficult to speak with an animal that I couldn't see and with which I'd not yet made any connection. I had no idea what a donkey looked like. I decided to focus on the goats because I knew what they were. I tried and tried and eventually, just as my head had begun to spin and I could feel my lunch rising back up my gullet, there was a break-through.

*Hello, goats.*

*Who are you and what are you doing in my head? I don't have time for this. There are dragons here!*

*I'm a beast-speaker, standing outside the barn. I want to rescue the girls that are in there. The dragons are my friends. They've promised not to eat you or the donkey. They're here to help me.*

*Yeah, so you say. How do we know you're not one of the dragons?*

*Do I sound like one?*

*No, but everyone knows you can't trust a dragon.*

*I don't have time to argue with you. Please tell the donkey that we're not here to bother you or him.*

*Tell him yourself.*

*I can't. I've never met a donkey, so I can't see him in my head.*

'What's happening, Seeger?' Felix asked.

'I'm trying to reassure the goats and the donkey that the dragons mean them no harm. They don't believe me.'

Felix put his hand on my arm. 'They'll soon find out. Tell the dragons to begin an assault on the barn without using their fire.'

I pointed to Shadreer. 'He can hear what you're saying, you just can't hear his reply.'

Felix didn't question me, he simply turned to Shadreer and said, 'My apologies. Would you please tell your friends to begin to pull this barn apart?'

Shadreer inclined his head and then began clawing at the barn door. Felix began to rip the roof tiles off. We could hear Hizaree and Azree thumping on the back wall. The men inside the barn began to shriek and yell. The girls were silent.

Riff said, 'The girls better be all right.'

Asher had his arms folded across his chest. I had never seen such a thunderous look on his face before. Kieran stood next to him, his arm around the Record-Keeper's back. Riff still held the kitchen knife in his clenched fist.

Once more, Felix called to the men. 'There are four dragons pulling this barn apart. Unless you come out now, and the girls are unharmed, we cannot guarantee your safety once the dragons break through.'

'You lie!' came the reply.

'This is your last chance,' Felix said. 'I don't want to tell these creatures to use their fire.'

'You're just throwing rocks on the roof. You can't frighten us.'

Some of the men inside seemed to be arguing with their leader. I could hear them shouting at each other but, as they were all yelling at once, I couldn't make out the words. Then, Fitzee broke through. He crouched down, so that he was almost lying across the rest of the roof. His head was angled on the side so that he could see into the hole he'd made. Then, he reached in with one front leg.

There was a blood-curdling scream and then Fitzee was holding a stranger up in the air. His legs were kicking and blood streamed down from his shoulder and arm, where Fitzee held him with his talons. The red dragon held the man over the edge of the roof and dropped him. His victim landed in a crumpled heap near Felix and me. He was still alive. He started to pull himself up, saw Shadreer peering over him and fainted. Riff and Kieran quickly moved him away from the door. Asher sat on him while Kieran tied the man's hands and feet with some twine.

'Where'd that come from?' Asher said.

'I found it in the drawer next to the knives,' Riff said.

*Don't do that again, Fitzee,* I said. *They'll be prepared for you this time. They could hurt your leg.*

*Very well,* he said, *but I have to say, I enjoyed that very much.*

*Can you see the girls? Are they all right?*

He angled his head down again but then had to pull back, just as an arrow whizzed up past him.

*I saw them. They are tied up in a corner, near the donkey's stall. They have cloths stuffed in their mouths. They are unharmed. However, that donkey keeps kicking the wall that they are leaning against. If it breaks through, it could land a hoof on one of their heads. The poor beast seems crazed with fear. I cannot make it see sense.*

*I'll go in,* Joffre said. *They won't think twice about a bird fluttering around in a barn.*

Before I could say anything, he'd flown up and through the hole that Fitzee had made.

*Can you see the raven, Fitzee?*

*He is perched up on a rafter. The men have not noticed him. There he goes. He has landed on the donkey's back. He is walking up to the chap's head. Oh dear!* There was a bellow of rage. *He pulled a hair out of the donkey's ear! Well, that has got the fellow's attention.*

For a short time, I waited, frustrated that I couldn't see what was happening inside the barn.

*The donkey has calmed down,* Fitzee said. *He is still making that terrible racket, which I am sure you can hear, but he has stopped kicking his stall. Now the bird has hopped into the goat's pen. Ah! The goats tell me they have decided to believe our assurances.*

Once more, Felix called to the men. 'Come out and I promise you, on my honour, that nothing will happen to you. You can collect your injured companion and leave this farm with no harm done.'

'Yeah, and what if we don't want to?' a voice shouted.

'Then I will leave you to the dragons,' Felix said. 'They happen to be very fond of the two young ladies you have in there with you.'

'They ain't no ladies,' the voice replied. 'Ladies don't knee a fellow in the family jewels.'

Joffre flew back out and settled himself once again on my shoulder. I grinned at Riff, who waggled his eyebrows at me.

'Young Bernard here was in tears!' the voice continued.

'Aww, don't tell them that!' another voice shouted. 'I never was.'

'Yes, you were. We all saw it,' the first voice said. 'Ain't no shame in it mate.'

'Hurry up,' Felix said, 'the dragon is growing impatient.'

Shadreer dipped his head down low and sent plumes of smoke under the door. Then, just as another shriek came from inside the barn, he began to growl. The others joined in. It was a terrifying sound: a deep rumbling that seemed to come from the bowels of the earth.

'We ain't coming out if one of those things is on the other side of the door.'

# Twelve

'Very well,' Felix said. 'We'll ask the dragon to move back. However, if you aren't out by the count of ten, he will have my permission to break in and do what he likes with you.'

Shadreer backed away and Felix began to shout, 'ONE. TWO. THREE ...' He got all the way up to nine before the door slowly opened.

# Thirteen

The men, cowards that they were, pushed Riva and Rimini out the door first. Kieran and Riff ran to the girls and led them away. They gently pulled the gags out of the girls' mouths and untied their hands. Riff hugged Riva and kissed her. The strange thing was, I didn't feel jealous.

Rimini looked around, frowning, so I said, 'Boyd's inside, guarding Luka.' That seemed to reassure her.

Then the men sidled out. One of them, clearly the leader, glared brazenly at us but two of the others looked more embarrassed than defiant. The last two, one of whom walked slowly, wincing with every second step, looked terrified. He made sure that the rest of the gang was between him and the dragon. Shadreer hissed and puffed another plume of smoke and Fitzee leant down from the roof and did the same. The gang all jerked with surprise and tried to lean further away.

'Be grateful you aren't dead,' Felix said. 'Leave this property now and if we meet again, you'll regret it.'

# Thirteen

The bandits collected their injured companion and, edging past Shadreer, they set off past the barn and up the road that led to the hills. Occasionally one or two would look back and then their steps would quicken.

Riva wanted to kick them but Riff held her back. Rimini smouldered with anger.

'Which one kneed them in the groin?' Felix said.

Rimini put her hand up. 'I told him not to touch me but he didn't listen.'

Felix grinned. 'Good for you.' Joffre landed on her shoulder and rubbed his head against her face. 'He was worried about you,' Felix said.

Rimini rubbed the top of the raven's head with her forefinger. 'I'd have escaped. It was just a matter of time.'

I thanked the dragons and asked them to wait. I wasn't sure what we were going to do next but I felt better when they were around. The others all went back into the house but I went into the barn, to meet the goats and to finally see my first donkey.

What a beautiful creature! He had long ears—now minus one hair—soulful brown eyes, and sturdy legs that ended with hard hooves, quite unlike the soft pads of a camel's foot. It also had a barrel-shaped body that was marked with a dark brown line across its shoulders and down its back.

*That mark looks like the sword of Sed!*

*That's because we're special to him,* the donkey said. *He used to ride us when he was here.*

*I didn't know that.*

*I'm not surprised. You're only young. I expect there's a lot you don't know.*

I rubbed his long ears and he dipped his head closer to me. It's funny how most animals love having their ears fondled. Then I gave the goats a good scratch. They were very polite animals and they said that Luka treated them well.

*I'm sorry we gave you such a fright,* I said. *I'm going into the house now but I'll probably see you soon.*

*Take your time,* the goats said. *No rush.*

I hurried inside and found the others circled around Luka, who was still sitting tied up in his chair. Rimini, with the raven perched defiantly on her shoulder, stood close to Boyd and glared at the old man. Her fingers were twitching at her sides so I don't think it would have taken much for her to attack him. Joffre also studied Luka, his head tilted to the side and his hackles raised.

Luka was talking to Asher. 'Look, I'm sorry. I just needed to make some money. I'm still paying this property off. Don't forget, I'd planned it so that you wouldn't be hurt. You're family.'

'You planned to sell these young people to slave traders!' Asher said.

Luka shrugged. 'Everyone does it.'

'You know better than that,' Asher said. 'These are people, not pieces of baggage or furniture to buy and sell. If your mother could hear you now ...'

Kieran coughed politely. 'Excuse me. Are we still going to look for Maraed?'

Asher slapped his forehead. 'You idiot, Ash! I'm sorry, Kieran, it'd slipped my mind in all the kerfuffle. Felix, get the donkey cart ready.'

'No need,' Luka said.

Asher strode over to the base of the stairs to retrieve the recorder's bag which had been left where Luka had dropped it.

'I know where she is,' Luka said.

Felix walked through the kitchen to the door. 'We won't be long,' he said.

126

# Thirteen

'I KNOW WHERE SHE IS!' Luka shouted.

We all turned to stare at him. Felix froze, his hand still on the door handle. Asher walked back to Luka's chair, carrying the bag.

'I beg your pardon?' he said.

'I checked the records when I got your first message,' Luka said. 'I was curious.'

Asher flopped down in the chair facing Luka. 'You were going to let me go all the way into the city ...'

Riff said, 'He needed to get you out of the way, Ash.'

Asher nodded and then ran his hands through his hair. He stood up, unclipped the fancy cloak that Luka had loaned him and threw it over the back of the chair, before slumping back down into it.

'So, where is she?' Kieran said.

Luka turned to him. 'Your sister was bought by the tavern-keeper of the Rusty Anchor, in the town of Portsmouth. It's on the edge of the coast where the river Anx meets the sea. The Slave Master noted in her details that she was a good singer. Is that right?'

Kieran nodded.

'Well, that's good news for you,' Luka said. 'He'll have bought her to entertain his customers with her singing. Hopefully, it wasn't for anything else.'

Joffre leant forward and squawked at Luka, *You nasty man!*

Riva walked over to Kieran and put her hand on his arm. 'Don't think about it. I'm sure she'll be all right.'

Rimini snorted, turned away and went to stare out of the window. Joffre was still perched on her shoulder, making soothing chirruping sounds in her ear. Felix let go of the kitchen door and re-joined the group.

'I know where that is,' he said. 'I think we can get there by nightfall if we leave now.'

'Very good,' Asher said standing up. 'Seeger, are the dragons still here? Good. Everyone, gather your things and let's go.'

He dumped the recorder's bag on Luka's lap and then went to collect his own kitbag from the pile against the wall. The rest of us followed suit. I guessed I wouldn't be seeing the donkey again. I would have liked to spend time getting to know him.

Once we were all ready to leave, Felix untied Luka.

'Farewell, Asher,' he said. 'No hard feelings, hey?'

'Goodbye, Luka,' Asher said. 'I doubt we'll see each other again.'

Luka watched him stride out of the house, his mouth hanging open in shock. He seemed genuinely distressed by Asher's attitude. All I could think was that he'd lived too long in Forabad.

As we were mounting the dragons, Luka came to the door and shouted, 'You won't get her back, you know. It's a lost cause.'

Felix was right. By the time the sky was streaked with pink and grey, and the sun had begun its daily slide downwards, we could see the mouth of the Anx where it met the sea and the town of Portsmouth clustered at one side. It was spread out along one side of the river, with a small bay a little to the left of the river mouth. As we began to dip down, I could see a few ships lying at anchor.

The dragons let us off on the other side of the river mouth, so that they wouldn't be seen by the townspeople. Then they moved back a short distance and lay down, huddled together to keep warm as they snoozed. Once it was dark, they would look like a mound of rocks.

Those of us who had weapons took them out of our bags.

# Thirteen

Asher took out his coin bag, tipped some of the money into a smaller bag and gave it to Felix. He tucked it in the pocket on the inside of his jacket. We left the rest of our gear with the dragons. I wondered how we'd get across the water but Felix had that in hand.

'There's a sandbank that stretches across the river just before it meets the sea. At low tide, we can easily walk across. Just take your boots off, so they don't get wet.'

That explained why the ships were all anchored in the bay and not along the river. 'When is low tide?' Asher said.

'Now,' Felix said, as he bent down to pull his boots off. 'Come on. Get a move on.'

We all sat down to remove our boots and then, holding them up so they wouldn't get wet, we followed Felix out into the water. He was right. Although, in the poor light the water looked deep and menacing, when we stepped in we found it was barely above our ankles.

Once on the other side, we rubbed our feet dry with the grasses that grew on the edge of the river and then put our boots back on. In the distance, we could see some lights and hear music and voices talking, laughing and shouting.

'That's the Rusty Anchor over there,' Felix said.

'How are we going to do this?' Boyd asked.

Felix shrugged. 'I guess we go inside and see what we can find out. I don't know about you but I could use a meal.'

'What about the girls?' Asher said. 'Perhaps they should wait outside.'

Rimini took a step towards Asher, her fists clenched. Joffre leant forward; his head tilted on the side as if he was querying Asher's statement.

'What are you talking about?' Riva said.

'You remember what Luka said about—'

Riff elbowed Asher in the ribs. 'He just wants to be sure you'll be safe.'

'Oh, for goodness sake,' Riva said. 'I've been looking after myself since I was three. Rimini is a soldier. We don't need you to wrap us up in baby blankets. Thanks all the same.'

Rimini nodded, drew a sharp knife out of her tunic pocket and held it up.

Asher held his hands up in surrender. 'Very well. No offence meant.'

Felix told Riff and Kieran to check out the stables and the back of the tavern, to see how things were set out.

'It wouldn't surprise me if Maraed is locked away somewhere, when she isn't performing,' he said. 'If we're in luck, it won't be in the main building. Hopefully, there'll be a room or small hut out the back somewhere.'

'Perhaps I should go with Riff,' I said. 'There might be some animals I can talk to. Kieran's the only one who knows what Maraed looks like, so he should stay with the group.'

Felix and Asher thought that was a good idea, so it was decided that Riff and I would see what we could find out from checking the outlying buildings, while the others got a table inside. If at any time Maraed should go to the privy, then Riva and Rimini could follow her there and let her know our plan.

'And, what is that plan?' Kieran said.

'To take her with us, of course!' Asher said. 'Use your brain, son.'

Kieran nodded but he leant over and whispered to me, 'That's a goal, not a plan.'

'One more thing,' I said. 'I don't think Joffre will be allowed inside the tavern. He can come with us.' I turned to Rimini. 'Is that all right with you?'

She nodded. Joffre flew over and settled on my shoulder. *I'm a great spy,* he said. *I can do lots of clever things.*

*I know,* I said. *You already have.*

We set off towards the Rusty Anchor. We could hear a band playing but no one was singing. Every now and then, raucous laughter would spill out into the night air. When we reached the front porch, Riff, Joffre and I went around the side of the building while the others, led by Felix, headed inside.

'Act and look as though we're meant to be doing what we're doing,' Riff said. 'No creeping or sneaking. If we act as though we belong, people are less likely to notice us.'

'And if they do notice us?'

'Let me do the talking.'

I shrugged. 'You're the older brother.'

Riff sighed. 'Don't start that nonsense now, Seeger. Please?'

*Don't worry,* Joffre said, *I'll protect you.*

Towards the back of the tavern, but still at the side, we could see the stables. Riff pointed towards them, I nodded and we went inside. We stood still for a while, just inside the door, to let our eyes adjust to the poor light. There didn't seem to be any lamps inside the stable but there was enough ambient light from the last gleam of the sun as well as streaming out of the tavern's windows, for us to see the walls of the stalls and the general layout of the building.

I focused my mind and could soon sense the presence of several animals. I whispered to Riff, 'There are some donkeys here and a couple of griven. I'll see what they can tell us.'

He nodded. He no longer questioned what I could do with my beast-speaking ability. Joffre left my shoulder and did a lap of the stable. He landed on the door of one stall.

*This is the chap to talk to,* he said. *He lives here. The others belong to people who have just flown in for a short stay.*

I walked over to the stall and saw a donkey, chewing on some straw. *Good evening, sir,* I said.

He looked up at me. *Evening, young fella.* He leant forward and sniffed me. *Been consorting with dragons, have you?*

*How do you know that? Have you ever met a dragon, before?*

*I've had a few close calls,* he said. *There's a couple that live up in the ranges, to the north of here.*

There are other dragons! I couldn't wait to tell Shadreer. Maybe they were some of the young ones that left Draageer after the Xanthi's murderous raid?

*I promise you that my dragons won't cause you any harm. They're my friends.*

*Ah,* he said. *You're a dragon-friend and a beast-speaker. Well, well, well. I thought I'd seen and heard everything.*

*I'm here in search of my friend's sister. She was stolen from her family and sold to the owner of this tavern.*

*Just like me!* the donkey said.

I scratched my head while I thought about it. *Well, yes, you could say that. We want to take her back home. Will you please help us?*

*Not much I can do, young fella. I'm stuck here in this stall.*

Joffre squawked. *You can talk, can't you? You know what goes on here.*

I said, *Do you know where the tavern-owner keeps his humans when he's not making them work?*

Riff, who'd been keeping watch at the window, hissed, 'Seeger, I think someone's coming.'

'Hurry!' I said. 'Come hide with me in here.' I quickly god-spoke to Sed, asking for his protection.

Joffre fluttered up and perched on a roof beam. He became part of the shadows. Riff hurried over and we squeezed ourselves down in the back of the donkey's stall. I figured that it was less likely that someone would try to take him out, seeing as he belonged to the place, and I was right.

Someone came in, holding up a lantern. I held my breath and stayed as still as I could. Riff was huddled up next to me. I heard the footsteps lead away from us, towards the other end of the stable. Then I heard a stall door open and someone murmured to their animal, 'There, there. Stand still while I put your harness on. That's it. Good boy! Out we come.'

We heard a clip clopping sound—I assumed it was the sound of a donkey's hooves on the cobblestones—the barn door creaked open and then the lantern light left the room. I could see it bobbing past the window and then all was in darkness again. Riff and I both breathed out. Joffre swooped down and landed on my shoulder.

*Good boy, my fat butt,* the donkey said. *That fellow should hear what his beast says behind his back.*

*Can you help us or not?* I said.

*My master has a small herd of humans that help him in the tavern but he only owns one. She has her own stable out near the little room where the humans pass water and poop. I feel sorry for her. On a warm day, when the wind is coming from the east, the smell must be awful.*

*Is she free to come and go?*

*No. The big man locks her in.*

*Do you know where he keeps the key? Does he carry it with him?*

The donkey shook his head. *It's not on his belt. I don't know where he keeps it.*

*All right. Thanks, anyway.*

*She sings like a caged bird, poor thing. I hope you can get her out of there.*

I told Riff what the donkey had told me and he said we'd better have a look. He edged the stable door open and peered out. Then he beckoned me with his hand. I thanked the donkey once more and, with Joffre snuggled up against my neck, I crept up to Riff's shoulder. He had another quick look and then went outside with me close on his heels.

We walked further on, down past the end of the stable. We turned a corner and went behind the tavern. I could see the privy standing on its own. There was a lantern hanging outside the door, to help customers find it in the dark. To the right of it was a rough wooden shed with one small window and a door. That must be where Maraed was kept.

There wasn't any light on, so I guessed that Maraed was already in the main building. Surely he wouldn't make her sit there in the dark? I ran up to it and peered in through the window. Joffre flew off, saying he'd see if there was another window on the other side. It was too dark to see much. I could just make out a few shapes that were probably a bed and a small table and chair. Just as I was heading back to Riff, a man came around the corner.

'What are you two doing out here?' he said.

Riff turned around, with his hand on his hip. 'More importantly, what are *you* doing?' he said.

The fellow stopped in his tracks. 'Err, I'm going to the privy. Is that all right with you?'

Riff nodded. 'Of course.' He waved him on. 'Help yourself. We're done.'

He began to walk back towards the tavern and I scurried after him. As I passed the stranger, I bobbed my head and said, 'How do?'

The fellow stared suspiciously at us for a moment, shrugged and then went into the outhouse.

# Thirteen

Joffre swooped over our heads and landed on the windowsill near the back door of the tavern. He peered in. *Hey, fellas. I can see a big key hanging on the wall. If you could open up this space, I could fly in and get it.*

*Stay there, Joffre,* I said. *We'll see what we can do from inside. It might not happen until most of the people have left.*

*I can wait. We ravens are patient birds.*

# Fourteen

## Boyd Speaks

Seeger has panic attacks! I suppose I shouldn't have been surprised but I was. He'd never mentioned it and I'd never seen it, so ... Well, well! The great dragon-friend has a weakness like the rest of us.

I knew that Fingle, the sadistic mongrel, had beaten him but I figured that it wasn't much compared to the public flogging I'd endured. Maybe there was more to his story than I'd realised. I was shocked to hear Riff describing Seeger curled up in a ball and trembling all over. I could tell from Seeger's face that it was true. Of course, Riff was right: it's not a sign of weakness or cowardice. It just means a person has endured something beyond what their body and mind can cope with.

Knowing Seeger was like that, in some strange way made me feel better about myself. I could tell he was embarrassed so I didn't say anything to him but I began to pay more attention.

# Fourteen

At the start of our journey he was still besotted with Riva. Seeing her with Riff must have been hard to take. However, while we were at Luka's place I noticed that he didn't pay her much attention at all. When we first left Seddon, he would constantly stare at the couple and at any sign of affection he'd wince or his mouth would settle into a grim tight line. But at the farm, when Riff cuddled Riva and kissed her, Seeger didn't even twitch. I'd say he was definitely getting over his infatuation.

I also noticed that he'd volunteer for everything, even though there were plenty of us who could do the same thing. I used to think he was showing off; big-noting himself as the group's resident hero. Now, I'm not so sure.

I used to be jealous of his ability to beast-speak but, even though I still tease him about it, I can see it can be a burden as well as a blessing. After all, in Midrash it nearly got him burnt at the stake. It often meant he'd have to be in the forefront of the action, even if he didn't want to be.

When I was guarding Luka—the treacherous villain—and the others all ran outside to rescue the girls, I saw Seeger hesitate at the door for a moment. He looked back at me, almost wistfully, as if he'd like to change places with me.

I realised I'd misjudged my old friend. I'd lost faith in him but he'd never lost faith in me. I was determined to be worthy of such a friendship.

As usual, when we got to Portsmouth, Seeger volunteered to take Kieran's place and his explanation made sense but I could tell Kieran was a little miffed about it. When Riff and Seeger walked away from the group, I leant close to the Outer Islander and said, 'I bet you can't wait to see your sister again.'

He blinked, wrenched his gaze off Seeger's retreating back and looked at me. 'It'll be amazing,' he said.

I nodded and whispered, 'He wanted to give you that.'

'What?'

'He wanted to let you be the first to see her.'

'Oh. Right.' He smiled. 'Well, let's get in there!'

Before Felix or Asher could say or do anything, Kieran shoved the tavern door open and strode in. The rest of us followed. We walked into a wall of noise and warmth. The air smelled of sweat and roast meat. A small band—a drummer, three fiddlers and two men with fifes—was in the corner playing a lively tune. Several of the tavern's customers were standing around in front of them, waving their beer mugs in the air and bellowing the words. There wasn't a female leading the sing-along, so I guessed Maraed was somewhere else for the time being.

Felix pushed his way through the crowd and found us a table. Once we were all seated, he leant forward and shouted, 'I'll get us some food and drink. Stay here.'

I sat where I could get out quickly if need be and studied our surroundings. The Rusty Anchor was a busy, popular place. Despite Luka's warning about the treatment of females, and Asher's fears, there were plenty of women sitting or standing around in the crowded tavern. The only thing that stood out was that a lot of women were wearing head scarves. I wondered whether Luka had made that up about the restriction on women in Forabad to make sure the girls stayed behind on the farm, or if things were just more relaxed down on the coast.

Everyone seemed to be having a good time. Some of the men leaning on the bar looked as though they might be sailors off the boats in the harbour. The group that was gathered in front of the band looked more like locals. Of course, I could have got that completely wrong. It's just that their faces had that tinge of red on the cheeks and nose and on the back of their necks that farmers get. Some of the groups seated at tables like us, were couples out for a night's entertainment, or townsfolk finishing the day with a few pints.

Rimini leant into my shoulder and said, 'The sailors could be trouble but I don't see any trained soldiers in here.'

I nodded my agreement. Kieran also scanned the crowd, looking for his sister. Riva sat next to Rimini. She kept glancing at the door, waiting for Riff and Seeger to reappear. Asher drummed his fingers on the table.

'Now that sets my feet a-tapping,' Kieran said. 'What say you, Ash? Are you up for a little dance?'

Asher shook his head. Riva and Felix, who'd just come back to our table, stared at him.

'Are you all right?' Felix said. Asher shrugged. 'It's not your fault your cousin was a fraud,' Felix said. 'Come on, cheer up.'

'I know what'll put a smile on his face,' Kieran said, as he stood up.

Before I could say anything to him like, 'Don't draw attention to yourself!' he was up and jigging about in the space between our table and the next. The other patrons cheered and clapped, which only egged him on. I was embarrassed at first but then ... Oh my goodness that lad can dance! Asher, clomping about in his house, was full of fun and enthusiasm but Kieran ... Kieran was fire and passion and sparkling brilliance. The noise gradually died down as the crowd watched him leap and twirl and tap and slide. They could tell they were in the presence of brilliance.

The drummer shouted, 'Wahoo! From the top, fellas.'

The customers began to clap in time to the music as Kieran jigged his way in and around the tables and chairs. Then he leapt up onto the biggest table, his feet a blur of movement and sound. The band built the tune up into a crescendo and then, in a snap of an instant, both the music and Kieran's tapping came to an abrupt halt.

Everyone cheered. He bobbed his head in acknowledgement of the applause and jumped down from the table. As he walked back to our table, breathing heavily but smiling as though he'd finally worked out how to do it, the band began a gentle ballad. Then a voice like liquid amber rose in a lament.

'Farewell fair Marella, shining star upon the sea.

Those who leave will miss you and their hearts will ne'er be free.'

Kieran stopped dead still. The colour left his face. He whirled around and looked for the singer. She was standing just inside the doorway but near the band so that she didn't block the entrance. It was the same door that the waiters were coming in and out of, so I guessed it led to the kitchen. The woman had flaming red hair and sea-green eyes. It was the same colouring as Kieran's but she made it look beautiful.

Rimini nudged me. 'That's got to be Maraed.'

Felix grabbed Kieran's arm and pulled him back towards our table. 'Sit down,' he said. 'Don't make a fuss.'

Kieran yanked his arm away. 'That's my sister!' he hissed.

Felix smiled. 'If you want to help her, sit down and pretend you don't know her.'

'But ...?'

'It's all right, son,' Felix said. 'She knows it's you. Why else would she be singing, *Marella's Lament*?'

Kieran stared wistfully towards the band but he slowly nodded. 'I just want to grab her and run.'

'I know, lad,' Asher said, 'but don't worry, we'll get her. Now's just not the time for it.'

# Fourteen

We listened to the rest of the song in silence. Riva kept wiping her eyes and Rimini sniffed. I was going to laugh at their woeful expressions but out of the corner of my eye I saw Asher give a quick shake of his head. So, I turned back and watched Maraed pour her heart out, standing next to the drummer.

When she finished, you could have heard a pin drop in the silence. Then, the place erupted with shouts and whistles and boots stomping on the floor. The crowd began to chant, 'More! More!' One of the fiddlers started a tune, livelier than the last and when the rest of the band joined in Maraed began to sing again. I could have listened to her all night.

A fellow with an apron tied around his waist came to the table with two large platters: one was covered in roasted meat and the other had piles of roasted tubers. He slapped them down in the centre of the table, muttered, 'Enjoy' and left. He was closely followed by a young woman carrying a tray of mugs, three were filled with ale and the rest with tapanj juice. I guessed that meant I was getting juice.

We'd just begun to tuck in—that is, all of us except Kieran who just sat staring at his sister—when Riff and Seeger joined us. They'd wisely left the raven outside.

# Fifteen

## Seeger Speaks

We walked into the tavern. No one turned around to look at us. The place was packed.

'There they are,' Riff said. 'Come on.'

As we drew near to the table where our group was sitting, I saw two large platters of food in the middle. My stomach rumbled in approval. Everyone was helping themselves to the meal except Kieran, who sat staring down the room towards the band. I followed his line of sight and there she was: Maraed. Her hair was a halo of fire in the lantern light and she was singing a cheerful song about drinking too much. My gut clenched. I'd never seen such a beautiful girl before.

We sat down and before I could say or do anything, Riff leant forward and said, 'We know where she's kept at night. The key is hanging on the wall inside the back door. Now all we have to do is figure out how to get it.'

I grabbed a couple of slices of meat and tucked them into my trouser pocket. Boyd looked at me with his eyebrows raised.

'It's for the raven,' I said.

He nodded and passed me a mug of juice. I noticed that Riff got ale. Rimini must have heard me because I saw she also put some meat aside. I grabbed a drumstick for myself and for a while we all concentrated on eating.

Felix nudged Kieran and said, 'Eat, boy. It might be quite a while before we get a meal like this again. You'll be no use to her if you're faint from hunger.'

A man at the next table laughed and shouted to Felix, 'Looks like your lad's in love!' Everyone around us laughed and cheered. Felix nudged Kieran again and Asher waggled his eyebrows at him. He got the message and managed to look embarrassed. He smiled at the table and shrugged his shoulders. The crowd laughed again. Then the band struck up a song that everyone seemed to know and they all began to sing. The attention was no longer on Kieran and our table.

Felix leant in and beckoned us to do the same. 'There's nothing we can do now. We'll come back when the place is closed and no one's around. Meanwhile, we blend in. Don't draw any more attention to us. Now, lean out and laugh as though I've just told the funniest joke you've ever heard and then keep eating. Right? Good. Laugh.'

We all leant back and roared with laughter. Asher wagged his finger at Felix. Riff slapped him on the back. Kieran even joined in the merriment. Then, gradually, we went back to eating, occasionally chuckling and shaking our heads.

We stayed until the food was gone and most of the patrons had left the premises but we made sure we weren't the last to leave. The look on Maraed's face as we got up to go, was heart-breaking. I wish we could have told her that we wouldn't abandon her. I suddenly had a flashback to the clearing on the Outer Islands, when the Islanders left Brianna tied to the pole as a sacrifice to the dragon. She had the same look on her face.

We went outside and Felix began to lead us away. I said, 'Wait! I need the privy.'

'Very well,' Felix said, a little louder than usual so that any hangers-on could hear, 'hurry up. We'll wait here.'

'I'm going, too,' Kieran said.

We both set off around the corner of the tavern. I heard footsteps hurrying after us. I glanced over my shoulder and saw Rimini and Boyd.

'We also need to go,' Boyd said.

When they caught up with us, Rimini shoved into my hand the meat she'd collected for the raven. We hurried on down past the stable and turned the corner. The privy still had the lantern lit and hanging on a hook near the door. Rimini went in first, while the rest of us waited.

Joffre flew down and landed on my shoulder. I tore strips off the meat and fed him a piece at a time.

*Thanks, pal,* he said. *You're a good fella.*

*Not a problem,* I said, as I handed him another scrap. For a short time, he ate greedily, fluffing his feathers and making soft burbling noises. Then, he stopped still and tilted his head to the side.

*Someone's coming,* he said. He snatched the last piece of meat out of my hand and flew away onto the roof of Maraed's hut.

The tavern-keeper—big-bellied but with arms that could crush stone—came out of the back door, holding onto

Maraed's arm. He headed towards the little shed he kept her in but stopped dead when he saw us.

'What are you lads doing here?' he said.

'Waiting our turn to use the privy,' Boyd said. 'Our sister's in there at the moment.'

The man frowned. 'Really? Why don't I believe you?'

'Don't know sir,' Boyd said.

We all shrugged and tried to look innocent. Just as the big man was about to say something else, Rimini came out of the privy and called, 'Next!'

Kieran hurried past her saying, 'About time! Why do you women always take forever?'

The tavern-keeper must have decided we were harmless because he pushed Maraed towards the shed. With one pleading look over her shoulder, she went inside and he locked her in.

'Why did you lock her door, sir?' I said. Boyd nudged me, as if to say, 'Shut up!'

The tavern-keeper folded his arms across his belly. 'So she doesn't run off and so no one takes her. I paid good money for her and I protect my property. What's it to you?'

I shrugged. 'Just curious, sir. I didn't know she was a slave. She didn't sing like one.'

The man tilted his head and looked at me as if I were some special sort of stupid. I let my mouth drop open, to reinforce his thinking.

'And what does a slave sound like when they're singing?' he said.

'Seeger, shut up!' Boyd said. 'I'm sorry, sir. My brother's a bit thick.'

The man nodded.

I scratched my head. 'I guess I thought they'd sound really, really sad.'

Kieran came out of the privy and Rimini gave Boyd a shove. Kieran said, 'Your turn, brother.'

'Hurry up, lads,' the man said. 'I'll wait here until you're done.'

He was as good as his word so first Boyd and then I did the business, and then we all hurried back to the others who were waiting out the front.

As I went past the stable I heard Joffre say, *I can get the key, pal. Just wait until it's dark and the place is still. Come back then.*

*Are you sure?*

*I'm a raven, aren't I? Course I'm sure.*

I told the others what he said, so we walked away down the road that led into the rest of the town. Boyd was annoyed with me but I laughed it off.

'I did no harm,' I said.

'You were an idiot,' he said.

Felix suddenly turned down a side street that came to a dead end. On either side were brick walls, with one large door on each side.

Felix said, 'This is a service lane. No one will come down here at night. It's as good a place as any to wait.'

We sat down, our backs against the wall and waited. We could hear the town slowly shutting down for the evening. It seemed to take forever.

While we waited, Felix said, 'I'll take a smaller crew with me to release Maraed. Asher, you and Riff take the others to get our gear and the dragons. Fly them back and meet us on the road leading out from the Rusty Anchor.'

'Good idea,' Asher said. 'Then all we have to do, once you've got her, is fly away. They'll never catch us.'

Finally, when the moon was high and the only sounds we could hear were our own breathing, Felix stood up.

146

'Let's go,' he said. 'If we pass anyone on the street, we're just a bunch of lads out having fun and taking too long to get home. All right?'

We all nodded and followed him out onto the main road. There was no one around so our acting skills weren't called upon. When we turned down towards the tavern, Felix said, 'This is where we part company. Asher, you take Riff, Riva, Boyd and Rimini and get the dragons.'

Boyd bristled. 'Why can't I go with you?'

'The more there are of us, the noisier we'll be. We must be quick and quiet. Kieran needs to be there to reassure his sister, Seeger is the only one who can talk to the raven and I'll be armed and on guard. Just in case.'

Asher and Felix nodded. Riva, Boyd and Rimini didn't look too happy but Felix ignored them. 'Right,' he said. 'Let's go.'

He strode off towards the Rusty Anchor, with Kieran close on his heels. I ran after them, talking to Shadreer as I went, explaining what was about to happen. I looked back, once, and saw that the others were hurrying down the riverbank towards the shallow water where we'd crossed earlier that evening. But then, I saw two figures branch off and run back towards us. They soon caught up.

'What's going on, Boyd?' I said.

Felix and Kieran stopped and turned back when they heard what I said.

'Rimini and I have been on plenty of night raids,' Boyd said. 'How many have you been on, Seeger?'

Felix walked up to the two rebels. 'I thought I told you to go with the others.'

'We're on this trip because we're experienced soldiers,' Boyd said. 'Isn't it time you used our expertise?' He glared at Felix, his hands on his hips.

Felix sighed. 'We haven't got time for this. All right, come on and keep quiet.'

All the lights were off in the tavern. It looked as though the owner had gone to bed. We tiptoed down the side of the building, past the stables.

*It's about time,* the raven said.

'Where's the key?' Felix whispered.

'Hanging on the wall inside the back door,' I said.

'Right, Boyd and Rimini stay on guard back here,' Felix said. 'The rest of us will go around the back and try to find a way in.'

'I could probably jimmy open the kitchen window,' Kieran said.

'Let's see,' Felix said.

We left Boyd and Rimini standing in the shadows at the corner of the building. The rest of us crept around to the back window.

*I can do it,* the raven said. *I'll fly down the chimney and get the key.*

*Are you sure you can manage it?*

*I'm a raven, pal. I can do anything I like.*

I told Felix and Kieran what Joffre was going to do and the three of us waited by the window.

*Going in,* Joffre called.

For a short moment, there was silence. All I could hear was the thumping of my heart and my breath wheezing in and out. Then there was an almighty racket, a dreadful screeching.

*Joffre,* I called. *What's going on? Are you all right?*

*Owwww! I nearly lost my tail!*

*How?*

*There's fire at the bottom!*

Boyd came running around the corner. 'What's that noise?' he said.

'The fire is still burning in the hearth,' I said. 'The bird singed his tail. Look,' I pointed up towards the gutter, 'there he is. I guess we're not getting the key that way.'

'Let's keep the noise down,' Felix said. 'Kieran?'

Kieran took a small knife out of his trouser pocket and reached up to the window. He'd just begun to wedge it under the bottom end of the frame when the kitchen suddenly lit up and the door was flung open. We all hurriedly stepped back. Standing in the doorway, holding a lamp aloft in one hand, and a long-handled axe in the other, was the tavern-keeper.

'Well, well,' he said. 'Look who we have here. Back to use the privy again, lads?'

The four of us moved even further away from the door and the keeper followed us.

'I knew you were up to no good,' he said. 'So, the love-sick pup thinks he can steal himself a sweetheart. Not going to happen, lads. I knew what was going on, so I sent a message to the Watch asking them to send a squad around. They should be here any moment. You want a girl? Go buy one for yourselves.'

Kieran stepped towards him. 'They're not pieces of furniture, or animals, mister. They're people. How do you think they became slaves ... volunteered? They're stolen from their families. How would you like it if that happened to you?'

Felix pulled Kieran back. 'Easy son.'

The tavern-keeper sniffed. 'That's not my problem. Now, you can clear off before you get arrested or you can stay and maybe lose a limb or two to my trusty axe.'

Felix raised his bow, an arrow notched ready to fly, and said, 'I don't want to hurt you but I won't let you get in our way.'

'Who are you? His dad? What, he can't find a girl on his own, so you're going to help him steal mine?'

While they were speaking, I watched the raven fly in through the open door and shortly afterwards, fly out again with the key dangling from his beak. He flew up and landed on the gutter again.

*You get him sorted,* the bird said, *and then we'll get the lady out.*

*Good job, Joffre!*

Then I saw a slight movement in the shadows: Rimini! She slipped into the kitchen. Felix must have seen her as well because he took a couple more steps back, drawing us with him, so that we were quite close to Maraed's shed door. The tavern-keeper stepped with us.

'I guess we're at a bit of a stalemate,' Felix said.

Suddenly the tavern-keeper exclaimed, 'OOF!', dropped his lamp and axe and, his hands between his legs, dropped to his knees. Then Rimini, standing behind him, whacked him over the head with a heavy frying pan that she must have taken from the kitchen. The poor man toppled over sideways, his hands still clutching his groin, and lay there with his eyes shut and his mouth open.

'Did I kill him?' Rimini said.

Felix ran to the tavern-keeper, turned the lamp upright, and stuck two fingers against the man's neck.

'No, lass,' he said. 'You've just knocked him out. He'll have a nasty headache in the morning, as well as other aches and pains. Now, quick, grab the key.'

'No need,' I said.

The raven landed on my shoulder with the key still firmly held in his beak. I gave it to Kieran, who ran to unlock the door. Then he slipped inside. We could hear him talking to Maraed and then he came back out.

# Fifteen

'She's just got to get dressed,' he said.

We stood in a little huddle, admiring Rimini's handiwork while we waited.

*Please look for me, Seeger?* Joffre said. *Is my tail a mere stub?*

*No, it's all there. I think you just singed the ends of a few feathers.*

*Just? What do you mean, just?*

He flew over to Rimini and perched on her shoulder. She rubbed his head and he tucked in closer so she could do it better.

'Good work, Rimini,' Boyd said. 'You saved the day.'

'How did you—?' I said.

'I was just going to smack him over the head,' Rimini said, 'but he stood there with his legs akimbo so I thought, why not? I kicked him good and hard between the legs.' I winced. 'It's my specialty.'

'Hurry up,' Felix called to Maraed. He looked at us. 'We don't know whether or not he was bluffing about the Watch.'

We nodded and shuffled our feet. My legs began to tremble. I found myself straining to hear the marching feet of the Watch coming up the road. The slightest creak or flap of breeze and I'd twitch.

*Some men have just turned the corner from the town onto this road.* Shadreer called. *They are carrying weapons. I suggest you hurry.*

*We're coming!* I said.

'Shadreer says the Watch has turned into the tavern's road and are on their way,' I said. 'Hurry!'

Rimini tucked Joffre down the front of her tunic.

'Maraed?' Kieran called. 'We're leaving.'

She ran out of the tiny shed, without even a glance at her former master lying curled up on the ground. He'd begun to moan, so it wouldn't be long before he'd be properly awake.

'Let's go,' she said.

We ran down past the stables and there, in front of the tavern, were the dragons and the rest of the team waiting for us. She stopped in her tracks.

'Oh my!' she said.

'Trust me, they're friendly,' Kieran said. 'Come on, climb up.'

We heard the men of the Watch shouting in the distance so we ran to the Flight, got on with the help of our friends, and then in two hearty wing-flaps we were air-born. We soared over the heads of the Watch, who stood looking up with their weapons hanging loosely in their hands. One fellow at the back of the squad had dropped his pike.

*Where to now?* Shadreer said.

*I heard there were some dragons in the ranges to the North of here.*

*Then that is where we will go.*

# Sixteen

It was still night when we reached the ranges, so the dragons found a wide clearing in which we could all get some sleep. They lay down in a large circle and we curled up in the middle. Kieran had packed an extra blanket for Maraed in his kitbag and Riva shared her bedroll with her. We chatted quietly for a while but it wasn't long before, one by one, we drifted off to sleep.

In the morning, just after we'd finished eating and Riff was kicking dirt over the small fire we'd made, the dragons lifted their heads up, their throats stretched in a straight line and began calling: a high-pitched trilling sound that echoed around the clearing.

'What are they doing?' Asher said, his hands over his ears. 'Are they trying to deafen us?'

I shook my head. 'They're calling to the dragons that live in these ranges.'

'Dragons?' Asher said. 'No one said anything about other dragons!'

The others all looked at me, surprise or confusion etched

on their faces.

'Didn't I tell you?'

They all shook their heads. Oh dear. I keep forgetting that other people can't hear the conversations I have with animals.

'I'm sorry,' I said. 'The donkey in the tavern's stable said that he'd seen dragons in these ranges. I mentioned that to Shadreer when we left last night so that's why we're here.'

'You should have said something,' Riff said.

'I'm sorry. There wasn't really any time.'

'You could have told us when we were waiting in that alley in town!' Boyd said.

I rubbed my forehead. The dragons' trilling was giving me a headache. I could also sense a faint reply, coming from somewhere to the left of me.

'I know. I should have, but ...' I said, making circles on my temples with my fingers. 'Anyway, they've heard and they'll be here soon.'

'What?' Boyd said.

'I suggest we move back and give them some room,' I said, walking unsteadily towards the tree line.

Joffre flew alongside of me. *I'm keeping out of the way of those big lizards,* he said.

Dragon emotions were swirling around in my head. It made me feel dizzy and sick. When I reached the shelter of the trees, I clutched the trunk of a young sapling, leant forward and vomited. As I'd barely eaten in the last couple of days, there wasn't much to show for my effort, apart from the dry bread I'd had for breakfast. I wiped my mouth, kicked dirt over the mess and then found a spot to sit down with my head between my knees.

'What's wrong with you?' Boyd said.

# Sixteen

Riva began to rub my back. 'I've seen him like this once before. He gets drawn into the dragon's emotions and they overwhelm him. After all, they're huge, ancient beasts and he's just one young lad.'

'Can't he just not listen?' Boyd said.

Riva shrugged. Joffre flew onto Rimini's shoulder and peered at me. *You all right, fella?* he said.

'I'm still learning,' I said. 'There's still a lot I don't know and there's no one who can teach me. I haven't met any other dragon-speaker and the only ones I've heard of were killed by the Midrashi over a hundred years ago.'

The others sat down near me and watched the Flight growing more and more excited. I was the only one who could feel the emotions swirling around the clearing but it was easy to tell by the dragons' behaviour that something was happening. They were still trilling but they'd also begun to sway and shuffle their feet. It was like they were both dancing and singing to welcome the new dragons into their midst.

Then, we could see two beasts flying in over the trees. They were both blue but a lighter shade than Azree. Where he was the dark blue of the ocean on a summer's day, they were the bright, light blue of the sky in spring. As they dipped closer, I could see that the back of one of them was more the shade of the lavender of which my mother is so fond. They were singing as they flew in and their song was pitched higher, so that it harmonised with the trilling of the Flight.

As well as their lighter colour, there was something different about these two dragons. They were smaller than Shadreer, even smaller than Fitzee, and their wings glistened with silver. Then, as they began to circle overhead before landing, I noticed they were missing something else that our dragons had.

'They're female,' I said.

'How marvellous,' Asher said. 'Aren't they just lovely?'

I clutched my head and groaned. I wanted to leap up and run around the clearing. I wanted to find somewhere to hide. Bile kept rising in my throat and then sinking back down again. I clenched my teeth, wrapped my arms around my knees and rocked from side to side.

I could feel the raven trying to speak to me but he was just a faint, annoying tapping on the edge of my mind. I knew that the others were saying something but I couldn't make out the words. The last time I was swamped by dragon emotions, Fingle nearly beat me to death. At least I was safe from that happening again.

Then someone lifted me up from the ground and, carrying me in their arms, they began to run through the trees. I screamed and flailed my arms. Was Fingle's ghost tormenting me?

I heard a deep voice say, 'Don't worry, lad. I've got you. You're safe.'

The deeper we went into the trees and the farther we were from the clearing, the better I began to feel. Gradually the tsunami of emotions ebbed away and my headache began to fade. Eventually, I was back in my right mind. I realised Felix was carrying me, and some of the others were running alongside of him. Joffre was flying overhead.

'You can stop now,' I said. 'I'm all right.'

Felix pulled up near a paperbark tree. The others gathered around. Poor Maraed bent over, her hands on her knees, gasping for breath. I guess she hadn't got out much for the past couple of years.

'Are you sure?' Felix said. 'You gave us all a fright back there.'

I nodded. 'I'm sorry. I've just got a bit of a headache now.'

## Sixteen

He put me down. I looked around at my friends. Rimini, with Joffre now perched on her shoulder, seemed impassive but she stood very close to Boyd. He was frowning. Riva smiled at me. She was with me the last time this happened and it looked as though she'd taken it in her stride. Kieran and Maraed stood a little further back, behind Boyd and Rimini. Maraed's gorgeous green eyes were wide open and she was clutching Kieran's arm.

'I'm so sorry I upset you,' I said, looking at Maraed. 'Where are Asher and Riff?'

'They're back at the clearing, watching the dragons,' Felix said. 'Does this happen often?'

I shook my head, immediately regretting it. It stirred up the headache that I thought had almost gone. I rubbed my temples and took a few deep steadying breaths.

'No,' I said. 'It's only happened once before.'

Riva rubbed my back again. 'It was when the dragons learned of their betrayal by the Midrashi.'

'They yodelled and danced like that, back then?' Boyd said.

'No,' I said. 'They wept and then they went silent. They didn't move and didn't make a sound for days. It was eerie.'

I dropped my head as the memories swarmed back.

'When they first formed a circle and began crying,' Riva said, 'Seeger got swept up into their grief-storm. It left him helpless. That's when Fingle, the Beast-Master, beat him. He didn't just flog his back, like he usually did. He whipped him everywhere. He even beat his head with the handle of his whip. Jarl couldn't stop him. At first, we thought Fingle had killed him but Seeger's tougher than he looks and, after being unconscious for a few days, he finally woke up. He took a while to recover. He was still getting over it when we escaped.'

I could feel the heat in my face. I didn't want to look at the others, in case they pitied me. The raven flew to me and crooned his comfort as he perched up against my neck. Then he took off, heading back towards the clearing.

'Flaming heck, Seeg,' Boyd said. 'I had no idea. I mean, I knew he beat you but …'

I flapped my hand. 'Water under the bridge,' I said. 'You've had worse.' I smiled at him. He smiled back.

'Cock-a-doodle-do,' he said. We grinned at each other.

'You two are weird,' Kieran said. 'The dragons didn't carry on like that when they met Fitzee, so why are they doing it now?'

'I suppose it's because the new ones are female,' I said.

Felix took charge. 'If you're feeling better, we should head back. Hopefully the dragons have finished getting to know each other and we can get on our way. Don't forget, there's an army waiting for us.'

Maraed leant in closer to Kieran and whispered something. He patted her hand, where it lay on his arm, and whispered something back. She nodded at him and then spoke to Felix.

'I'm coming with you,' she said.

Felix shook his head. 'Oh no, young lady! We rescued you so you could go home.'

'I'll get there eventually,' she said, putting her hands on her hips, 'but not before the mission is complete. I can be useful.'

'No, no, no!' Felix said. 'Definitely not!'

Anger swept over her face like a cloud blotting out the sun. She stamped her foot. 'Yes, yes, yes, definitely yes. I'll not have any man telling me what to do any more. Understand?' She poked Felix in the chest with her finger. 'I'm a free woman, by all that's holy, and I intend to stay that way.'

# Sixteen

She folded her arms and glared at Felix. He looked at Kieran, who shrugged. 'What about your parents, son?'

'I'm sure we could send them a message,' Kieran said. 'They'd be happy just to know she's no longer a slave.'

Just as Felix was about to reply—he'd opened his mouth and taken a deep breath—Joffre flew down and landed on Rimini's shoulder.

*The big lizards have finished their warbling and are nuzzling each other. I felt sick watching them. Can you come back now and tell them to stop?*

'The raven says the dragons have settled down, so we can go back,' I said.

'Good,' Felix said. 'Let's go.'

I saw Maraed look at me with a frown on her face and then she whispered again to Kieran. He muttered something back, so I guess he was explaining my gift to her. Whatever Kieran said, she stopped frowning and nodded. I suppose she'd pegged me as the freak of the group.

We followed Felix back to the clearing.

Joffre was right: the dragons were taking it in turns to rub faces with the newcomers. I'd never seen the Flight so affectionate before.

'It's a shame you missed most of this,' Asher said. 'It was fascinating.'

*Shadreer,* I said, *are you going to introduce us?*

*Hatchling! We have found two of the females who escaped the Xanthi slaughter. This young female is Silvana—she* inclined her head—*and that one*—pointing to the one with the pinky blue colouring on her back—*is Fiddha.*

The second female was standing next to Azree, who was nuzzling her neck while making a sound that could only be described as "purring".

*Azree?* I said. *What's going on?*

*We have bonded,* he said. *The Great Dragon has given me a mate.*

Fitzee and Hizaree were watching the courtship of Azree and Fiddha with great interest. Hizaree seemed excited and a little confused but Fitzee was jealous. I could feel his frustration and irritation bubbling away just below the surface of his restraint.

*Don't worry, Fitzee,* I said. *I'm sure there is a female out there waiting for you, the Red Peril, to find her and sweep her off her talons.*

He turned his great head to look at me. *I expect you are correct, hatchling,* he said.

*Shadreer, is Silvana your mate?* I said.

*No, hatchling. She is too young.*

*Are you sorry that Fiddha bonded with Azree and not you?*

*Bonding is a mysterious process. It happens or it does not.*

I thought of me and Riva. *You say true,* I said. *Well, I'm happy for Azree. He has always wanted to father his own hatchlings. But, for now, we need to get moving. It's a long way to Midrash. Are you ready to go? I assume the ladies will come with us.*

*We are ready,* he said. *Just say the word.*

I turned around and addressed the group. 'Everyone, these two dragons escaped the Xanthi slaughter and have been living down here on their own ever since. The female standing next to Shadreer is Silvana and the one being nuzzled by Azree, is Fiddha. Azree says that she's the mate he's been longing for.'

'Congratulations, old chap!' Asher said. 'How lovely! She's very beautiful.'

Azree lifted his head and winked at Asher. We all laughed.

'They'll be coming with us,' I said. 'They're ready when we are.'

'Right,' Felix said, taking charge, 'get your gear. Rimini grab that bird. Mount up and let's go.'

According to Asher, once we were airborne we headed North-east. It took us three days of solid flying—only stopping at midday and then at twilight to make camp— before we saw the city of Boron to our left. We didn't fly over it but it was a good reference point. I felt that, at last, I had some idea of where we were.

The next major stopover was in the abandoned city we'd found on our long march to Midrash last year. There was no sign of the sand devils we'd met on that journey but that didn't mean they weren't there. I suppose with six dragons in our party, they'd decided it was prudent to stay hidden. It was a good spot to refill our water supply and for the dragons to have a long soak. Joffre went hunting. Before he left, he asked if anyone would like him to bring back a mouse or two, but no one accepted his offer. Silvana and Fiddha said that they remembered the place. They had rested in the empty streets on their flight south, over a hundred years ago. It was abandoned then, as well.

Asher was delirious. 'I wonder how old this place is. How exciting! Oh, I do wish I had time to study it properly. One day, Kieran, we'll come back with the proper equipment and we'll map the whole town. Who knows what treasures we'll find here!'

That evening, as we sat around the fire, Maraed sang an old Outer Islander ballad about yearning for home. It told the story of a fisherman out on the high seas, trying to land a catch of blue fins to feed his wife and children, who are back in the harbour. All the time he's out there, scanning the water for signs of the big fish, his heart is yearning to walk the streets of his town all the way up to his front door.

When she'd finished, for a moment no one said anything. Her voice was honey in the air. The fisherman's grief at being so far from his loved ones was a gentle ache in my chest. Riva sniffed and wiped her hands across her face. Joffre chirped his approval and landed on her shoulder.

Asher sighed deeply. 'That was perfect, my dear,' he said.

*Hatchling,* Hizaree said, *would you please ask her to sing again?*

I cleared my throat. 'Maraed, Hizaree would like you to sing another song.'

She smiled and a lump suddenly formed in my throat. I swallowed hard, to try to clear it so that I could breathe properly.

'Which one is that?' she said.

'He's the one over there,' I said. 'His skin is the light green of an unripened tapanj.'

I pointed at him and I swear, if it were possible, you'd have thought that he was blushing!

She turned to the young dragon. 'Hizaree, I'd be delighted,' she said. 'I'll sing, *The Loving Cup*. It's an old favourite at weddings on the Island.'

She sang and it was as if the stars themselves leant down to listen. I couldn't take my eyes off her. Because I knew Kieran, and I'd met his parents, I thought I had a good idea of what Maraed would be like. I was totally unprepared for the real thing.

In the distance, I could hear the low purring rumble of Azree and Fiddha cooing to each other. Somehow it fitted well with what Maraed was singing. I heard Fitzee snort and then he launched himself into the sky.

*Fitzee?* I said.

# Sixteen

*I am going hunting. I will be back.*

*Shadreer,* I said. *Fitzee's—*

*Do not worry, hatchling. He can look after himself.*

While Maraed was still singing, Rimini stood up and loudly announced, 'I'm going to bed.'

Boyd nodded; his eyes still glued to Maraed's face. I hadn't realised he was such a fan of traditional Islander music. Maraed's voice faltered and the song faded into silence.

Boyd said, 'Go on, Maraed. Don't stop.'

She picked up where she'd paused and Rimini stomped off, Joffre flapping alongside of her. However, once Maraed had finished the song, Felix said that Rimini had the right idea: it was time to settle down for the night.

Fitzee returned to us just as Asher had begun to snore. I heard the other dragons welcome him so I said, *How was the hunt?*

*Go to sleep, hatchling.* He grunted and settled down next to Hizaree.

I was going to say something but Boyd began screaming in his sleep and the moment passed. I went over to Boyd and gave him a shake. That seemed to do the trick.

# Seventeen

In the morning, as we were sitting around the fire eating the last of the cheese and dried fruit and Joffre was off hunting for his breakfast, I heard Shadreer telling Silvana and Fiddha where we were going, and why. They weren't at all happy with what he was saying.

*You want us to go to the nest of our betrayers?* Fiddha said. *You think we will get help there? Are you mad?*

*We have defeated their leader and their army,* Shadreer said. *It is now ruled by a Rigoni, our ally. It is not the same place.*

*Two-legs are the same wherever we go,* Fiddha said. *They cannot be trusted. Silvana and I do not understand why you are with this clutch of humans.*

*They are our friends. Seeger, the dragon-speaker, revealed the Midrashi's treachery to us. We, the Flight, love him.*

*We trust the dragon-speaker,* Fiddha said. *His thoughts are open to us. However, we do not know what the others are thinking. Why are we with them?*

*These two-legs have agreed to help us free Draageer from our enemies.*

Silvana snorted. *These few two-legs are going to wage war for us?*

*There is a band of warriors waiting to join us at Midrash. Besides, you would be surprised what these two-legs can do. Although they are small and weak, they are brave and loyal. You will see.*

'Seeger?' Riff said. 'What's going on?' I blinked and turned to look at my brother.

'You've got that look on your face,' he said.

'The newcomers don't want to go to Midrash,' I said. 'They don't think we can be trusted.'

Asher and Felix nodded. Riff and Kieran frowned. Maraed looked from person to person, as if she didn't understand. Riva looked sad.

'I'm ashamed of my people,' she said.

Boyd and Rimini kept their heads down, not looking at anyone. Then Rimini cleared her throat, looked across at Asher and said, 'I don't want to go there, either.'

'Boyd?' Asher said. 'What about you?'

I could see Boyd's fists were clenched and his mouth kept puckering as if he was chewing something sour.

'Boyd?' I said.

He looked at me and his eyes were pools of misery. 'I don't care if I never see that place again,' he said. 'It could sink into the sand and disappear forever and I'd be the first to cheer.'

'Why didn't you say something sooner?' I said. 'Why did you come on this trip?'

For a moment, he sat staring over my shoulder at something in the distance. Then he rubbed his nose and sighed.

'I thought I could do it,' he eventually said. He looked at Rimini. 'We needed something to change in our lives and this seemed the perfect solution. Right, Rimini?'

She nodded. He flicked a glance at me and then went back to studying the horizon. 'The closer we get to that place the sicker I feel. I can't sleep. At night, I'm visited by the dead. I know I'm weak. You did it, but I don't know if I can.'

I moved over so that I could sit next to him. 'I understand. When we went back to rescue you, I couldn't stop my legs from shaking. I constantly felt as if I wanted to be sick.'

He turned to look at me. 'Then, how did you do it?'

Suddenly, I felt salt water pooling in my eyes. How embarrassing! I slowly breathed in and out and flicked the water away with my fingers.

'I found it was all right, once I was doing something. When we were in the thick of the action, there wasn't time to think about what I was feeling. I just got on with it.'

He nodded. Rimini sniffed. Salt water was running down her cheeks. Joffre dropped the dead rat he'd brought back with him and settled close to her ear, making soothing twittering noises.

'There's no shame in admitting your fear,' Riff said. 'We all know what it's like to be afraid.'

'What happened in Midrash?' Maraed said, looking from Boyd, to Rimini, to me and back again.

Kieran leant against her shoulder. 'I'll tell you later.'

Felix picked up his bow and quiver and his kitbag. 'It may be that some of our troops are staying outside the city, near to where we camped last year. You could stay with them and not go into the city at all.'

Asher stood up and brushed the dirt off the back of his pants. 'We don't have to decide anything now.'

'Let's pack up the camp,' Felix said, 'and get our gear together, while the dragons decide what they're going to do.'

Riva said, 'I don't blame the females. They watched as humans slaughtered most of their family. I wouldn't trust us, if I were them. We humans can be vile creatures. I'm going to speak to them.'

She got up and hurried over to where the Flight were huddled. I followed her so that I could interpret if she needed me to. She addressed the two females.

'Silvana, Fiddha, I can't imagine the grief you must be carrying. You've seen atrocities that go beyond my imagining. I was born in Midrash and so your pain was caused by some of my people. Even though this happened several generations ago, and today our people do not know this story, it doesn't change our guilt. I am so very, very sorry.'

Both females lowered their heads towards Riva. Fiddha spoke. *You two-legs are cruel and untrustworthy.*

I told Riva what the dragon had said. She bowed to both, with her hand over her heart.

'You say true,' she said. She straightened up. 'Even worse, we're not just cruel to animals or birds, we're also cruel to each other. The dragon-speaker here and those two young people ...' She pointed to Boyd and Rimini. 'They were stolen from their homes by the Midrashi and forced to join their army. Seeger was sent to the stables, where he met me and the Flight, but Boyd and Rimini were forced to fight. They were even forced to kill.'

The dragons' eyes flared and their ears twitched. Riva didn't need me to tell her that they were shocked to hear that.

'All three of them were physically abused and terrorised by my people. They were about to burn Seeger on a bonfire, when the Flight rescued him. I escaped with him because I have the ability to speak with some animals—camels and grivens—and if they found that out, then I would also have been burned.'

*So far,* Silvana said, *you have only proved to us that we should stay away from Midrash.*

Once again, I translated. I watched Riva's face as I spoke. She closed her eyes for a moment and whispered, 'Sed, help me.'

I put my hand on her arm. 'Let me speak.' She nodded.

'It's true that many of us are wicked, faithless and cruel,' I said. 'However, we're not all like that. There are also many who are honourable and kind. We're here because the Flight asked for our help. We're happy to give it because they're our friends. It's true that the Xanthi killed your hatchlings, but the Midrashi, their allies, stole our children and forced them to join their army. Many of those children were killed; some on the battlefield and some by the Midrashi because they were too young, too scared or too weak. Many others were seriously injured and emotionally damaged. You're not the only ones who have lost their young.'

*Is this true?* Fiddha said.

*The hatchling speaks true,* Shadreer said. *To my shame, I helped the Midrashi steal those children. Then, when we realised that the Midrashi had not honoured their contract with us and had lied to us, we left them. We joined forces with the two-legs from Seddon, Seeger's nest, and some others from Boron and Rigon. We defeated the Midrashi, burned their city and rescued the children who were still captive. Two-legs and dragons fought side by side. They were honourable allies.*

Riva whispered, 'Seeger, what's going on?'

'Shadreer is speaking on our behalf.'

*Now,* Shadreer continued, *we go to Midrash to meet up with some warrior two-legs from Seddon. They are coming with us to defeat the growing army of Midrashi and Xanthi, and free*

*Draageer of their presence. We will have our homeland once more.*

'That's right,' I said. 'Even though that city reminds us of our suffering, and our hearts are failing at the thought of being there again, we're ready to face it because it's a necessary step towards helping you win back your homeland.'

'We will fight despite our fear,' Boyd said.

I jumped at the sound of his voice. He'd walked up behind me in that stealthy way he had and I didn't know he was there. Riva softly giggled. I stuck my tongue out at her.

'We've given our word,' Boyd said. 'You can count on us.' He moved up to stand next to me. 'That's what friends do,' he said.

'You aren't the only ones who have suffered.' I jumped because this time Rimini spoke and, again, I hadn't realised she'd also joined us. I glared at Riva, daring her to laugh again.

'A dragon stole me from my home,' Rimini said. 'My mother died of grief, while I was gone. The Midrashi men hurt me, over and over and over again. Just to hear the name, "Midrash" is enough to give me nightmares. I don't want to go there ... but I will. I've given my word.'

*What's your problem, you big scaredy lizards?* Joffre said. *Don't make me fly up there and teach you a lesson! These two-legs rescued me from a gruesome death. They're helping you even though they don't know you. We're going to save your territory. If you can't be bothered, then fluff off. We'll do it without you.*

*There is no need to be so hasty,* Fiddha said. *We accept the two-legs' apology.* Her long tongue flickered. *They seem genuine. We will stay with the Flight. However, if any two-leg proves to be treacherous or lacking in honour, we will deal with them.*

I translated what Fiddha said. Everyone nodded. Riva bowed to them again. Rimini flashed a quick smile. It completely changed her face! She's really quite pretty when she isn't scowling.

*Joffre,* I said, *you had a nerve challenging a dragon. What could you have done?*

*I could have put its eye out,* he said. *Never mess with a raven.*

Felix, who was kicking dirt over the fire, called out, 'All settled? Very good. Let's go.'

We ran to collect our things and then to mount our dragons. I helped Maraed climb up behind her brother. She smiled at me and I swear I forgot how to breathe. I finally remembered and gasped a lungful in, just as the world was turning black.

She put her hand on my arm. 'Thank you, Seeger. I'm sorry for what happened to you. I guess I'm not the only one who was stolen from her family. I think you and the others are all very brave.'

I felt the heat in my cheeks and mumbled something incomprehensible to her. She giggled. Kieran laughed. 'You'd better get moving, Seeg,' he said. 'Shadreer's looking impatient.'

'Yes. You're right. Of course,' I said, slowly backing away from the flame-haired vision.

As we soared over the desert, I thanked Shadreer for speaking on our behalf.

*It was necessary,* he said. *Silvana and Fiddha left Draageer during a violent and frightening attack, when they were still young. They have not had contact with any other two-legs since then. They have not had a chance to know you as we do. They will learn. It will be well.*

*I hope so. Azree and Fiddha seem very happy. I would hate to see that spoiled.*

# Seventeen

It was late in the afternoon when we finally saw the city of Midrash up ahead. We couldn't see any encampment outside the city, so we flew over the Citadel area. There, near the old barracks, we could see some tents set up in the training arena. It looked as though the Seddonese troops had settled in there, although it surely couldn't be all of them. The Flight circled overhead, landing one at a time to allow their human passengers to alight, and then took off again. Only Shadreer landed near the dragons' pool. He said that the others would stay out in the ranges to the south of the city, while he would come inside to visit with Jarl and Myrmee.

Just as we were heading into the stables area, through the door that led out to the pool, I heard a shout from inside the complex. A figure burst through the door.

'Hey, hey! The gang's all here!'

'Sergeant Grimm!' I said.

'It's captain now,' he said.

'Congratulations!'

He flapped his hand as if brushing away a fly. 'Mika's just being kind to an old soldier. Rog's here, too. We've already restocked our water supply and food rations and we're ready to go.'

The others walked inside, followed by Shadreer, who was keen to see Myrmee again. I went in last, walking down the corridor with Grimm so that I could ask him some questions.

'Where's the army?' I said. 'Where are the animals? Apart from the tents in the training arena, there's hardly a sign that you're here.'

Grimm looked sideways at me, as he scratched his head. 'Well, lad, you see ... Well, the fact is ...'

'Spit it out, Sergeant ... sorry, Captain.'

He held my elbow and led me down to the kitchen area. 'I'd rather wait until everyone can hear.'

# Eighteen

## Boyd Speaks

Talk about surprises! There we were, eating breakfast and feeling rather pleased with ourselves. We'd rescued Maraed with no loss of life, despite Asher's cousin-friend trying to double-cross us and the large tavern-keeper threatening us with his axe. I confess that I hadn't felt that good in a long time.

Then Seeger drops the bombshell that there are other dragons in the area and they're about to join us. How could he forget to tell us that? There were plenty of opportunities to let us know this momentous news and it slipped his mind? Really? He stood there looking at the rest of us as though we were the weird ones, not him. I mean ... more dragons! I was still getting used to being so close and friendly with the ones we already had. Dragons might be everyday creatures like cats and camels to him, but they're strange, fierce beasts to the

# Eighteen

rest of us. And now, there were going to be more of them?

Shortly after he'd decided to tell us that gem, two new dragons flew into our clearing. We'd moved to the tree line to give them room. As far as it's possible to think that dragons can be beautiful, those two were stunning to look at. They were a pale shade of blue and their wings sparkled as though they were shot through with silver thread.

Our Flight were warbling and shuffling about, obviously excited to see them. I watched them greet the newcomers. It was touching. These must have been some of the dragons that fled the slaughter by the Xanthi. I saw another side to these huge beasts. They could be tender and affectionate. Who knew?

Then I heard Seeger retching. His face was ashen, his eyes looked sunken and he was hugging his knees, rolling on the ground and groaning.

'What's up with Seeger?' I said.

Riva said she'd seen him like this once before and said something about him being overwhelmed by the dragons' feelings. That didn't seem right to me. Why couldn't he just stop listening to them? I know he doesn't hear everything they say because he chooses not to listen in, so I didn't see the problem. However, Riva said this was different. Watching him roll about like that, making those terrible noises, I felt so helpless. If only there was something I could do.

Felix must have had the same thought because he suddenly scooped Seeger up in his arms and charged off into the forest, with Riva running alongside him. Seeger thrashed about, his arms flailing all over the place. He sounded frightened. I couldn't have that, so I immediately chased after them. Rimini, my shadow, was only seconds

173

behind me. Later I realised that Kieran and Maraed had also joined us. I don't know what they thought they could do to help. They should have stayed behind with Asher and Riff.

We ran for a while but eventually Seeger asked us to stop. I could see that he had some colour back in his cheeks and he looked better. Felix put him down and asked what had happened back in the clearing.

Riva explained the situation. Seeger had his head down and his blush could have lit up a room. His cheeks glowed with heat. That's typical of Seeg. He doesn't like to talk about himself.

When Riva told us what Fingle did to him, I felt my face and hands grow cold and my stomach churned. I knew he'd been beaten. I remember Idris telling me about it when I was recovering from the flogging Fingle had given me. I thought it was like that for Seeger. I had no idea the old Beast-Master of Midrash had gone so far. He really was a twisted piece of work.

When I confessed to Seeger that I had no idea how bad it was, once again he made light of his suffering saying it was water under the bridge and that I'd also been badly treated. I remembered what he used to say, "We're small but we're wise, we're terrors for our size." I smiled and he smiled back. Perhaps we hadn't moved as far apart as I thought we had.

I remembered our promise to each other to be fighting roosters, so I said, 'Cock-a-doodle-do.'

The flash in his eyes told me he knew what I meant as he repeated the refrain to me. Kieran said we were weird but we didn't care. It was just something between me and Seeger.

We went back to the clearing and he seemed all right. Whatever had been going on with the dragons that had caused such a strong reaction in him was now over. We were introduced to the two new dragons: Silvana and Fiddha. Honestly, the names these dragons give themselves! Am I the only one who finds them funny? Anyway, we were now accompanied by six dragons instead of four.

The dark blue dragon, Azree, was clearly enamoured of the pinky-blue newcomer, Fiddha. It was also obvious that the red dragon, Fitzee, was consumed with jealousy. Poor old fellow.

Late the next afternoon we landed in an old abandoned town. From what the others were saying, they'd discovered it when the army from Seddon was on its way to Midrash last year. Asher, Seeger and the others keep forgetting that Rimini, Maraed and I weren't with them for most of their adventures. Most nights I had to explain to Rimini what they were talking about, to help her keep up. She relies on me far too much. I wish she'd make friends with the others, instead of clinging to me like a limpet to a rock.

When Maraed sang to us as we sat around the campfire, I got lost in her voice. There was something about the way that she sang that drew me in and enveloped me with warmth and hope. Rimini ruined the mood by announcing she was off to bed. Why didn't she just go without making it such a drama? Maraed's song faltered and then stopped. I told her to keep singing. I don't know what Rimini was playing at. Why'd she have to spoil it for the rest of us?

The next morning, we were sitting around the fire eating breakfast. I was sick to death of cheese and figs and was thinking of creamy porridge and fried fish, when I noticed that Seeger wasn't eating. He had that gormless, dreamy expression on his face again. He gets like that every now and then. It makes him look as though he's a fence short of a paddock. From what he said to Riff I finally figured it out: he gets like that when he's listening to the dragons talking.

It turns out they were arguing about going to Midrash. The newcomers weren't too happy about it. I don't blame them. I wasn't so keen either. The night before, I'd had another one of those dreams in which all the dead and injured paraded before me: Idris, Drebbin, Tam, the kids who were killed when we attacked Ludlum, Luda and Rasman who never made it past their first day in training, and all the others I'd known who'd died because of Midrash. One after the other, they all pointed at me and said, 'It's your fault.' I'd plead with them. I'd say I was sorry. I'd scream, 'Go away!' But they'd keep coming, keep pointing, keep bleeding ...

The closer I got to that cursed city, the worse the dreams had become. I didn't know if I could hold it together much longer. How did Seeger do it? That place messed him up, too, yet he went back to rescue me and now he was going there again. Does he get nightmares? I don't think so.

Then Rimini said she didn't want to go there either and everyone was looking at us. I told them what I thought. I hoped that Asher or Felix would say that we could bypass Midrash and head straight for the Dragons' homeland.

Instead, Seeger asked why I'd volunteered for the trip. I couldn't say, "I had to get out of Seddon before my father beat me to death" so I made a vague reference to needing a fresh start, or something like that. Then, before I could stop myself, I told them about the dreams. I looked at Seeger, calm as always, and I asked how he did it. He confessed that his legs shook and he felt sick! No one would have guessed that. Riff said that there was no shame in being afraid. I didn't agree with him then but later, thinking about what Seeger said—that he didn't think about it, he just got on with what he had to do—I realised that he was right. Being brave doesn't mean you don't feel fear; it means you do what's right, what's needed, even though you're afraid. Seeger does that all the time. I've always thought that he was braver than me.

Then, while I was chewing on all that, and wishing people would stop looking at me, Riva suddenly races off to the dragons. She began to apologise to the females. I couldn't believe it. I'd totally forgotten that Riva was a Midrashi. I thought of her as one of us. It made me think not all Midrashi are bad. Lorik was all right, even though he was a soldier. Jarl is a good man. There were others I'd met that were just like the people of Seddon.

I could tell that the dragons were listening to her. Then Seeger began to interpret what they were saying. They didn't trust any of us. I remembered what Seeger once told me about dragons: honour is everything to them. I knew I had to tell them that, despite my fear, I would keep my promise to help them get their land back. Then Rimini joined in.

I felt a flash of annoyance when she first spoke but when she revealed some of her story to the whole group, I couldn't stay cross with her. It was the first time she'd let them in, a little, to the pain she carried in her heart. She was brave to do that and I think the dragons could see it and respected it. I respected her a bit more, too. I remembered that she wasn't just someone who clung to me. She was a fellow soldier who had endured far worse at the hands of the Midrashi than I had.

Later that same day we were flying over the circular city of Midrash. I couldn't see any army camped near it. Where were the Seddonese? Had we got there before them?

# Nineteen

## Seeger Speaks

The others were already seated around the kitchen table and Jarl was busy serving everyone with a hot drink. He put the ladle down to hug me in greeting.

'It's so good to see you again, lad,' he said. 'You should have seen the two dragons greet each other. I swear they had tears in their eyes.'

'It's always good to see you, Jarl,' I said. 'Where are the dragons now?'

'They've wandered down to the end room. Myrmee's moved in there. He can use the tunnel to go outside after the sun has sunk below the hills and get some fresh air without upsetting anyone.'

I nodded. 'How's Myrmee's reading and writing coming along?'

Jarl ladled some serves of warm milk into two mugs and gave one each to Riff and Riva.

# Nineteen

'I'm astounded at how quickly the old dragon has learned his letters,' Jarl said, scooping up another ladle of milk and pouring it into a mug for me. 'He's been reading everything I can find to bring him and he writes every day. We can converse now. He's a wise old fellow.'

I sat down at the table and sipped my drink. Jarl sat next to me. Grimm sat opposite me, next to Felix. For a while there was silence as everyone quietly drank their warm milk. Well, I say "everyone" but Asher was a slurper. Every now and then Maraed would frown and flick a glance at him.

Then, Boyd said, 'So when's the army getting here, Grimm?'

'Ah, yes,' the captain said, 'about that …'

Asher put his mug down and leant sideways over the table, past Maraed, so that he could see Grimm's face. 'I've been wondering the same thing. I was sure they would have got here before us.'

Captain Grimm scratched his head and grinned nervously. 'Now, I don't want you getting upset but …'

'Spit it out, Grimm,' Felix said.

The captain nodded and pushed his mug away from him. 'There is no army.'

'What?' Felix leaped up from the table, knocking his chair over. 'The Commander promised!'

Grimm flapped his hand at him. 'Yes, yes, don't get excited. General Mika has sent help, just not a whole army. The logistics of moving that many men so far north without a guaranteed supply chain was too risky.'

'I don't understand,' Asher said. 'We promised the dragons—'

'Don't worry,' Grimm said. 'I've got a crack squad of seasoned fighters. There's a troop of experienced archers that will be led by Felix and a small band of well-keepers led by our old friend, Rog.'

I didn't like the sound of that. 'Just how many are there altogether?'

'About a hundred or so.'

'Is that all?' I said. 'What can a hundred people do against Blunt's army?'

From the uproar that ensued around the table, everyone else was as shocked as me. Asher kept shaking his head, muttering to himself. 'No, no, no. This isn't good enough. Not good enough at all.'

Grimm held his right hand up. 'Now, now. We have fifty archers, forty soldiers and ten well-keepers, plus a few healers, a couple of cooks and a few others. Success doesn't always lie in numbers. You'll see. Tell them, Felix.'

'It is possible for a small attack force to beat a large army,' Felix said. 'It depends on the strategy. I assume Mika instructed you, Grimm?'

'Well,' he said, scratching his head again, 'as we don't know what sort of terrain we'll be working with, she left a lot of it up to me.' He beamed at us as we sat around the table staring at him in shock. 'I have the utmost confidence that we will succeed.'

'And the animals?' I said.

'There are four griven, which will haul our supply and equipment wagons. No camels.'

Shirra wouldn't be happy about that. I'd promised her we'd meet up in Midrash.

'We're walking to Draageer?' I said.

'It won't take long,' Grimm said. 'Think of it as a grand adventure.' He turned to Asher. 'Do you have any maps of the area, Ash?'

The Record-Keeper looked miserable. 'Not many. Not

many at all. I've never been there so I haven't made any myself. I found a few old maps of the Xanthi kingdom that includes the mountain range the dragons live in, but I'm not sure how reliable they are.' He looked up at Grimm. 'I'm very, very disappointed. The dragons will be devastated when they hear this news.'

Felix picked up the chair he'd knocked over and sat on it. 'Don't worry too much, Asher. There are benefits in being a small force. We'll move quicker and more easily. We'll be more flexible in our movements and we'll stay undetected for much longer. Surprise will be on our side. It's not all doom and gloom.'

'Where's Rog, now?' Riff said.

'He's been working with the Midrashi to sort out a problem with their culverts,' Grimm said. 'Tatum asked him if he could help. He should be finished by this evening.'

'What about Tatum?' Asher said. 'Has the Rigoni added any of his men to our force?'

Grimm shook his head. 'No, but he's been very generous with water, foodstuffs and other supplies.'

He looked around the room and saw the same worried and confused faces that I saw.

'Each one of our force is equal to ten less talented fighters,' he said. 'I suggest that we rest up tonight, enjoy the meal Jarl is preparing for us and try to get a good night's sleep. We'll have a planning session tomorrow morning before we head out. All right? Good.'

He got up and left the room. Felix asked Asher if he had the maps handy. Ash pulled them out of his kitbag and they began to pore over them. Riva helped Jarl pack up the mugs. Riff and Kieran were muttering to each other. Boyd and Rimini were doing the same. Their conversation looked a little more animated than that of the other two. Rimini kept shaking her head. I turned to Maraed, who seemed to be trying to fade into the wall.

'Would you like to come meet the camels?' I said. 'Although they're a bit rough and ready, they're good-hearted creatures. And then there's old Myrmee. He's a delight.'

'Myrmee?' she said, standing up from the table.

'The old dragon. I'll introduce you.'

She nodded. 'So many dragons!' she said. 'To think that only a couple of days ago, I didn't believe they existed.'

I led her down the passage to the camels' quarters. 'What, not even when you were tied to the stake in the clearing?'

'I admit I believed back then,' she said. 'I was terrified. But then, when the men from Forabad turned up and there was no sign of the beast, I decided that dragons were just an invention of the mayor, Sed curse his soul.'

I laughed. 'If you only knew! Fitzee, the red dragon, was living in a cave just above the clearing the whole time. He always hid when the drumming and singing began. He didn't like the noise.'

She laughed with me. 'I wish I'd known he was there. I'd have called for help.'

'He loves to swoop in and save the day. He calls himself, the Red Peril.'

She grinned. 'How wonderful. I wish I could talk to them like you do.'

We'd reached the door to the camels' stalls. 'I wish I could sing like you.'

We walked into the room and immediately the camels began to call, *Seeger, mate! Long time no see, young feller-me-lad! Still got a girlie with you, hey?* and so on. I introduced Maraed to Bob, Gerald and the rest of the camels. Before I could stop her, she curtseyed to them, which they all loved.

*She's smart as well as cute,* Gerald said.

I told Maraed what the big camel said and she giggled. I told them that she was a singer and, of course, they wanted to hear a song.

*Does she know a song with camels in it?* Bob said.

I passed on the request. She thought for a moment and then said, 'There's an ancient song about a caravan. Would that do?'

Of course, it did. Gerald said, *Everyone knows a caravan is a flock of camels on a long trek. Sing away, young lady.*

'It goes something like this,' she said.

She began to sing and all the camels moved up to the rails of their stalls to watch and listen.

Let's take a caravan to the motherland,

It's a long way to go, so hold my hand.

When we reach the land where we were born,

The darkness will end with a golden dawn.

Let's take a caravan, it's a golden caravan.

Let's join the caravan of love.

There was more along those lines but I won't repeat it all. All right ... I say true, I can't remember the rest of it. As Maraed said, it was an ancient song so I didn't know it. However, her voice did its usual magic, filling the room with love, warmth and hope. I could tell the camels loved it, even without listening to them. Their eyes shone and several even drooled. When Maraed had finished singing, for a moment the only sound in the room was our breathing. The camels sighed. Then Bob gurgled his approval and the others joined in.

'What are they doing?' Maraed said. 'Why are they making that noise?'

'They're applauding you,' I said.

'Oh!' She curtseyed again. 'I'm glad you liked it.'

'I'm taking her to meet Myrmee now,' I said. 'I hope I'll see you again before we leave.'

*Thanks, mate, and thanks young lady,* Bob said. *We'll never forget this. You stay safe, you hear?*

I led Maraed back down the passageway to the large chamber at the far end. It was the room that had the doorway leading to the secret tunnel. I told her what Jarl had said about Myrmee moving in there, and that the old dragon could then go outside the walls during the night and wander around without frightening anyone. She thought it was sad that he felt he had to hide away, never going outside in the daylight. I agreed.

Shadreer and Myrmee were standing facing each other, their foreheads pressed together.

'What are they doing?' Maraed said.

'Sharing memories.'

I walked over to Myrmee and hugged his chest. He and Shadreer pulled apart and Myrmee clutched me to him with a front leg.

*Seeger, dear hatchling, it is so good to see you again,* he said. *You will never guess what I am doing these days. Go on. Try to guess.*

'I have no idea,' I said. I stepped back and turned to Maraed. 'He wants me to guess what he's been doing lately.' I turned back to Myrmee. 'This is Kieran's sister, Maraed. We rescued her from slavery in the town of Portsmouth, near the river Anx in the south-west.'

Myrmee inclined his head in greeting. *Delighted to make your acquaintance,* he said, *and congratulations on gaining your freedom.*

I told Maraed what he said and she blew him a kiss.

# Nineteen

Shadreer threw his head back and bugled. Maraed was startled and looked at me to explain. I told her that the dragon was laughing. She grinned.

'I never knew that animals could laugh,' she said. 'Well, I never!'

*Go on, hatchling. Guess,* Myrmee said.

'I've no idea what you've been doing, Myrmee,' I said. 'You'll have to tell me.'

*I am writing my memoirs!*

'You're writing your memoirs?' I said.

Maraed clapped her hands. 'How wonderful!'

'You've lived a very long time, Myrmee,' I said. 'So, it'll take a long time to write it all down.'

*I know!* Myrmee said. *I make sure I write a few pages every day. It will be a long process but I believe it will be worth it. I have seen a lot of interesting things in my lifetime. I would like to pass on my experiences and the wisdom I have gained.*

'If you want to give it to the next generation, you'll have to teach them to read and write, too,' I said.

Myrmee frowned and turned to look at Shadreer, who inclined his head towards the old one.

'I have confidence in you,' Maraed said. 'I'm sure you can do whatever you put your mind to do.'

*I like her,* Myrmee said.

*So do I,* I said, *but don't tell her.*

*Ah. Once bitten, twice shy?*

*How did you know about—*

*Shadreer showed me when we shared memories.*

'It's time to go, Maraed,' I said. 'I'm not sure how far we have to walk tomorrow but we need to be prepared for a long trip. Goodbye, Myrmee. I hope we'll meet again soon.'

The old dragon leant forward and nudged my cheek with his snout. I patted it before turning to leave.

*I will walk with you,* Shadreer said. *There is something I want you to help me talk to Jarl about.*

When we left the chamber, I sent Maraed back to the kitchen to ask Jarl to meet Shadreer and me by the soaking pool. We didn't have to wait long. In hardly any time, he hurried out to meet us, wiping his hands on his apron.

'I was just finishing getting the meal ready for everyone,' he said. 'I hope this won't take long.'

'Shadreer wants to talk to you about Myrmee. He's worried about him and has a suggestion he'd like you to consider.'

'Of course! I'm happy to do anything that'll help the old fellow. What do you have in mind?'

It was a short conversation but at the end of it, as Jarl and I hurried back to the kitchen—he was worried that the meat would burn—we grinned at each other as we ran.

'That dragon is a clever beast,' Jarl said. 'It'll be fun.'

# Twenty

The next morning, before we'd even had breakfast, Joffre had set off on a tour of the city. He'd found a small flock of pigeons who'd promised to show him the sights. Asher, Felix, Grimm, Jaxon the archer, Rog, Riff, Boyd and I met in Jarl's kitchen. Asher's maps of the northern area were spread out on the table in front of us. Kieran and Rimini were off restocking our small group's supplies of food and water, even though Grimm had said we were welcome to share the army's provisions. Riva and Maraed were having a session with the Citadel's wardrobe mistress. Riva said something about Maraed's gown not being suitable attire for our mission. I didn't know what the fuss was about. I thought she looked wonderful in it.

'Shouldn't we have invited Shadreer to be a part of this?' I asked. Everyone looked at me as if I'd suddenly spoken in a foreign language. 'He's the leader of the Flight and it's his homeland after all. He and the other dragons are the reason we're going there in the first place.'

There was a mixed reaction to what I said: some frowned, some let their mouths drop open and one—Asher—smiled ruefully.

'Seeger, lad,' he said, 'he wouldn't fit in here.'

'Then we should meet with him outside.'

Grimm looked steadily at me. 'Not now, Seeger.' He looked around at the rest of the group with an expression that seemed to say, 'He's just a kid. What would he know?'

Felix said, 'He has a point.'

'Now look,' Rog said, 'I don't think we need worry about what a few animals think.'

At that Riff sat up in his chair and scowled at his former leader. 'Tell me you don't really think that Rog!'

'They just do what Seeger tells them to,' Grimm said. Everyone around the table, apart from Rog, glared at him. 'Don't they?'

'Underestimate them at your peril,' Asher said. 'They're very clever and very proud beasts.'

There was more heated discussion but I didn't listen. I could feel a gentle tugging in my mind.

*Hatchling,* Shadreer said, *I am listening.*

*I'm very sorry that no one thought to include you in the planning session, Shadreer.*

*Do not be concerned. I am used to the ways of the two-legs. They assume that they are the only creatures that can think.*

*It's only Grimm and Rog. They don't know you like the rest of us do.*

*They will learn,* Shadreer said. *Be patient.*

'… and that stupid look on his face!' Grimm shouted.

I found everyone staring at me. 'What?' I said.

'What did the dragon say?' Riff said.

Grimm stuck his tongue between his lips and made an airy, squelching sound, while throwing his hands up in the air.

188

Asher frowned at him. 'Don't be so childish, Grimm!' he said. 'Go on, Seeger, what did he say?'

'He'll listen in through me. I can pass on anything he has to say.' I stared at Grimm. 'He's used to humans ignoring him and thinking he's a dumb animal.' I glared at Rog. 'But he knows exactly what's going on, so don't be fooled. He also has an excellent memory.'

Asher, Felix and Riff all nodded in agreement. I looked at Boyd, who smiled and shrugged. Grimm and Rog were frowning but Rog had pulled one of the maps towards himself and was studying it. Finally, I turned to Jaxon.

'Weren't you the fellow who escorted Riva and the camels out of Midrash?'

He nodded. 'That's right. Nice to see you again, lad. They were interesting times. Those dragons of yours made all the difference in the fight.'

Grimm turned to look at Jaxon, still frowning but not so angrily.

'They're not my dragons,' I said. 'I don't own them. I don't control them. I'm their friend.'

'Fair enough,' Jaxon said. 'I'm looking forward to seeing them in action again.'

'This is all well and good,' Grimm said, 'and I'm sorry if I've offended you, Seeger, but let's get on with planning our mission, shall we?'

He pulled the other map towards him.

'Have you been up north before, Captain?' I said.

He shook his head.

'So, you don't know much about the terrain then. Do you know where Blunt has his army?'

Again, he shook his head.

'Does anyone at this table know where it is?'

Everyone shook their heads. Felix's mouth began to curl in a sly grin.

'I know someone who knows the terrain intimately and can not only tell you where Blunt has his army, but he could lead you right to it.'

Grimm sighed and ran his hand over his head. 'We've no time for your games, lad.'

Felix smiled at me. 'Don't be so hasty, Grimm. We don't want to go up there blind. Tell us who the informer is, Seeger.'

I stretched back in my chair. 'I don't know … I don't think Captain Grimm is interested.'

Asher looked from Felix to me and then back again to Felix. I saw the light turn on in his eyes. 'Oh, of course!' he said.

'Stop teasing him, Seeger,' Riff said.

'Very well,' I said, 'I'll ask Shadreer to tell me what he knows and I'll then translate for you.'

Grimm frowned and looked as though he was about to say something but Felix didn't give him a chance. 'That's great. Let's spread out the maps so all of us can see and then, Asher, you find the places that Shadreer, via Seeger, will describe.'

Grimm and Rog spread the maps out in the middle of the table and everyone stood up, to get a better view. I asked Shadreer to tell me all that he could remember and then I began to share that with the rest of the group.

'The dragons have retreated to the highest peaks of the mountains of Ylani, the dominant range in the area,' I said.

Asher pointed to a curving line of mountains up at one side of the map. 'These must be the ones he means,' he said. 'They're in the north. There are other lower hills scattered around but, as these are the highest and most prominent, I can't see what else the dragon could mean. Of course, the locals might have another name for them.'

I continued. 'Blunt has taken up the area in the middle of the largest valley, alongside the Sayle River that runs through it. The river flows from West to East, with its source up in the slightly smaller range of mountains that are covered by the forests of Bjorn.'

Asher pointed to the spot on the map. 'It looks as though the river is quite wide. I'm surprised Blunt thinks he's got room in that valley to grow an army.'

I relayed his comment to Shadreer and then I repeated the dragon's reply. 'It's not wide anymore. Shadreer says that the Xanthi built a big wall up in the mountains to turn the river into a lake. What is left is just a trickle compared to the original river.'

'Have they now?' Rog said. 'We might be able to work with that. That's very interesting.'

'Shadreer said that there are farms along the valley's edge, mainly on the northern side near the foothills of Ylani.' I said. 'They would have once faced right onto the river but now, since the building of the wall, they have more land to farm. There are channels that come from the river to water their crops and livestock.'

Grimm nodded. 'I bet Blunt counts on them to help feed his troops.'

Felix, Riff and Boyd all agreed.

'Blunt's troops,' I said, 'are on the southern side of the river.'

'This is wonderful information,' Felix said. 'Where does he think we would best dig in, when we get there?'

'Shadreer says that there is a natural fortress in the hills at the Eastern end of the valley. He's showing me what looks like a rocky escarpment at the top of a steep rise, at the end of a short canyon. Can you find it on the map, Asher?'

The team all eagerly scanned the map. Asher felt it might be something that was marked as a ravine on the map but he wasn't sure.

'Shadreer says he can fly you over the area once we get near and you can see for yourselves. There are some small caves in the same area.'

Grimm nodded again. 'That's good to know. We're going to need somewhere to store equipment and make repairs and so on. I have a feeling we're going to rely a lot on the bowmen to win this battle, so we have to ensure a good supply of arrows.'

'We've brought some fletchers with us,' Jaxon said.

Everyone nodded but I had no idea what a "fletcher" was. Felix must have noticed my confusion because he said to me, 'That's an arrow-maker.' Well, why didn't they say that in the first place?

Asher said, 'We also need to find a way to turn the locals against the Midrashi. We have to convince them that they can co-exist with the dragons. I know very little about the Xanthi. Can anyone enlighten me?'

Everyone shook their heads.

I said, 'They used to have a reputation for being fierce warriors and for eating their enemies. However, that was a long time ago before they became farmers.'

Jaxon spoke up. 'I suggest we send a small crew into the area, in disguise, to get to know some of the farmers. There's nothing better than first-hand knowledge.'

'I agree,' Felix said. 'Perhaps we can sow a few seeds of distrust of Blunt among the locals.'

'I have an idea,' Boyd said.

Everyone turned to look at him. He hadn't said a word so far.

'We should use the talents we have on hand. Kieran is an amazing dancer and his sister, Maraed, sings like an angel.

Why don't we send them, plus a few extras like Asher and Riff, disguised as travelling minstrels? They can put on a little show to entertain the farmers. Country people always welcome such visits as they rarely have a chance to get to a city.'

Asher clapped his hands. 'That is a lovely, lovely idea, Boyd! Oh well done you!'

'You'd make a great story-teller, Asher,' Rog said. He smiled. 'Folks love to hear a good tale by the fire at night.'

Felix said, 'I suggest the non-combatants go with Asher. That's Seeger, Kieran, Maraed, Riff and Riva. They could take one of the wagons, after we've downloaded our stuff. They'd look more authentic travelling that way.'

'Wouldn't you need Seeger here to work with the dragons?' Boyd said.

I held my breath. I knew they didn't need me but I wanted to stay with them, instead of being shunted off to the side with all the other civilians.

'I'm sure we'll manage for a few days,' Felix said. I breathed out. I don't know why I bothered to hope. 'But,' he continued, 'you'll need some musicians.'

For a moment everyone thought about what he said. He was right, of course, but I couldn't think of an answer and it didn't look as though anyone else had an idea either.

Then Jaxon slapped his forehead. 'Where's my brain? Nikluss has a tin whistle with him and Angus carries a bodhran around. They could go with you. They'd be a bit of protection, as well, if needs be.'

I whispered out of the side of my mouth to Asher, 'What's a bodhran?'

'A hand drum,' he whispered back.

Grimm rubbed his hands together as a grin spread across his face. 'This is more like it!' He rolled up the maps. 'Thank the dragon for his help, please Seeger. We can discuss tactics on the journey up there.'

'Shadreer said the Flight will fly on ahead,' I said. 'They'll meet with us again at the base of the southern ranges. They want to visit with the other dragons while they have the opportunity.'

*See you soon, Shadreer,* I said. *I hope all is well with the others on the mountain top.*

*Thank you, hatchling.*

'I assume,' Felix said, 'that at first we'll be making short forays into the field to sow doubt and fear among Blunt's troops? Steal some stuff, attack supply wagons, kill a few sentries and so on?'

'While that's going on,' Rog said, 'I can take the well-keepers up to the dam wall and wreak some havoc. If we can break through it, the resulting flood would cause a lot of damage.'

'I like it,' Grimm said. 'You should take a couple of archers with you, in case the wall is guarded.'

'Rimini and I will go with them,' Boyd said. 'We can fight if necessary and we'd like to be useful.'

Grimm looked at Rog, who nodded his agreement. 'Very well,' he said, 'Asher, can you figure out where we should head, using these old maps?'

'Of course!' he said. 'And once we're there, we can always fly with the dragons to get an overview if we get stuck.'

'Very good,' Grimm said. 'Sort out who you're taking with you, then talk to Jarl, organise your food and water and we'll get going.'

'Right!' Asher said, looking rather vague. 'Err ... right. We'll ... err ...'

'Don't worry, Asher,' Riff said, 'Kieran and I will soon

get us sorted.'

After several days of walking north with the griven—Trevor and Harvey, and Chops and Biff—pulling two wagon loads of supplies, we finally reached the foothills of the mountain range that formed the southern boundary of the Sayle River valley. We set up camp near a water hole. The animals were grateful but the mosquitoes were fierce and the next morning we were all keen to move on. Even the raven found the insects annoying. I'd hoped he'd eat them but he wasn't interested. However, Grimm wouldn't let us leave. He said he wanted a couple of the dragons to take himself, Rog, Felix and Asher on a flight over the area so that they knew what they would be dealing with, before moving further in.

While waiting for the dragons to find us, I went to where the griven were grazing. Trevor and Harvey had grumbled the whole way there. They took turns complaining to me about the food, the length of the journey, the weight of the supply wagons, the heat of the day, the cold of the night, the way the wagon-drivers spoke to them, the way the dragons looked at them ...

*Honestly, you are a pair of miseries,* I said.

*I don't understand what you mean,* Harvey said. *We're never miserable.*

I stared at them, my mouth hanging open.

*What?* Trevor said. *What?*

*You are the most grumpy, depressed, negative creatures I have ever met!*

Trevor and Harvey looked at each other. Then they looked at me. They blinked several times. Harvey shook his head and Trevor flicked his ears.

*Ridiculous!* Trevor said. *You wound me with that accusation.*

*We're always positive,* Harvey said.

I laughed in disbelief. *Oh yes,* I said. *You were positive that Timkins and Rawnsley were going to beat you to death. You were positive you would die of thirst on the journey to Midrash. You were positive the Midrashi would shoot you down in a hail of arrows and you were positive the dragons would eat you.*

*Exactly!* Harvey said. *Positive, positive, positive.*

Trevor shook his head and snorted. *We've always known that you two-legs don't understand us griven. We're doomed to suffer because of your ignorance.*

*And we're positive about that,* Harvey interrupted.

They turned their backs on me so I hurried off to find some company with others who were in a better temper.

Joffre, who had sat on my shoulder listening to the grivens' litany of woes, said, *What's their problem?*

*They can't help it, Joffre. They were born depressed.*

*Maybe it's because they can't sing. A little caw or two, a short trill in the upper registers and the sadness soon lifts. Poor things. It's a shame they can't be birds like me.*

*If they were, they wouldn't be able to pull the wagons for us.*

*I don't know about that. We ravens could do it … if there were enough of us.*

*That would be an unkindness.*

*What's unkind about ravens pulling a wagon for you, if they want to do it?*

*Nothing, Joffre. That's the name we give a group of you. You know: a parliament of owls, a flutter of sparrows and an unkindness of ravens.*

*Humph! I don't think much of that. What do you call crows?*

*A murder of crows.*

*Well, you got that right!*

We passed Riva, Rimini and Maraed who were taking it in turns to braid each other's hair.

# Twenty

'Good morning, ladies,' I said. Rimini simply nodded but Riva and Maraed both said hello. 'Riva, the griven are miserable as usual,' I said. 'Do you think you could visit them, once you're done here?'

'Of course,' she said.

'We'll all go,' Maraed said.

Rimini nodded again. 'I like your hair like that,' I told her. She blushed.

Shortly after Joffre and I had found Boyd and Kieran, and we'd begun a game of knuckle bones, the dragons came winging in. Azree and Fiddha were missing but Jondalee was back with the Flight.

Azree and Fiddha had chosen to stay with the remainder of the dragons on the mountain top. Azree would replace Jondalee as the only flame-breather, while Fiddha enjoyed her reunion with the few remaining females. Silvana, however, wanted to help in the fight with Blunt. I'd noticed that she'd begun to follow Fitzee around, staring at him with an adoring gaze when he wasn't looking, so it didn't surprise me that she'd chosen to stay wherever he was. He seemed oblivious to her adoration.

Shadreer and Fitzee took the men up for their reconnaissance flight, while the other dragons settled down for a short nap. I hugged Jondalee's face as he lay there next to Hizaree and I told him I'd missed him. He said he'd missed me, too, and the rest of the Flight. Things had been rather grim up on the mountain top, with so many dragons now dead or missing, and the responsibility of protecting the few who were left was a huge burden for him to carry. He was looking forward to being in the action again.

I introduced him to Joffre. *How very interesting,* Jondalee said. *I have been learning about the local two-legs while I was waiting for the Flight to return. I think you will be surprised to hear what they think of ravens.*

*What are you suggesting, pal?* Joffre said.

*I do beg your pardon if I have offended you. That was not my intention. No, no. You are a very important bird.*

*You've got that right!* Joffre said. *I can see you're a dragon of great intelligence. I think we'll be good friends.*

He flew off my shoulder and perched on Jondalee's. He tucked himself up against the dragon's neck just below his ear and after preening himself he settled down to sleep. I smiled at the sight. Jondalee winked at me. It brought back memories of Azree and Midnight, the cat.

I was sitting by the campfire with Kieran, Boyd and Riff, when Shadreer and Fitzee returned with the men. They jumped down off the dragons' backs, thanked them for their help and then ran into Grimm's tent. The four of us leapt up and hurried in after them.

In the tent, Grimm, Rog, Felix and Asher were already leaning over a map that was spread out on the table between them.

'Here's the river valley,' Asher said, pointing to a spot on the bottom third of the map. 'The dam's up here.' He pointed to the left.

I could see the ranges and the woods but there was only a mark where the river came down out of the hills onto the plain. The others all nodded in agreement so it looked as though Asher was right.

'The caves and that interesting ridge that the dragons showed us are here.' He pointed to the right-hand side of the map, just below the course of the river.

Felix traced a line along the upper edge of the river, near the foothills of the northern side of the valley. 'There were some farmsteads along here,' he said. 'That's where you should head, Asher.'

'If I were you,' Grimm said, 'I'd take your party up along the eastern end of the valley, circling around the base of the ridge. I think there was a ford here ...' he pointed to a place where the river narrowed, '... where you could cross over. You should be far enough away from Blunt's army, down there.'

'How long should we take?' Asher said.

'I think it'll take you a day to get to the ford from there,' Grimm said. 'Then allow three or four nights to visit the nearest farms. Come back via the ford and up into the hills down here ...' again he pointed to the map '... where we'll be camped. Don't worry, we'll have lookouts posted. We'll find you.'

'How big is Blunt's army?' Riff said.

Grimm pursed his lips and looked up at the top of the tent. 'Hmm. I reckon there'd be around a thousand men. What do you think, Felix?'

He nodded. 'It'll be around that number. Maybe a hundred or two more.'

I'm sure I wasn't the only one whose stomach sank towards his boots. My left leg began to jiggle.

'Sed help us!' Boyd said. 'We won't have a hope.'

Felix slammed his fist down onto the table. 'Stop it! I won't hear such negative talk. If you keep that up you'll be beaten before you even try.'

'What do you want the dragons to do?' I said, changing the subject.

Rog turned around and looked at me. 'I was going to talk to you about that,' he said. 'I'm hoping that a few of them would transport me, my crew and our equipment, up to the face of the dam. I'm not sure what we'll find there but I know we'll need help dismantling that wall. Once we're done, they can fly us back to join the rest of our fighting force at the eastern end. Otherwise it would take us a seven night, perhaps longer, to walk there and another to walk back and we don't have the time for that.'

I nodded. 'I'm sure they'd be happy to help.'

'Excellent!' Grimm said. 'I have some ideas on how the dragons could help us harass Blunt's army and give him some headaches. They'll do what I say, won't they?'

'Just remember to ask them instead of ordering them,' I said. 'They aren't pack animals who can't think for themselves.'

Felix said, 'It would be wise to not let the Midrashi know we're connected to the dragons. Let them think they're still wild. That will keep our presence secret for a while longer.'

'Yes, yes,' Grimm said, 'I agree. Excellent suggestion, Felix.'

'I think, for safety's sake,' Boyd said, 'Rimini and I should also carry some weapons. Maybe a sharp knife or two, or a sword?'

Grimm pointed at Boyd. 'We can fix you up but don't go looking for trouble.'

'No, sir.'

I said, 'The raven might go with Rimini or he might stay with the dragons.'

'It doesn't matter what the bird does,' Grimm said.

'I wouldn't be so hasty,' Asher said. 'I have a vague feeling, niggling away at the back of my mind, that there's something I should remember about ravens.'

Grimm shrugged. 'It's just a bird. Now let's get busy.'

# Twenty-One

We travelled together until we reached the trail going up into the rocky hills. Once there, we unloaded the supplies from Trevor and Harvey's wagon. Some of it went to Chops and Biff's wagon and the rest was distributed between the troops for them to carry. Asher, Riff, Riva, Kieran, Maraed, Nikluss, Angus and I threw our bedrolls and cooking gear onto the now empty wagon. Riff took the reins, Asher sat next to him, the girls rode in the back and the rest of us walked alongside. We waved goodbye to the others and set off around the foothills, heading towards the river. Joffre chose to stay with his new friend, Jondalee.

*What's going to happen to Chops and Biff?* Harvey said. *Will they be abandoned, left to fend for themselves amongst the rocks? I suppose, if the two-legs don't eat them, they'll wander about, slowly starving before falling down a ravine and dying an agonising death of hunger and broken bones.*

*Nothing quite so dramatic,* I said. *Once their wagon is unloaded up amongst the hills, they'll be led down the other side to the river. There's a large open area near the foothills that will be perfect for them to graze on until they're needed for the long journey home.*

*Hmph! So you say,* Trevor said. *We'll see. I noticed several of the two-legs licking their lips whenever they looked at us. I expect they're all longing for a big, juicy steak.*

*Don't worry,* I said. *We never eat our comrades.*

I don't think I convinced them. I walked alongside Trevor and we chatted about it for a while longer. I could hear Kieran talking with Nikluss and Angus and occasionally Maraed would join in, leaning over the side of the wagon bed. I think they were planning their repertoire. A bit later, Nikluss began a lively tune on his tin whistle with Angus thumping his bodhran in time. They were surprisingly good. The music made the journey go a little quicker.

We reached the ford just as the sun began to sink behind the distant forests of Bjorn, so we made camp on the southern side of the river. We didn't want to force the griven through the waters when it was dark.

As we sat around the campfire, Asher said we needed to discuss our strategy. 'We need to be consistent with our stories,' he said. 'The farmers may not be very friendly, so we must win them over.' We all nodded. 'I think all of you, except Nikluss and Angus, should call me, Father.' He turned to the two archers. 'You can call me, Uncle.'

'Why don't we call you, Pa?' Kieran said.

'Very well,' Asher said. 'That's fine.'

Riff shifted his position so that he wasn't sitting quite as close to the fire as he previously was. 'Will they believe we're all siblings? How will you explain Kieran and Maraed's hair colour? They're nothing like the rest of us.'

Asher shrugged. 'If anyone says anything, I'll just say they take after my dear departed wife. Anyway, travelling minstrels often have extended families with many adoptees included in the mix. I don't think anyone will question the set up.' Nikluss cleared his throat. 'Yes, Nik, you want to say something?'

'I think we should all be clear on the roles we're going to play.' He fiddled with the whistle, running his fingers up and down the stops as if he was already playing it in his mind. 'These travellers usually have the jobs sorted out and everyone knows what their responsibility is and what part they play in the scheme of things.'

Asher frowned. 'What are you getting at?'

'Well, you're the father, the patriarch so to speak, so you're the leader. You'll also be the story-teller, correct?' Asher nodded. 'Angus and I are the musicians and the hunters for food on the trail. That explains our quiver full of arrows.'

Again, Asher nodded.

'Maraed is the singer and Kieran is the dancer. They should also have other jobs like helping set up the campsite,' Nikluss said.

'We already do that, Nik,' Kieran said.

Nikluss rubbed the back of his head. 'Yes. Right. I guess Riva is the cook, responsible for all the cooking gear, for getting the fire started and maintained, and for serving out the food and cleaning up afterwards.'

Riva didn't look too pleased about that. She folded her arms across her chest and glared at the archer.

'Riff is the driver,' Nikluss continued, 'and, obviously, he'll oversee the care of the griven. But, then there's Seeger. What's his role?'

Everyone turned to look at me. I frowned back at them. He was right. What *was* my position in this caravan? I really had no skills to offer. The silence dragged on for quite some time. I stared into the flames and listened to the pop and hiss that came from the logs. I had never felt more useless in my life.

Then Maraed spoke. 'I have an idea.' Everyone turned to look at her. 'I don't want to offend anyone, or speak out of turn so ...'

Asher beamed at her. 'No, no, dear girl. Speak up, speak up! You're part of the family now.'

She smiled back at him and then reached over and patted his hand. 'Thank you ... Pa.'

He grinned. 'Seeger's specialty is conversing with animals. Correct?'

Everyone nodded and murmured their agreement although, to me, it didn't look as though Nikluss and Angus were convinced.

Maraed continued. 'I assume that, on our travels, Seeger will talk to as many animals as he can to see if he can pick up any information that we might miss.' She looked at me. 'Correct?'

'That's right,' I said. She bit her bottom lip. 'Go ahead,' I said.

She tugged her sleeves down as if they didn't already cover her wrists. 'Please don't be offended.'

'Oh for Sed's sake,' Kieran said, 'spit it out, sis!'

'Well ... it's just that ... well ... When you talk to the creatures, Seeger, you often get a sort of blank look that makes you appear somewhat of a simpleton.'

Oh nice! I looked around the circle and everyone seemed to agree with her. Flaming heck, what must people think of me? Then snatches of previous remarks came flooding into my mind. I squeezed my eyes shut as I heard several voices saying: 'What's wrong with that child?'; 'Every now and then, he goes a bit doolally', and, 'That stupid look on his face!'

I covered my eyes with my hands and god-spoke to Sed, 'Please open up the ground and let me fall in.'

I heard a rustle of clothing and then felt a body sit down next to me. An arm went around my shoulders. 'Seeger,' Maraed said, 'I didn't mean to hurt you.'

I shook my head, my eyes still covered. 'S'all right,' I mumbled. 'Just bein' honest.'

'Get a grip, Seeg!' Kieran said. 'She didn't say you were stupid. She just said you sometimes *look* it. Right, sis?'

'You're not stupid!' she said. 'I think you're very brave and clever. It's just that most people aren't aware of the special gift you have. When you're concentrating on the conversation going on in your head you can look a little blank.'

I put my hands down and looked across the fire at Riva, her arms still folded, leaning up against Riff. 'You can talk to camels and griven and you don't ever look weird.'

'Yes, she does,' Riff said. 'It just doesn't happen as often, or last as long as it does for you.'

I had another sudden flash of memory: I was lying on my straw bed in the loft in Midrash. Riva was helping Jarl nurse me back to health. There'd been a sudden blank look on her face as she tried to talk to the camels in the stables below and I'd thought, 'So that's what I look like!'

I sighed. 'Very well, I often look like I'm stupid. So what?'

Maraed gave my shoulder a little squeeze. 'We can use that to our advantage. I think when we're with strangers, let them think you can't speak. Be Pa's feeble-minded son, who's fascinated with animals. That way you can spend as much time as you like gathering information in the special way you can and no one will wonder why you're with us, when you're not musical or skilled like the rest of us. You'll be overlooked when the Xanthi are talking among themselves because you won't seem a threat.'

Nikluss and Angus had begun nodding their agreement when Maraed first said we could use my apparent stupidity to our advantage. When she'd finished, Nikluss said, 'Brilliant! That's an excellent plan. Of course, he can still do some of the menial jobs around camp: lifting stuff and helping serve out food and so on.'

These archers seemed very keen that other people did all the lifting and serving!

Asher smiled. 'Good thinking, Maraed. I agree. What do you think, Seeger? Will you play the simpleton while being our spy?'

I closed my eyes and nodded. 'It sounds like it's a role that will come naturally to me.'

*I have confidence in you, mate,* Trevor said. *You'll be brilliant at being stupid.*

*We're positive about that,* Harvey said.

Cheeky beggars! I opened my eyes and looked at the group of concerned faces around the campfire. Maraed gave my shoulder a final squeeze and took her arm away. Riff nodded at me, Riva smiled and Kieran held up his thumbs. I had no idea what that meant.

Asher said, 'It won't be easy, Seeger. Some people are unkind to simpletons but we'll do our best to protect you. There'll be times when you'll be tempted to retaliate or, at the least, to say something back. You must be brave and keep quiet no matter what. Can you do this?'

I thought about the picture he'd painted and I wasn't sure if I could carry it off. I was going to say I'd rather be the cook's assistant but Maraed spoke first.

'I know you can do it, Seeger,' she said. 'We'll all help you play your part and I know the animals will help as well. You'll have the most important role to play in this mission. You can do things that the rest of us can't.'

Well, what could I say after that? I smiled at her. 'Thanks,' I said. 'I won't let you down.'

'Now I suggest we get to sleep,' Asher said. 'I want to try to reach the first farmstead by mid-afternoon tomorrow.'

There were plenty of bushes for us to use as a privy. Riva and Maraed went to the right and we men went to the left. The girls made up their beds in the back of the wagon and the rest of us lay out our swags around the fire. It wasn't long before we were all settled comfortably.

'Maraed,' Kieran called, 'please sing us a lullaby.'

She began to croon a sweet, low tune.

> The stars in the night sky are showing the way.
> The birds in their nests and the goats in the hay.
> The sun has gone down and the moon now shines bright.
> It's time for the weary to put out the light.

I remember hearing her voice, soothing and caressing, but I can't remember what else she sang. I was asleep before the second verse.

The next morning, after breaking our fast, we quickly put out the fire and rolled up our swags. Everyone seemed to know what their job was and we worked together as if we'd been doing it all our lives. Once everything was loaded onto the wagon, Riff picked up the reins and I went to walk next to Harvey as we crossed the ford. It was easy going in the daylight because the animals could see where they were putting their hooves and the water was quite shallow. It didn't even reach my knees.

We were through the ford and up the other bank in no time at all. Then Asher pointed to somewhere in the distance, Riff nodded, and away we went. I still walked alongside Harvey as he was keen to chat. He and Trevor had thought of a long list of disasters that might await us. The only thing they weren't worried about was my ability to appear simple. I wasn't sure if that was a compliment or an insult.

We found a dirt road heading towards the mountains. Asher said he was sure it would pass by the farmsteads in the area. We stopped for a quick lunch and a short rest at midday and Maraed, Kieran, Nikluss and Angus finally decided on the program they'd present to the farmers. It all sounded pretty good to me.

By late afternoon, we approached the first farm. As we walked the wagon in through the gate, the farmer and a couple of his workers greeted us with pitchforks held out in front of them like pikes.

'Stop right there!' the farmer called.

Riff pulled on the reins and the griven halted. Asher stood up, with his legs pressed against the back of his seat. He held both his arms up in the air.

'Gentlemen,' he said. 'We mean you no harm. We're an honest family of minstrels come to entertain you. If we could please camp in your field for the night, we will regale you with story, song and dance. What say you?'

The farmer looked at his two men and then stared at us, his face dark with mistrust. 'How do we know you're not spies?'

'Why would anyone spy on you?' Asher said. 'Are you at war?'

The farmer frowned. 'Not exactly. But these days we can't be too careful.'

Asher slowly lowered his arms. 'Quite so but you have nothing to fear from us. Maraed, could you give us a quick tune?'

Maraed stood up, curtseyed to the men and began to sing *Marella's Lament*. The men's mouths dropped open. She'd just begun the second verse, when the door to the farmhouse swung open and out came a woman wearing a dirty apron stretched across her imposing chest, followed by some small children.

'Dirven, where's your manners, man?' she called. She wiped her hands on her apron and then beckoned us closer. 'Come on in and share a meal with us.'

Dirven, the farmer, turned to glare at her but he also slowly nodded. 'Fair enough,' he said, turning back to us. 'Park your wagon over there.' He pointed to a small paddock to the left of the gate and just down from the house. 'We don't get much company out here so it'll be good to get some news of the wide world.'

*Harvey. Trevor. Behave yourselves and see if there's any animals you can chat with.*

*Bless his heart,* Trevor said, *the poor simpleton thinks he can give us orders.*

*Don't push your luck, pal,* I said.

'What's wrong with your lad?' Dirven said.

'He's a bit simple but he means no harm,' Asher said. 'The poor boy was born with a few goats missing from the top paddock, if you know what I mean.'

We all trooped into the house and settled ourselves around the huge table. The farmer's wife was already bustling around near the fire, just like Mother would have done. I had a sudden pang of homesickness.

As she served us hot drinks and prepared a platter of sliced cold meat, cheese and cooked vegetables, I let the conversation waft over me as I concentrated on seeking out any listening minds. I found some goats in a far field, too far away to hear them properly. I was thrilled to discover there were some donkeys in a paddock behind the barn. I couldn't wait to go chat with them. There were also some cats somewhere else in the house. I called to them and they wandered into the kitchen to find me. There was a big ginger that smooched up against my legs and a smaller black and grey one leaped up onto my lap. I heard the woman gasp.

'I've never seen Caspar and Juno take to a stranger like that before!' she said.

'Seeger has a way with animals,' Asher said. 'I think it's God's gift to him to make up for the things he lacks.'

She beamed at me. 'Well, ain't that lovely?'

'Would you mind if he wanders about and meets your other animals?' Asher said. 'He knows not to leave gates open and he means them no harm. They seem to understand him and it gives him great pleasure.'

Dirven thought for a moment. 'Very well, but I'll send one of the lads with him just to make sure.'

Asher put his hand on my arm. 'Seeger, you can visit the animals if you want. Take some food with you and listen to the man. Only go where he lets you. All right?'

I nodded, grabbed some meat and cheese and immediately hurried outside, with one of the farmhands following me. As I ate the food I'd grabbed, I'd occasionally drop pieces of meat for the two cats who trooped behind me.

*I'm Caspar,* the black and grey said, *and he's Juno. They think you're stupid but you're not.*

*Hello,* I said. *I'm Seeger. I prefer to talk to animals. They make more sense.*

*Then you're verrry smart,* Juno, the ginger cat, said.

The farmhand, the cats and I headed down the side of the barn towards the paddock where the donkeys were waiting. From what I could see, the Xanthi farmed in similar ways to the Midrashi and even the people of Forabad. There were a

210

few minor variations, probably influenced by the weather and access to water, but I wish people could see how much they have in common instead of fearing the differences.

One thing that stood out was the decoration of the buildings. There were carved and painted black birds over every doorway. Joffre would have said they were ravens and it's quite possible he'd be right. I was more used to the marine decorations in Sed but I liked the look of the birds; it seemed friendly. These Xanthi, so far, were nothing like the fearsome people I'd been told about.

We reached the back paddock. The donkeys ran towards us, wheezing their funny cries in welcome. The cats jumped up and perched on the top railing. The farmhand put his hand on my shoulder and said, 'Stay on this side of the fence.'

*Greetings, donkeys,* I said. *Would you like me to scritch your ears?*

*What's that?* the one on my left said.

*It's like scratching but gentler.*

*Yes, please,* they both said.

*You're too kind,* the one on my right added.

They stretched their necks over the fence and lowered their heads so that I could reach. I gently rubbed my nails up and down their ears and they sighed.

*My name is Seeger. Who are you?*

*I'm Pepper,* the one on the left said, *and that's Herb. Could you just move your fingers down a little? Mmmm, yes that's the spot.*

*Are these people kind to you?*

*Oh yes, we can't complain,* Herb said. *They do their best. Mind you, they sometimes get a bit distracted these days.*

*They can't help it, Herb,* Pepper said. *They say there's a war coming and it's making everyone nervous.*

I moved closer to the fence and Pepper leant his head on my shoulder. I stroked his neck, while still rubbing Herb's ears. Caspar, the black and grey cat, leaped onto Herb's back. I smiled at the farmhand and then turned back to the donkeys. The man reached out and stroked Herb's neck.

*What war is coming?* I said.

*They say the drrragons are coming,* the ginger cat said.

*Coming from where and why?*

*They live up on old Ylani,* Herb said. *I've only ever seen one or two flying past, way up high. They've never bothered us. Could you please scratch the top of my head between my ears? Thanks.*

I shifted my hand to the new position. *If they've never bothered you before, why is everyone worried?*

Pepper lifted his head and snorted. Then he tucked his head back on my shoulder. *Some silly two-legs from down south have got everyone in a stampede. They're making an army to go fight the dragons. There's lots of shouting and marching around. Silly nonsense.*

*I wouldn't be surrrprised if the drrragons get sick of it and then they'll rrreally come to fight,* Juno said. *The humans might find they've bitten off more than they can chew.*

*I hope not. I don't want anyone to get hurt.*

The farmhand put his hand on my shoulder. 'I think you've had enough now, son. Time to get back to the others.' I frowned at him and shook my head. 'Don't be stubborn now. They'll still be here tomorrow, so you can see them again.'

*I'll talk to you again soon,* I said to the donkeys. *It was lovely to meet you.*

*Thanks for the scritches,* Pepper said.

I turned around slowly and trudged back to the farmhouse, the two cats once more following close behind.

I frowned and occasionally slid a morose glare at the farmhand, playing the part of a sulky child.

Just before we went back into the house, I bent down and picked up Caspar. As I did, I asked the cats, *Why is the house decorated with black birds?*

*They're meant to be rrravens,* Juno said. *The silly humans believe a rrraven is their god visiting them. It's rrridiculous! If God ever visited them, he'd obviously come in the form of a cat.*

*So, the raven is a sacred bird?*

*Yes. Stupid humans.*

*I have a raven friend but he's just a bird.*

*I'm not surrrprised,* Juno said.

We walked back into the kitchen and found that the meal had ended. Riva and Maraed were helping the farmer's wife clean up the dishes. The men were huddled around a map that Asher had spread out on the table. From what they were saying, I gathered that Asher had been asking them for directions to other farms.

I sat down at the end of the table, still cradling Caspar, and Juno leapt up onto my knee. I kept my head down, looking at the cats as I stroked them. Not long after I'd sat down, Asher rolled up the map and thanked the farmer for his hospitality.

'We'll get ourselves settled and then we'll prepare for tonight's performance,' Asher said.

The farmer grinned and clapped his hands. 'Great! I've sent Sven and Jurgen to invite our nearest neighbours to join us, so there should be a good crowd tonight. I'll help you string up some lamps, I've got some spares in the barn, and I'll see if we can rig up some seating.'

His wife turned around, a plate and dishcloth still in her hand. 'I'm so looking forward to this,' she said. 'It's been ages since we've had any fun.'

# Twenty-Two

While Dirven, Nikluss and Angus strung up lamps on poles, and Riff and Kieran set up rows of planking stretched between old fruit crates, Asher pulled me behind the wagon.

'What have you so far?' he whispered.

'People from the south have stirred up everyone to wage war against the dragons. They're training an army down in the valley. The local farmers keep them supplied with food. The donkeys say they don't know why this is happening because they've never been bothered by the dragons. I don't think there's been a dragon attack in these people's lifetime.'

'So, the right word at the right time might help some of them see sense,' Asher said. 'Anything else?'

'The raven is sacred. They think it's their god appearing to them in the form of a bird.'

'Now that *is* interesting,' he said, scratching his chin through his beard. 'Excellent. Good work, Seeger. Try to circulate through the crowd tonight and see if you can pick up anything else.' He raised his voice. 'Now I want you to help the girls set up the stage. Just do as they tell you. All right, son?'

I nodded. I turned to go and bumped into Dirven's generous stomach. I ducked my head and slipped past him.

I heard Asher say, 'Sorry about that. He doesn't mean anything by it.'

Thank Sed, Asher saw the farmer's approach. If he'd heard any of our conversation my little subterfuge would have been over.

I helped Riva unhinge the sides of the wagon and drop it down. We then put chocks around the wheels to hold it steady because it would be the platform for the evening's performance. I untied the reins and Riff and I led the two griven into the neighbouring paddock.

*You should be fine in here, boys,* I said. *You'll have a good view of the concert, too.*

*I suppose the thumping and caterwauling will go on all night and we'll not get a wink of sleep.*

*Be fair, Trevor! You think Maraed's singing is lovely. I know you do.*

*She's all right, I suppose, but the rest of you are rubbish.*

I patted Trevor's rump and Riff and I left both griven chewing morosely on some dry stubble as we went back to the stage area. I could hear Nikluss playing some scales on his flute and Maraed was making some odd noises: meee, meee, meee, maaa, maaa, maaa, mooo, mooo, mooo ...

I watched her for a while, trying to work out what she was doing. Kieran came up and stood next to me. 'She's warming up her throat, ready for the performance,' he said.

I stared at him, mouth agape.

'It's the same as Nikluss is doing. He's warming up his instrument, the flute, and Maraed is warming her instrument, the throat.'

I slowly nodded and he patted me on the shoulder before going to where we'd stored our sleeping gear. I assumed he knew what he was talking about but it sounded peculiar to me. She'd been talking all day. I'd have thought her throat was plenty warm enough!

I walked over to the gate and climbed up on the fence next to it so that I could watch the neighbours' arrival. Juno and Caspar jumped up and perched on either side of me. The three of us sat companionably, watching the crowd gather and listening to the hum of human anticipation. For a short while, everything seemed peaceful. Then, something hit me between the shoulder blades and a voice called, 'Hey, stupid face!'

I craned my head around, looking over my shoulder. Standing behind me, with a large clod of dirt in his hand, was a chubby, red-faced boy who looked as if he had about twelve years. He laughed and threw the dirt at me. Thank Sed, it fell short. The cats arched their backs and hissed at him.

I frowned and tilted my head in puzzlement. Why would he do that? I climbed down from the railing and slowly walked towards him, my hand held out in greeting. The cats walked with me, still hissing at the boy.

'Get away from me! Stupid creep,' he yelled, backing away.

The strange thing was, although he sounded frightened he didn't look it. His grin was mocking and his eyes were alight with menace. What could he be playing at? I stopped still, my hand still outstretched, and waited.

He stopped walking, leant down and found something else to throw at me. This time it was a rock. I lowered my hand and edged backwards. I didn't want him to miss his target and hit one of the cats.

*Be careful, you two,* I said to them. *I don't want him clocking you with that rock. Get behind me.*

*He's a bully,* Juno said. *He often thrrrows things at us. We should scrrratch his eyes out.*

'Oooh, stupid face is scared,' the boy said. 'He's blanked out, like that'll help him.'

He laughed and threw the rock. I tried to duck but his aim was slightly off in the first place so, even though I bobbed down, the rock also dipped and got me on the forehead. Blood began to drip into my right eye. I pressed the cut closed with my fingers. It hurt like the blazes.

What was the boy's problem? I hadn't done anything to him. The cats were standing on the tips of their toes, their backs arched and fur up, and they were spitting and hissing like wet coals in a fire. If I hadn't told them to stay with me, I'm sure they'd have charged the lad and used their claws to shred his nasty face.

Still chuckling, the boy bent down to pick up another rock. However, he couldn't see what I could see over his bent back: Dirven was running to my rescue. Just as the lad curved his arm, ready to launch the next missile, the farmer grabbed it.

'What do you think you're playing at, Marlo?' he said. 'Say you're sorry and get yourself over to your parents.'

The boy glared at me. His chin stuck out as if he was asking me to punch it.

'Drop the rock, Marlo,' Dirven said.

The boy opened his hand, let the rock fall to the ground, and then yanked his arm away from the farmer. The cats stopped hissing and began to curl themselves around my legs, trying to comfort me.

'My dad'll hear of this,' he said. He curled his lip and stuck his hands in his trouser pockets.

'He certainly will,' Dirven said, 'because I'll tell him. If I catch you bullying this lad, or anyone or anything else on my property, I'll get one of my farmhands to take you home. Got it?' The boy grudgingly nodded. 'Now be off with you.'

The lad sauntered away as if he didn't have a care in the world.

Dirven walked over to me and held my chin so that he could check my face. 'You all right, boy?'

I nodded. Blood flicked out and landed on his sleeve.

'You've got a nasty cut there but it won't kill you,' he said. 'Here, press this on it.' He handed me a folded cloth that he'd taken out of his pocket. 'Don't worry, it's clean.'

He bent down and stroked Juno and Caspar. 'Well done, boys.'

He straightened up and looked at me again, concern etched into the lines on his face. 'The cats looked like they were ready to spring to your defence.'

I must have looked worried because he chuckled and said, 'Don't fret, you're not in any trouble. Marlo is a bully. He enjoys terrorising people and creatures that seem weaker than him. He made a mistake with you, though.'

I raised my eyebrows in query and instantly regretted it because the cut stung.

'There's more to you than meets the eye, I think,' Dirven said. 'Marlo has no idea that the whole of the animal kingdom would have rushed to your defence.' He nodded and smiled. 'I'd have liked to see that. I reckon your two griven would have pushed the fence down and trampled him. From the way they're snorting and pawing their hooves, they might still do it.'

*Thank you, Harvey and Trevor. I'm all right now.*

*That boy hurt you. You might be a simpleton but you're our simpleton!*

*I'm not a simpleton!*

*You keep telling yourself that, if it helps.*

'... and then the cats would have danced on his flattened body,' Dirven said. He laughed. 'Keep the cloth. I suggest you find a safe spot to watch the show and keep out of trouble.'

I changed hands so that I could hold the cloth with my left, put out my right hand and he shook it. I nodded at him and, the cloth still pressed to my head, I walked over to find Asher behind the wagon.

He fussed and fluffed about, which was embarrassing. He made me sit down and told Riva to fetch me a drink of water. Then, he cleaned the cut and wrapped gauze across the wound and around my head, pinning it tight just behind my right ear.

'We're asking too much of you, Seeger,' he said, laying his hand on my cheek.

'I'm fine,' I whispered into my cup. 'Don't make a fuss. Once the concert has begun, I'll wander about at the back and see if I can hear anything useful.'

'Very well, lad,' he said as he took my cup and absentmindedly put it in his gaping cloak pocket. 'But the first sign of trouble, you come running.' I nodded. 'You'll be all right? Excellent. I'll find the others and get this show started.'

He hurried off and I stayed where I was for a while. My head was throbbing. The two cats were still by my side. It seemed they'd assigned themselves as my bodyguards.

Asher climbed up onto the wagon and called the crowd to attention. 'Welcome everyone to our little show. Let's all relax and have a good time.'

Everyone cheered. Nikluss and Angus began a lively jig that had most people's feet tapping before the first verse was over. Asher climbed down and Maraed took his place. She clapped along to the rhythm of the dance and within moments the crowd was beating time along with her.

I got up and wandered out from behind the wagon, my two feline escorts close behind. My first thought was to put some distance between me and the music. My head was still sore and my stomach was doing strange things. The cats and I strolled down alongside the crowd until we were at the back of the audience. Some of the farmhands, who'd obviously missed out on a seat, were standing there clapping and whistling at Maraed. The man who'd escorted me to the donkeys saw me and waved me over.

'Hello, lad. What happened to you?' he said. 'You all right?' I nodded. 'She's a looker, your sister.'

For a moment I had no idea who he was talking about. I nodded, frowning, but then I remembered he meant Maraed. I glared at him.

'I've never seen hair the colour of fire before,' he said. 'It looks really pretty in the lamplight.'

It certainly did. Mind you, it looked pretty in daylight, too. When the jig was over, Maraed began to sing.

Let's take a caravan to the motherland,
It's a long way to go, so hold my hand.
When we reach the land where we were born,
The darkness will end with a golden dawn.

My friend the farmhand sighed. 'She's wonderful!'

Others standing around us murmured their agreement. Some had begun to sway in time to the tune.

Let's take a caravan, it's a golden caravan.
Let's join the caravan of love.

A voice behind me said, 'A caravan of love, eh? I'd like to see that.' Others shushed him and he went quiet.

The cats decided I was in good company so they wandered off on secret cat business. Juno murmured something about mice in the fields. I looked around to see if I could spot Marlo and I eventually picked him out, sitting with two adults who must have been his parents. I felt safer once I knew where he was. Despite what Dirven had said to the boy, I didn't think it would take much to get him to attack me again. I moved back and sat down in the shadows of an old tree behind the men. They were so engrossed with Maraed's performance, they soon forgot I was there.

No one spoke while she sang but they chatted away in the breaks between the acts. As I'd hoped the main topic of conversation was the army, the southerners in charge of it and the future battle with the dragons. It seemed the local farmers weren't that convinced that a war was necessary.

One yellow-haired fellow, who towered over his friends said, 'Those dragons ain't been any bother in my lifetime. Any of youse been attacked by one? Anyone had their stock taken? Nah, I reckon the dragons are just an excuse for something else. Mark my words, it won't end well.'

He handed the large ceramic jug he was holding to the man who stood next to him. The fellow's beard hung past his waist and his pants were held up with some string that went from the front of his trousers, over his shoulders and then was attached at the back of his pants. I guess he couldn't afford a belt.

'I don't know, Ralf,' the bearded man said. He tipped up the jug, drank from it, wiped his mouth and then passed it along. 'Dragons be fierce beasts and can't be trusted. They're up there on old Ylani. I've seen 'em flyin' around.'

A lanky, weedy young lad, who didn't look much older than me, reached for the jug but was refused. He stuck his bottom lip out and kicked the dirt with his boot. When the jug continued around the circle and no one would give him a swig he said, 'What do you make of that priest? The one with the cloak made of ravens' feathers. We got to pay attention when a holy man says it's important. Don't we?'

The tall man who had spoken first said, 'I don't know about that, Ferdie. Ravens are holy, right? We treat 'em with respect, right? So how is it a holy thing to slaughter enough of 'em to make a cloak? That don't seem right to me.'

'Good point, Ralf,' the beard said. 'Besides, this priest, this Lorik person, he ain't one of our priests. He's come up from the south with the other foreigners. I didn't think they knew about the raven down there.'

Could it be there were two people with the Midrashi called Lorik or was this Boyd's old friend? If it was him then there was nothing holy about him. The Xanthi were being duped.

'You don't know everything,' skinny Ferdie said. 'They might know the raven down south. When was the last time you were down there, Ralf? Lars? I don't reckon you've been outside this valley?'

Ralf pulled out a large, checked piece of cloth from his trouser pocket and blew his nose. When he'd finished, he vigorously rubbed it with the cloth, carefully refolded it and stuffed it back into his pocket.

'I don't like what's going on,' he said. 'Taking all our able-bodied men away from honest work and making 'em march up and down all day. Farms around here are short-handed and harvest will be on us soon. The blacksmith lost his apprentices and is struggling to keep up with his workload. Some of the smaller shops, up near the mountain pass, have closed. It's ridiculous.'

'You be careful, Ralf,' Lars said. 'Some people might accuse you of treason.'

Ralf snorted. 'Don't be stupid, Lars. Everyone knows I'm a proud Xanthi through and through. I just have a hearty suspicion of southerners.'

The musicians struck up a rousing jig and down on the wagon-stage, Kieran began to tap, leap and twirl. At first there was a stunned silence but then people began to whistle and clap as he danced his way across the wagon bed.

My head was still aching and the men had stopped chatting, so I sat leant my back against the trunk and made myself more comfortable. As it felt as though my stomach could turn on me at any moment, I thought I'd just have a little rest and then I'd go back down behind the wagon. I knew Asher would be very interested in what I'd just heard.

Something fell on my head; the sudden pain and shock jolted me awake. I rubbed my sore head and groaned. Above me, hidden amongst the leaves, someone giggled. I looked up but I couldn't see anything. It was too dark. Then, another rock smacked into my shoulder. I leaped up and stood back, still searching the tree for any sign of my assailant. The person laughed as another stone flew through the air and I knew who it was: Marlo!

I backed away, looking around for a friendly familiar face. The boy jumped down from the tree, pulled out another stone and juggled it in his hand. His pants sagged under the weight of the supply stashed in his right-side pocket.

'Hello, me old mucker!' he said. 'Pleased to see me?'

He threw the stone, which smacked against my cheek bone. I put my hand to my face and felt the gush of blood. I turned and ran.

He chased after me, laughing as I led him down the far side of the seating area. People were packing up and getting ready to leave. One of the neighbour's wagons was already moving out through the gate and onto the main road. Why couldn't it have been Marlo's family? Some of the farmhands chuckled and cheered us on, thinking we were playing a game.

'Watch where you go lads,' one called. 'Don't get in the way of the workers.'

I stared wild-eyed at the man but he'd already turned away. He didn't realise I was in danger. I couldn't call out to anyone and thus reveal my subterfuge. I had to maintain the semblance of a simpleton; simple of mind and unable to speak. I couldn't see Asher anywhere, nor any of my crew. I ran: my lungs straining to pull some air in and keep it there; my chest aching with the thump of my heart, and my head throbbing as the blood ran down my face.

*Over here!* Trevor called. *We'll save you.*

I made a beeline for the griven's paddock. Another stone whistled past the side of my head, clipping my ear as I went.

'I'll get you,' Marlo called. 'You can't hide from me.'

I reached the paddock and, wheezing and gasping, my legs and arms trembling, I pulled myself up and over the fence. I ran to the griven who were already plodding towards me. Their heads were lowered, presenting their double layered horns as a shield, and they were bellowing their anger at my attacker. I ran behind them and then stopped, resting my hands on my knees as, doubled over, I sucked air back into my lungs.

*The boy is sitting on top of the fence*, Harvey said. *We won't let him get in here. We'll save you, Seeger.*

*Thanks, fellas.*

*He's hurt you,* Trevor said. *You're bleeding. We don't like this boy. Can we stick our horns into him?*

*Don't do it, fellas. Keep the noise up and I'm sure someone will come to the rescue.*

Suddenly Harvey shrieked.

*What happened? Harvey, are you all right?*

*The little blighter's thrown a stone at me. It hit my cheek. It hurt me! Are you sure I can't stick him with my horns?*

*I'm sure. Perhaps you should move back?*

*No! We're going to charge him and see how he likes that.*

The two griven leaped forward and ran at the fence, thundering like demons out of hell. I had no idea they could be so loud or so menacing. Usually griven are placid, morose, unassuming creatures. I'd never seen them like this before.

Marlo screamed and leaped down from the fence. The griven pulled up short of knocking it down but their heads were in reach of the boy. They snorted and shook their heads and then bellowed again.

'Hey!' I heard a voice call. 'What's going on there?'

It sounded like Riff. I peeked out from behind Harvey. Riff and a couple of other men were hurrying towards the enclosure.

'What are you playing at, boy?' Riff called. 'Leave our griven alone.'

'Don't you mean, your griven should leave my boy alone?' a stranger said. He must be Marlo's father.

'Daddy!' Marlo called. 'The nasty animals attacked me.'

He ran over to his father. Several men, including Riff and Dirven, had gathered around. Several held up lamps. I came out from my hiding place.

'That stupid loony made the griven do it,' Marlo said, pointing at me.

I shook my head and then winced. I moved closer, into the pool of light thrown out by one of the lamps. The men gasped as they saw the blood. I later realised that, as well as my face, my shoulder and ear were also bleeding. At the time, all I could feel was the thumping of my head. I put my hands up to hold it steady. It felt as though it would fall off at any moment.

Dirven nodded. 'I thought so. You've been up to your nasty tricks again, Marlo.'

Marlo shook his head. His father put his arm around the boy's shoulder. 'I think you owe my son an apology, Dirven. He hasn't done anything wrong. Just a bit of high spirits, that's all.'

Dirven snorted. 'Look at that poor lad, dripping with blood. Look at how those beasts are protecting him. One of them is bleeding, too. Now look at your boy. Not a mark on him. His pocket's still bulging with ammunition. You're not fooling anyone, Ranald. Take your boy home and teach him how to behave.'

Ranald gave Marlo a brief, one-armed hug and then pushed him away. 'Go find your mother. I've got this.'

Marlo turned to grin at me and then he sauntered away, once again as if he hadn't a care in the world.

'Are you choosing strangers over your neighbours, Dirven?' his father asked. 'You'll be sorry. Mark my words.'

'Don't threaten me, Ranald,' Dirven said. 'Your boy is a bully. We all know it. He's abused my hospitality and attacked one of my guests. That's inexcusable. In the old days, I'd have had every right to skewer him and serve him for dinner. Now take him home while I still have my temper and we're still friends.'

The other men in the crowd murmured their agreement. Ranald nodded. 'Right,' he said. 'Fine!' He stormed off.

I could see that Asher, Nikluss and Angus had joined the group. Asher was wringing his hands together. I hugged both Trevor and Harvey and, before climbing the fence, thanked them for saving me. When I reached the other side, I put my hand out for Dirven to shake and then I walked over to Asher, who put his arms out and pulled me into his chest.

'I'm sorry about this,' Dirven said. 'Ranald will make trouble for you, now. I don't think this is a good time to be travelling around to the other farms.'

'Quite right,' Asher said over my head.

I'd begun to sag in his arms. The world was slowly spinning around and I thought it might be safer to lie down, in case I fell. Asher wouldn't let me go and pulled me in tighter.

'We'll pack up and go back over the river, first thing in the morning,' Asher said. 'Thank you for your hospitality, Dirven. We won't forget your kindness.'

Dirven shook hands with Asher. 'You and your family are welcome here any time, Asher, but for now it's wiser to retreat.'

I didn't quite hear what else they said. The world was spinning faster and I was afraid I was going to be sick all over Asher's tunic. Thankfully, everything went dark before that happened.

# Twenty-Three

## Boyd Speaks

After the "minstrels" left, we carried our gear up the narrow path to the rocky escarpment that would be our base. It was a natural fortress with a protective stony ledge in front, just like a castle wall. From that lofty perch I could see Asher's wagon and his team heading towards the ford in the river. Even though it was my idea in the first place, I still thought, *Lucky Seeger. Once more he gets the easy path, while I'll be in harm's way.*

Rimini stood next to me and saw what I was watching. 'I'm glad I'm not with them,' she said. 'Soldiering is much more straightforward than pretending to be something you're not.'

She patted my arm and wandered off to help the others get their gear sorted. She was right but I couldn't stop a pang of jealousy ripping a small hole in my heart. I turned my gaze straight ahead towards the river valley and Blunt's army. I saw the rows of tents, the wagons and little figures moving around between them. There were so many, compared to our small band.

Then I pictured the dam wall bursting open and all the water flooding out, sweeping down the valley and overwhelming the encampment. I told myself that what we were going to do was far more important than putting on a minstrel show.

The next day Rog and his well-keepers, Jaxon and two other archers, and Rimini and I climbed aboard Fitzee, Hizaree and Silvana. It was a bit of a squeeze fitting five on each dragon; especially with all the gear that the well-keepers were carrying. The dragon's backs are long enough but not all of the hide is suitable for sitting on. We bunched up and held on tight. The dragons headed off, veering slightly south for a while, so that we could then fly west with the low range of wooded hills between us and the river valley.

Apart from the dreadful realisation that there is nothing for a long way between you and the earth, it's quite amazing flying somewhere on dragon back. Even so, I kept my eyes shut for most of the trip. It would have taken us several days or more to walk to our destination. The dragons got us there in less than a day.

As twilight sent tendrils of shadow across the hills, we finally saw the dam wall up ahead. It was guarded but only by a handful of men. I suppose it hadn't occurred to old Blunt that anyone would bother with it. He wasn't as clever as he wanted everyone to think.

We landed in a clearing near the edge of the forest, not far from the wall. We could see it through the gaps between the trees. It towered up into the sky as if it were part of the mountain itself. We all stared at it in awe.

'It seems a shame to pull that down,' Rog said.

For a short while we stood there, admiring the work of the ancient Xanthi. I couldn't fathom how they did it.

'How did they keep the water out while they were building that?' I said.

Rog turned to me. 'Well, son, the water wasn't that deep when they started. It was just a normal river. They built the wall and then the water banked up behind it.'

'But there was still water flowing in the river, right?'

'Yes, they would have made sure that they kept it running. They've either got a spillway or they've got pipes or a tunnel somewhere. Just looking at it from here, I'm guessing there are a few earthenware pipes like the ones we saw in the abandoned city, spaced along the bottom of the wall. The wall looks as though it's just made with soil but I'm fairly sure there'll be a stony core. Whatever they've done, I'm very impressed.'

'Come on,' Jaxon said. 'Let's make camp and have an early night. It'll be a big day tomorrow.'

Once we'd unpacked our gear, the dragons took off to find a place to roost for the night. We ate cold rations, so as not to give away our presence to the small group of guards at the dam wall. I thought that if they hadn't noticed the giant dragons flying around, they probably wouldn't notice a small campfire that far back in the trees, but Rog didn't want to take any chances.

In the morning, Rog and his team crept through the trees to the edge of the forest, so that they could get a closer look at the dam's construction. I'd thought it would be a simple job to destroy the wall but Rog explained there were a lot of things to take into consideration. He wanted to do it in such a way that he and his men had time to make their escape before the wall gave way and the water broke through.

# Twenty-Three

Meanwhile, Jaxon and the other two archers were sitting together near our sleeping gear, having a fiercely whispered conversation. Rimini and I joined them.

'What's going on, fellas?' I said.

The men stopped whispering and moved over to make room for us. Jaxon said, 'We're discussing how to handle the guards. Adam thinks we should just shoot them and be done with it. Pete and I aren't happy about killing people who are merely protecting a water source. They're not enemy combatants. They're more likely ordinary Xanthi, just taking care of the dam.'

'Whatever or whoever they are,' Adam said, 'we need to get them out of the way so Rog can get on with wrecking that wall. The quickest and simplest thing to do is to shoot them from the shelter of these trees. They'd be dead before they knew what hit them.'

Rimini shook her head, glaring at Adam. 'Their lives matter, sir. They're not fighting us. Shooting them without giving them any warning, is a cowardly thing to do. It's a Midrashi thing to do. We're better than that.'

There was an uncomfortable silence in the group. Rimini kept glaring at Adam. He only held her gaze for a moment and then studied his fingernails. I looked at Jaxon, who shook his head and then turned to stare out at the forest around us.

For a while I sat and listened to the place we were in. There was a gentle breeze blowing, so I could hear leaves rustling, the occasional creak of a branch, the twitter of birds high up in the canopy and the sigh of the wind as it wafted through the forest and plucked at our clothing with invisible fingers. It was peaceful and soothing to the soul. Then the dirt around us began to spin in flurries and there was the sound of beating wings. The dragons were back.

Rimini ran to meet them and threw her arms around Fitzee's neck. I followed her there. The red dragon had lowered his head as soon as he saw her running towards him. The other two made a low rumbling sound and nudged her with their noses. If only I could feel as comfortable with the giant beasts as she did.

'I wish I could talk to them like Seeger does,' Rimini said.

I put my hand on Hizaree's neck. 'Me too.'

Rimini lowered her voice. 'We're not going to let them kill those guards, are we?'

'Not if I can help it,' I said.

We gave the dragons a few more pats and then walked back to the archers. Rog and the others joined our group shortly after we'd sat down.

'I've made my decision,' Rog said. 'It'll take a few days to set up but then, at the end, it will only be a matter of hours.'

'What's the plan?' Jaxon said.

Rog grinned. 'We're going to do what we do best. We're going to tunnel under the wall.'

I couldn't believe what I was hearing. 'How are you going to do that without the wall falling on you or the water breaking through before you're ready?'

Rog nodded at me. 'Excellent questions, Boyd. You should consider joining your brother, Randi, in the well-keepers one day.' He smiled.

That had never occurred to me before. It was worth considering. The best thing would be, I'd get to live in the barracks.

Rog said, 'We'll tunnel under the wall, shoring it up with timbers as we go. There's plenty of wood here in the forest. It's delicate work but I'm confident we can do it. My team are the best well-keepers in Seddon.'

The rest of his team smiled awkwardly and tugged their beards or scratched their heads, embarrassed by Rog's praise.

Rog continued, 'The tunnel will take a number of days, depending on how the wall is constructed. We won't find out what sort of material we're dealing with until we start digging.'

'But won't the water wash you away, if you dig through the wall?' Jaxon said.

'We don't need to dig all the way through,' Rog said. 'You'll see. Once the tunnel is done, we'll set light to the timber props. While they burn, we'll have time to make our escape. Once they're burnt through, the tunnel will collapse and then the wall will follow in a very short space of time.'

I could tell that the archers were just as impressed as I was. Those well-keepers are clever chaps.

'The first thing we need to do is to chop down some trees and fashion the timber props,' Rog said.

The dragons made a high-pitched warbling sound. We all turned to stare at them.

'What's up with them?' Rog said.

The beasts looked at the trees and then made the same trilling noise again.

'I think they're offering to help knock down the trees,' I said.

The dragons nodded. Well, fancy that! I got it right.

'What about the guards down there?' Jaxon said. 'They'll need to be out of the way.'

Rimini sat up straight and glared fiercely at Jaxon. 'We don't need to kill them!' She grabbed Rog's arm. 'Do we?'

He scratched his chin as he considered the situation. Then, he patted her hand. 'We can capture them and make them labour for us. The work will go quicker. Also, it'll give us a chance to talk with them. Perhaps we can get them to turn on the Midrashi.'

Rimini sighed with relief. Jaxon nodded. Adam looked disappointed but Pete smiled. I was pleased, too. I was sick of unnecessary killing.

'Let's get the dragons to knock a few trees down,' Jaxon said. 'While they're doing that, we'll pop down and round up the guards and bring them back up here.'

Rog slapped Jaxon on the back. 'Excellent!' He turned to his crew. 'Get your gear ready, while I go talk to the beasts.'

The well-keepers leaped up and hurried over to their packs. Rog walked over to the dragons. Jaxon, Adam and Pete went to collect their bows and quivers. Rimini and I looked at each other. She shrugged.

I said, 'Let's go with the archers.'

Capturing the Xanthi guards was far simpler than I was expecting. They were unarmed and it was obvious they weren't military. They were just farmers. Zeb, the oldest, was in charge and the youngest man, Artie, was his son. They said that all the Xanthi men took turns to mind the dam wall, to repair any possible leaks etc. Each male, over the age of sixteen, gave four seven nights of their time every two years to patrol the dam.

They told us that they'd never needed to do any repair work in their lifetimes, so they spent most of their time playing games of chance and telling each other stories around the fire at night. The young ones enjoyed the break from work but the older men resented having to spend time away from their properties. However, they all knew how important the dam was to their people, so no one tried to get out of their duties.

We led them back up to our campsite. Jaxon and his men kept their bows notched and their arrows aimed. Rimini and I had our knives at the ready but not one of them tried to escape. They came along quite happily. It was as if they enjoyed the change in their routine.

When we reached our campsite, they stopped dead in shock. Several trees were lying on the ground, their roots exposed to the air. Four well-keepers were sawing the largest tree into smaller pieces and the rest were sorting them into piles or chopping off any smaller twigs or branches.

'What the blazes …!' Zeb said.

The young man grabbed his arm. 'Dad! Look over there.'

He pointed, his finger trembling like a leaf in the wind. At the far end of the clearing, the dragons were taking a little nap.

'Are they …?' Artie said. 'I mean … are they …?'

'They're dragons,' Rimini said, 'and they're lovely. I can't believe you want to wipe them out.'

She ran over to the beasts and began to stroke Hizaree's face. He made a happy gurgling sound and gently pulled her in closer. The other two snuffled at her, sighed and went back to sleep.

'Well, cut off my legs and call me shorty!' Zeb said. 'That's something I never thought I'd see.'

'How'd you tame them?' one of the others said.

'We didn't,' I said. 'They're our friends.'

Jaxon poked one of the Xanthi in the back. 'Get over there and put your backs into it. We need these trees made into large timber posts as soon as possible.'

The Xanthi joined the well-keepers and began to carry the lumber from the newly chopped pile to the men who were doing the cleaning up. This freed some to begin work on the second tree. The Xanthi even offered to strip the bark off the posts and, when told that the bark was staying on, they couldn't understand it. They muttered amongst themselves, shaking their heads in disbelief. Later, one of the well-keepers explained to me that the bark would help the props catch alight much easier.

By the end of the day, Rog was satisfied he had enough timber for the task. We sat around the fire as two of the well-keepers prepared a hot meal and then served us all, including the Xanthi.

'Tell me, sir,' Zeb, leader of the guards, said, 'What is all this timber for?'

Rog was just about to put a spoonful of lentil soup into his mouth. He lowered it slightly and said, 'We're going to tunnel under the dam.' Then, he sucked the soup off the spoon.

The Xanthi all gasped. One dropped his soup onto his foot and leaped up, cursing and hopping on the spot. A well-keeper hurried over to help him.

'You can't do that,' Zeb said. 'It'll bring the wall down.'

Rog nodded. 'That's the plan.' He ate some more soup.

'No, no, we won't allow it,' the old man said. He stood up and the other guards stood with him.

In a flash, our archers were standing with their arrows notched and aimed at the group. I ran up, put my arm around the young man's shoulders and held my knife up to his neck. 'I suggest you all calm down. Let's not do anything silly.'

The young fellow swallowed hard. 'Dad?' he said.

'Don't hurt my son,' Zeb said.

'Then sit you down and Rog will explain everything,' I said. I looked at the well-keeper, my eyebrows raised.

Rog nodded and put his soup bowl down by his side. 'Sit you down, men.'

They did as they were told but they weren't happy about it.

'I know this goes against everything you've trained for,' Rog said, 'and, believe me, it gives me no pleasure to destroy this dam. I understand how you feel but this must be done.'

Rog told them how the Midrashi had fooled the dragons and used the Xanthi, many generations ago. He told them how the Xanthi had attacked the dragons, destroying their nests and killing their young.

When Rog described the massacre, all three dragons raised their heads and howled. The Xanthi looked nervously at them and shuffled in their seats. Rimini ran over to the beasts to comfort them. Rog told the Xanthi that the attack was orchestrated by the Midrashi.

He told them about the stolen children—including Rimini and me—forced to become soldiers. He told them how the dragons helped rescue all the children kept in Midrash. He described the fall of the great circular city and the retreat of Blunt. He told them that even now Blunt and his men were using the Xanthi for their own advantage.

He explained that, despite what the Xanthi had done in the past, the dragons were willing to coexist peacefully with them if they were given access to the river and were left alone. He said they were intelligent and honourable beasts, who would keep their word.

'How do you know what the dragons will do?' Zeb said.

'One of our company is a beast-speaker,' Rog said. 'He says the dragons understand everything we say. Isn't that right, Fitzee?' The red dragon roared and nodded his huge head. 'They just can't talk back to us.'

'Don't you have any beast-speakers among your people?' Jaxon said.

'There are a couple,' Zeb said, 'but, as far as I know, none of them have ever tried to speak with a dragon. We tend to keep our distance from the creatures.'

Everything went quiet for a moment as the Xanthi thought about what Rog had told them. Artie's mouth was agape. He kept flicking his gaze across to the dragons. Fitzee was sitting upright. Hizaree was crouched lower but his head was tilted slightly to the right so that he appeared to be listening closely and Silvana lay with her head resting on her front feet. All three were watching the Xanthi. Zeb and the other men glowered; their fists clenched while resting on their knees.

Finally, Zeb cleared his throat and said, 'That's some story, stranger.'

Rog smiled. 'Just because it's a story, doesn't mean it isn't true. You know that even now Blunt and his men are gathering together an army, down in the river valley.' They all nodded. 'He's stirring you up to go fight the remaining dragons. Correct?' They nodded again. 'After that he's going to lead the army south to retake Midrash and then go on to conquer other cities, including our own. I don't expect he's told you that part of the plan.' They shook their heads.

One of the Xanthi said, 'But there's a priest of the raven with the Midrashi. He's told us that the war with the dragons is what our god desires. It's a holy cause.'

This was news to us. The well-keepers and archers began to whisper amongst themselves. Rog looked to me.

'There was no priest of the raven with the Midrashi army when we were there,' I said. 'Was there, Rimini?'

She shook her head.

'As far as I can tell, they don't worship any god,' I said. 'Their temple is no longer used for prayers or rituals. It's a stable.'

Jaxon said, 'Sounds like this priest is a fake. Are you sure he's a holy man?'

Zeb looked troubled. The man next to him said, 'It always bothered me that the priest's cloak was made of ravens' feathers. That don't seem right.'

One of the other guards said, 'He said a hundred ravens had given him the feathers for the cloak.'

'I don't believe it,' Artie said. 'How would those birds live without their feathers? Can you see a hundred featherless ravens walking around naked? It's stupid.'

I asked the Xanthi, 'What's this priest's name?'

'Lorik,' Zeb said.

'What? Lorik has joined the priesthood?' I said. 'I don't think so.' Rimini and I laughed. 'He was just a corporal in the army when he left Midrash with Blunt.'

The Xanthi looked at each other, their brows furrowed.

I said, 'What would you say if I told you that our little troop has befriended a wild raven? He's especially close to Rimini and Seeger, our beast-speaker, and he's also become best friends with one of the dragons.'

It was the Xanthi's turn to look shocked. Zeb stood up again. 'Do you mock us, boy?'

'No sir. I speak true.'

'Do you keep the raven in a cage?' His face was black like thunder.

I put my hand on my heart. 'I swear, he is free to come and go as he chooses.'

'This is unheard of. We need to speak privately.'

The other Xanthi stood up. The group moved a short distance apart and, huddled together, they began to whisper heatedly. We watched as their arms flailed in the air, fingers were pointed and heads were shaken. Jaxon and his men watched the proceedings intently, their weapons ready if needed.

Finally, the men returned to the fire.

Zeb looked at the rest of the group and they nodded back at him. 'We'll help you but we ask a favour,' he said. 'Please let us warn our people about the coming flood. When the water breaks free from the dam, it will sweep everything before it. Everything! Give the farmers time to move their livestock.'

Rog dipped his head in thought. Everyone watched him. I was holding my breath and I don't think I was the only one.

At last he looked up at the Xanthi and said, 'Fair enough. But only the farmers. Jaxon and his men will go with you to make sure you don't warn the army. It'll take us three days to build the tunnel and it'll collapse on the fourth. I'm sorry I can't give you more time but we'll lend you the dragons. They can cover a great deal of ground in a very short time.'

'We couldn't fly on the dragons to our city or the farms,' one of the Xanthi said. 'They'll be shot down before we can give our message.'

I didn't know they had a city! Where was it?

'They're surprisingly difficult to kill,' Rog said, 'but I hear you. Nor do we want Blunt seeing them. Is there someone out there you can trust to help pass on the warning?' Zeb nodded. 'Then they'll fly you there and the rest is up to you. Agreed?'

'Yes, sir,' Zeb said. 'Thank you.'

Rog turned to the beasts and called out, 'Do you agree?'

The dragons rumbled and nodded their heads.

'Good,' Rog said. 'We'll begin first thing in the morning.'

Artie, the youngest Xanthi, stared longingly across at the dragons.

'Come with me,' I said, 'and I'll introduce you.'

# Twenty-Four

## Seeger Speaks

The next morning, Asher and Dirven talked together as the rest of us packed up our gear, ready to return to our company across the river.

Once all our gear was packed away, the campfire was out and the griven were hitched up ready to go, we sat down in the shade of the wagon's side and watched the two men. For a while it seemed as though Dirven was thinking about hitting Asher. He'd stiffened his back and his hands became meaty fists. But then, as Asher kept talking and occasionally dipping his head in a slight bow of apology, the farmer gradually relaxed again.

When the conversation was over, Dirven thumped Asher on the back and strode over to the rest of us. Asher was beaming so it must have been a good outcome. Dirven walked up to me and stuck out his hand. I stood up and shook it.

'I said there was something more to you than meets the eye,' he said. 'You're not simple at all, are you?'

The others laughed. 'That's a matter of opinion,' Riff said.

I stuck my tongue out at him.

'You're a beast-speaker?' Dirven said.

'Yes sir,' I said. 'It seems I can speak to most creatures. They say that if you can speak to dragons, as I can, then you can speak to all.'

Dirven smiled at me. 'I'd wondered if that was the case. There was the way the animals all took to you and then there was the look you'd get. I've seen that same blankness on my dad's face. He was a beast-speaker but he could only talk with our goats and donkeys. I always wished I could do it but the gift wasn't passed on to me.'

'Perhaps it'll turn up in one of your children,' I said.

Dirven pursed his lips and gazed past me towards Harvey and Trevor. 'I hadn't thought of that,' he said. 'Wouldn't that be something?' He looked back at me. 'Asher tells me the dragons have no desire to fight us. Is that true?'

'Asher speaks true,' I said. 'They know it's too late to get all their homeland back. They just want to be left alone. They'll keep to the mountains and the lands on the far side of the range and will leave you the river valley, provided they can have access to the river. They're an honourable species and they always keep their word. They could even become your friends if you let them.'

Dirven scratched the back of his head. 'Well, I never. Now that'd be something to see. All this talk about going to war with the dragons never sat right with me. I've never known or heard of a dragon attack in my lifetime and I don't think anyone else has, either.'

'You can't trust Blunt,' Riff said. 'He's using your people for his own ends.'

The rest of our group agreed with him.

'I grew up in Midrash,' Riva said. 'I know Blunt. He was one of the men who trained the stolen children to become soldiers. He used to kill the weaker ones, without turning a hair, as a warning to the others. Some of them only had five or six years. He lives to fight and to rule. He wants to use your people to help him win back Midrash and then to conquer other cities. He just wants to get rid of the rest of the dragons first, so they won't come to our defence. He can't be trusted.'

Dirven slowly nodded. 'I've had my suspicions and you've just confirmed them. I need to warn our people. Some, like Marlo's father, won't listen. They like the idea of returning to our savage past. But most of the Xanthi are happy to leave those days behind.'

Asher patted him on the back. 'That's good to know.'

'I'll try to pass the word along,' Dirven continued. 'Meanwhile, I still think it'd be wise for you to re-join your people. Even if you meant well, people don't like to think they've been fooled.'

Everyone glumly agreed with him. No one likes being lied to.

'Mind you,' Dirven said, 'you put on a cracking good show last night. You might be spies but you're talented ones.'

He laughed. 'I've never seen anyone tap the light fantastic like you did, fella,' he said to Kieran. He turned to Maraed, 'You, my dear, sing like an angel. And as for you,' he looked at Asher, 'you can spin a tale like a bard from the old days. You brought some joy and light into our lives last night.'

He then put his hand on my arm. 'I'm sorry you had a run-in with Marlo. If his parents don't wise up, that boy is going to grow into a dangerous, violent man. I'm sure that parts of his brain aren't wired right.'

I shrugged. 'He's a bully. One day he'll meet a bigger bully. God will bring justice.'

'Do you worship the raven god?'

'No sir. We worship Sed, the living message of the Most High. Do you really worship a bird?'

Dirven laughed. 'Good gracious, no! The raven is the form Rafnagud our god takes when he visits his people. Ravens are his servants. They're his messengers and spies.'

Asher's eyes lit up. 'This is fascinating. Perhaps, when this mess is over, I could come back and talk with you some more?'

Kieran leant into my shoulder and whispered, 'The things that man is planning to do ... I might not see Seddon or my homeland for a very long time!'

Dirven's wife came running out of their house, clutching something in her hands. 'Don't go yet!' she called. She ran all the way to us, calling out on every other step, 'Wait!' and, 'Don't go!' and, 'Hold up!'

When she reached us, her chest—which was considerable—heaved with the effort of regaining her breath. She beamed at us. 'I've got something for your journey,' she said, handing Asher a parcel wrapped up in a kitchen cloth.

'You shouldn't have,' he said.

She tucked behind her ears the strands that had come loose from the knot of hair on top of her head, and a flush of embarrassment added to the redness in her face. 'Oh, it's nothing much. Just some cake and biscuits.'

'That's not nothing,' Riva said, taking the bundle from Asher. 'Thank you.'

Dirven put his arm around his wife's shoulders. 'Gisella's a good cook.' She giggled. 'We'll let you go. Goodbye and may the raven be kind to you.'

Then, as they turned to walk back to their home, I felt a familiar tugging in my mind.

'Wait!' I said. 'Dragons are coming.'

Dirven's wife screamed. Dirven spun around. 'What?'

'They're carrying passengers,' I said. 'Does the name, Zeb, mean anything to you?'

Dirven came back, tightly holding his wife's hand. She was trembling like a palm tree in a high wind. 'Zeb, you say? We know him. What would Zeb be doing on a dragon?'

I shrugged. Asher put his arm around my shoulders. 'We'll soon find out,' he said. 'Be assured, we're in no danger.'

Gisella, Dirven's wife, shook her head. 'I don't believe you.'

Ash pointed towards Trevor and Harvey. They'd settled down on their haunches and were chewing their cud. 'See the griven? Do they look worried?'

'All the same,' Dirven said to his wife, 'you'd best go back to the house, love.'

I could see she was torn between staying with her man and running for safety. She hesitated for a moment, her gaze flicking around from us, to the griven, to her husband and back again. Then her chin went up and she shook her head.

'I'll stay with you,' she said.

How brave was that? It was easy to see that every fibre of her being was telling her to run.

'Don't worry,' I said. 'You'll be safe.'

A shout came from near the wagon. We turned to see who it was. Nikluss was pointing across the fields. 'Here they come,' he yelled.

In the distance, what looked like three large birds were heading our way. One was red, one was the light green of an unripened tapanj and one was a silvery blue. As they drew closer, I heard the farmer's wife gasp.

Now we could see their long necks, their enormous wings and their strong legs, tucked up against their bellies.

'Oh Dirven,' Gisella said, 'they're huge!'

It wasn't long before the dragons were flying over the field that the griven had grazed in, the night before. We could hear the passengers calling out, 'Hello the house!'

When they landed, several men clambered down. Jaxon and two other archers were with them. Some of the older ones staggered a little, as if their legs were unsteady, but a young one shouted, 'Yahoo! That was brilliant! Thank you, dragons. I'll never forget this.'

He ran towards us, grinning from ear to ear, while the older men followed more slowly behind him.

'That's Zeb's son, Artie,' Dirven said. 'Looks like he's enjoying himself.'

Fitzee angled his head towards the sky and screeched. Gisella screamed and grabbed Dirven's arm.

*Hatchling,* Fitzee said, *you are hurt. Who did this to you? They will pay.*

*It was just a child with some stones,* I said. *He isn't here. No one here has caused me any harm.*

'Seeger?' Asher said.

'They've noticed that I've been hurt,' I said. 'Nothing to worry about.'

I ran towards the three beasts and Riff, Kieran, Riva and Maraed followed on my heels. We all hugged and petted the dragons, who crooned their delight. I could hear the farmer and his wife exclaiming over our behaviour. The young Xanthi ran back and joined in, patting Fitzee's neck. It was obvious the dragons had won a fan in him.

*It is good to see you again, Seeger,* Hizaree said.

I rubbed his nose then turned to the red dragon. *Why are you here, Fitzee? Why aren't you with Rog and the others?*

*We were asked to carry these men here. They want to warn their family and friends about the coming flood. We will return to the forest near the big water, once we have rested. Unless you want us to stay with you? We could visit the boy with stones.*

*No, that's fine. You'll be needed to fly Rog and the others to safety, once they've done their job. Rest now while I go talk with your passengers.*

*Why do you want to help these people?* Silvana said. *They have shown their true nature by mistreating you. How can we trust them?*

*Not every Xanthi is cruel,* I said. *The people on this farm have been courteous and friendly. They don't want to kill you. They're willing to help us. If we do this right, it'll mean your people can live here in peace. Wouldn't that be good?*

She sniffed. *Of course, but we could also live in peace if we wipe all the Xanthi out.*

*No, you wouldn't,* I said. *Other humans would come to avenge them. The killing would just go on and on and on.*

We gave the dragons a final pat and hug and re-joined the others up near our wagon. One of the Xanthi—I guessed it was their leader, Zeb—was explaining things to Dirven and the others.

'We've got to warn our people,' the man said. 'The flood will be devastating.'

Dirven frowned. 'Your job was to protect the dam, not help to destroy it.'

Zeb nodded. 'We want to stop this Blunt person. Besides, the men promised they'd help us rebuild it once this trouble was over.'

Dirven nodded. 'Very well. I'll help you warn the other farms. I'll release the messenger birds and we can send news to our people in the valley with the next food deliveries, tomorrow.'

'Oh no,' Jaxon said. 'We won't allow you to warn the army.'

The other two archers who were with him, lifted their bows with arrows notched and ready.

'What about the city?' Dirven said.

'If it's not in danger of being flooded,' Jaxon said, 'then there's no need to tell them anything. Our orders are, only warn the farms. We'll ride with you when you make your deliveries, just to make sure.'

I looked at Asher, who seemed confused. 'City?' he said. 'You have a city?'

The Xanthi turned as one and stared in confusion at Asher. Kieran nudged me and whispered, 'I bet he'll want to see it!'

'Of course,' Zeb said. 'Our city, Xantar, is in the foothills of the northern mountains, west of Old Ylani. Surely you didn't think all the people in the army came from just a few farms?'

Nikluss stepped forward. 'This is the first we have heard of any city. The Midrashi have always given the impression that you were an uncivilised people.'

I think steam came out of Dirven's ears. Zeb flushed a deep red and the other Xanthi growled and bared their teeth. Maraed grabbed my arm, so I straightened my back and smiled reassuringly at her even though my heart had begun to race.

'I beg your pardon?' Dirven said.

'I'm sorry but I'm only repeating what I've heard,' Nikluss said, 'It's the Midrashi who represent you in this manner.'

Asher moved closer to the group of Xanthi, flapping his hands and making soothing noises. I speak true, he sounded as though he was calming down a flock of geese.

'Gentlemen, gentlemen,' he said. 'We mean no harm. It seems to me your allies, the Midrashi, don't respect you. Nothing is more important to them than themselves. They use who and what they want with no regard for the person, or creature, being used. I'm sorry but that is their nature. Help us put a stop to this, by defeating Blunt and his allies.'

The tension drained out of the Xanthi. Dirven smiled ruefully and nodded at Asher. Zeb's face returned to its usual colour and I could feel the atmosphere lighten. I patted Maraed's hand, to let her know all was well. She sighed and leant on me, letting go of my arm and holding my hand instead.

She was holding my hand!

I heard sniggering in my mind. *Trevor, is that you?*

*You look so soppy.*

*I do not!*

*Yes, you do.* He sighed. *It's all right for you. I don't have a sweetie.* Harvey *doesn't have a sweetie. No one loves us.*

I looked behind me to see what the dragons were doing. They'd curled up together and were already fast asleep. I turned back in time to see Dirven, Gisella and their Xanthi friends heading towards the farmhouse, followed by Jaxon and his men. Riff was climbing up onto our wagon, with Asher close behind him. Angus was helping Riva up onto the wagon-bed, while Nikluss was throwing our bedding up next to her.

'Come on, you two,' Kieran said. 'We're leaving.'

'What are the Xanthi doing?' I said.

'They can't waste any time,' he said. 'They've got a lot of people to warn and only a few days to do it.'

'I hope they leave Marlo's dad until last,' Maraed said.

I squeezed her hand and smiled at her. Her cheeks went pink. I took that as a sign of encouragement.

'Yes,' Kieran said, 'he could cause us a lot of trouble. Still, his livestock shouldn't drown just because he's a pain in the unmentionables.'

We hurried over to the wagon and I offered to help Maraed up next to Riva. She said she'd like to walk the first leg of the journey with Kieran and I, so I grabbed her hand again before she could change her mind.

Riff leant down towards the griven and said, 'We'd like to leave now, please fellas.'

The griven stood up, shook their heads and then began to pull the wagon out of the field and towards the open gate. Caspar and Juno sat on the fence and watched us go. I wished them well. We headed out onto the road and began the trek back to the Sayle River.

# Twenty-Five

As we neared the ford, I sensed the dragons flying overhead.

Hizaree said, *Yahoo!* as they passed by. Then, as they headed off towards the southern ranges Fitzee called to me. *Hatchling, there is a group of armed men heading towards you on the other side of the river. Be careful.*

I told Asher what the dragon had said so he called a halt to our progress. 'It's most likely they are part of the army on patrol,' he said. 'They're probably all Xanthi but we can't presume anything. If there are Midrashi amongst them, then Riva and Seeger are at risk of discovery.'

'Should we try to find another way back to our company?' Riff said.

Nikluss shook his head. 'There isn't another way back. We could stop here but that might look suspicious.'

We all thought about our predicament, while the griven took the opportunity to graze.

'Here's what we'll do,' Asher finally said. 'Girls, do you have any scarves with you? Yes? Then wrap them over your heads and across your face, like some of the women in Portsmouth did. Maraed, you should be sitting up here next to Riva.'

The girls immediately began to rummage in their things to find a scarf each. I, for one, had no idea why they'd even have such a thing in their kit but women have a different understanding of what it means to travel light.

'Seeger,' Asher said, 'come here. I'm going to cover the rest of your head with bandages. Then, climb up onto the wagon with the girls. Look sicker than you really are. We'll tell them you're the reason we're cutting short our visit to the north. Let's all remember that we're a family of travelling minstrels. Right? Good.'

Once our disguises were in place and I was sitting leaning against the side of the wagon bed, we set off again towards the ford. Thank Sed for the dragon's warning. As we crossed the Sayle River we could see the men approaching the wagon. They were all fully kitted out with helmets and breastplates, carrying shields and swords. Their faces were grim.

When we were through the ford, Riff tugged the reins and the griven stopped. As the soldiers neared us Asher called out, 'Greetings, gentlemen. Are you off to wage battle?'

The leader of the troop lifted his left hand and the men all stopped dead. They kept their shields up and their swords ready.

'Who goes there?' their leader said.

'Just a band of travelling minstrels,' Asher said, climbing down from the wagon and walking towards the soldiers. 'Friends to all, enemies of none. Who are you?'

He stuck his hand out in welcome but the stranger didn't shake it so he tucked it into his pocket. Then he pulled out the cup he'd put in there the night before and handed it back to Riff, who passed it on to Riva. If this startled or bemused the leader of the soldiers, he gave no indication.

'I'm Farkus, patrol leader,' he said, 'and these are my men.'

I heard Riva suck in some air as though she was startled. That name rang a bell in my mind. I'd heard it before … somewhere … I figured it'd come back to me when I was no longer thinking about it.

'Why are you so heavily armed?' Asher said.

'We're preparing for war,' Farkus said. 'Haven't you seen our encampment up in the valley?'

Asher shrugged. 'We're not from these parts, mister. We don't involve ourselves in politics. We sing and dance and tell stories to entertain folk who can't get to the big cities to see a show.'

He smiled and nodded at Farkus. The rest of us followed suit, smiling at the armed men. That is, all except the two girls and me. We were too wrapped up to show any emotion.

'What's wrong with him?' Farkus said, pointing at me.

'He ran into a little lad who was too quick to launch stones at a simpleton,' Asher said. 'We decided to take our talents elsewhere.'

Farkus pointed at Nikluss and Angus. 'Your men are armed with bows and arrows.'

I saw the archers shift their stance, just a little, so that they seemed relaxed but I knew they were ready to fire if needed.

'As well as being our musicians,' Asher said, 'the lads supplement our provisions with fowl and any other edible wildlife. One never knows when the opportunity to hunt will present itself.'

Farkus studied the archers for a while but then, his lips pursed, he nodded slowly. 'I see.'

253

'So, who are you at war with?' Asher asked. 'This area seems very peaceful to us, apart from the young stone-thrower.'

The patrol leader flicked his hand at his men and they shifted their stance: feet apart, shields relaxed and their swords down at their sides. Their quick and well-timed response to his gesture was impressive. Blunt, Lorik and company had drilled them well.

'The Xanthi and the Midrashi have combined forces to fight the dragons that live in the mountains in the north,' Farkus said.

Asher clutched his clothing at the base of his throat. 'Oh my,' he said. 'Dragons? Are there many? No, wait, there must be if you need a whole army to fight them. My goodness me!'

Farkus nodded, still watching us all suspiciously. 'Someone is in cahoots with them. We've had our supply wagons sabotaged and our sentries attacked. We're on the hunt for dragon-sympathisers.'

We looked at each other and then back at Farkus, as if we'd never heard of such a thing.

'My goodness gracious!' Asher said. 'How exciting!' He studied Farkus's face. 'You don't think ...? Why, you couldn't possibly think ...? We've just come from entertaining some farming families back there.' He waved his hand vaguely behind him. 'We didn't even know there was an army nearby. You could go and ask them, if you like.'

There was a moment's silence. Then, Farkus seemed to reach a decision in our favour. 'You'd best be getting along,' he said. 'Keep to the south-east and out of our way.'

'Yes, sir!' Asher said. 'Thank you and good luck.' He climbed back up onto the driver's seat next to Riff.

'Let's go, fellas,' Riff said.

The griven began to haul the wagon along the path that led away from the ford. Farkus and his men stood their ground, watching us as we left.

As we moved on up the track, Asher told the archers to strike up a tune. 'We told them we're minstrels,' he said, 'so let's prove it to them.'

They struck up an Outer Islands' jig, guaranteed to lift the spirits and set feet tapping. Because I was sitting in the back of the wagon, I could see the soldiers watching us as we left. Playing the role of simpleton, I waved to them as the distance between us grew. Not one of them smiled or gave any indication that they'd seen me or could hear the music. They didn't move until we had progressed quite a way up the path heading towards the range where the rest of our company were encamped. Eventually Farkus must have given the command to march because they set off again along the riverbank. They had no idea just how close they had come to finding their "dragon-sympathisers".

As I watched them leave, I said to Riva, 'Why does that name, Farkus, ring a bell?'

'He's a Midrashi,' she said. 'He and his brother often patrolled the corridors near the stables. If I wasn't wearing this head scarf, he would have recognised me.'

A cold shiver ran up my spine. What if the dragons hadn't been flying overhead when they did? What if I couldn't talk to them across a distance? It didn't bear thinking about.

Once again, we had to break the journey about halfway to the rocky escarpment. Out in the open, distances are so often deceptive. I could have sworn the range was only a short trek away.

As we set up camp, Asher told the girls to keep their head scarves on, just in case another patrol wandered by. Our brush with Farkus had left Riva, especially, very nervous. I didn't think I was in much danger of recognition because I'd rarely left the confines of the stable. However, Asher said that some of the Midrashi might remember the lad who rode on the back of a dragon during the siege of Midrash. I suppose he was right. Thank Sed, we had no more run-ins with Xanthi patrols and by late afternoon the next day we were at the base of the range.

Two dragons and a small black bird flew down the hill to greet us.

*You're back! You're back!* the raven called. *Why are you bandaged like that, Seeger? Tell me who did it and I'll take their eye out.*

He landed on my shoulder.

*Don't fret yourself about it, Joffre. It doesn't matter.*

*Was it one of these? That Nikluss looks like a shady character.*

He turned his head and glared over his shoulder at the archer walking behind me.

*No, it was a Xanthi child back over the river. It looks worse than it is.*

The bird huffed and puffed his feathers out but he accepted my answer and tucked himself up next to my jaw. *I'm sorry I wasn't there to protect you,* he said.

*Welcome back, hatchling,* Shadreer said. *Are you well?*

*I'm just a bit bruised and sore. I'll be fine.*

*Was the mission successful?*

*I believe so,* I said. *We'll soon know if it wasn't. What have you been doing while we were gone?*

*We flamed supply wagons and burned down a few tents. We carried soldiers out on reconnaissance flights. We helped transport some of their equipment. However, we are glad you are back. They forget that we can understand them and they treat us like tamed beasts.*

*Well, we can't have that!* I said.

The dragons landed and walked alongside us until we reached the narrow path that led up to the Seddonese hiding place. They then took off, heading higher up to perch along the top of the range. Trevor and Harvey carefully pulled the wagon up as far as the track allowed. Then, we unhitched them and parked the wagon in a shallow recess among the boulders. It was a tight fit so it took a bit of jiggling and shoving but, finally, it was done. The two griven waddled off down the other side of the hill to find Chops and Biff. Trevor mumbled something about "searching for their bones".

When we reached the cave system near the top of the escarpment, we found the place a hive of activity. Men were sharpening their swords with pumice stones, archers were fiddling with the strings of their bows, a small band of armed men passed us on their way down the hill and Grimm was inside one of the caves standing over a map.

We stood just inside the entrance to let our eyes adjust from the sunshine outside to the dim light in the cave. While we still stood there, Grimm noticed us and hurried over.

'I thought you'd be gone longer than this,' he said, 'but welcome back. Was it worthwhile? What did you find out?'

Asher, Riff, Nikluss and Angus walked back to the table with Grimm and, looking at the map spread out before them, began to fill him in on what we'd learned. Kieran, the girls and I went in search of something to eat. Joffre stayed with me, in case I found something he could have as well.

One of the cooks took pity on us and gave us each a small bowl of vegetable stew and a hunk of bread. We found a quiet spot towards the back of the cave and sat down to enjoy the hot food. I shared my bread with the raven. While we ate, I told the bird about the Xanthi's raven god and how important he was to them. He fluffed his feathers up and nodded proudly.

*They sound like a sensible group of humans,* he said. *It's perfectly understandable. We're special, as you know, unlike the stupid crows.*

Then I told him about Lorik, the false priest, wearing a cloak made of raven feathers. He dipped his head down between his shoulders and began to make a high-pitched keening sound, like an old woman wailing.

*Joffre?* I said. *What's the matter?*

*The men came with nets and killed so many of us.* He keened some more. *My mother, my father, my nest-mates are all on that cloak. They missed me but, if you hadn't found me when you did, I don't think I'd have lasted another day.*

*Oh Joffre, I'm so very sorry.*

*Why would they do that if we're sacred to them?*

*They wouldn't. That's the point. Lorik is a fake. He's fooled the Xanthi into thinking he's a holy man, when he isn't. He's just a soldier, playing a role to fool the locals into helping him and his friend, Blunt.*

*You're saying my family died so that he could tell a lie?* The bird sat up, a wild look in his eyes. *Right!* he said. *I've been making friends with the locals down in the southern forest. I'm going to have a chat with them. I think it's time I gathered an unkindness to help you in the fight.*

With that, he affectionately rubbed his head along my jaw and then took off, swerving around the people in the cave, dodging bows and helmets and eventually soaring off outside.

'Where's the bird going?' Kieran said.

'I told him about Lorik's cloak of raven feathers and it

upset him. He says those feathers belong to his family members.'

The girls gasped. 'That's awful,' Maraed said. 'The poor darling.'

'Is it certain that the feathers came from so far south?' Kieran said.

'I doubt they could kill so many ravens this close to Xanthi territory,' I said. 'Not with them being their sacred birds. I think Blunt and Lorik planned this not long after leaving Midrash. They've been very clever.'

Riva shook her head. 'So much misery for so many creatures, all caused by Midrashi. I'm ashamed to be one of them.'

Salt water leaked out of the corner of her eyes and trickled down her cheeks. Maraed put her arm around Riva's shoulders. 'Not all Midrashi are cruel,' she said. 'You're kind and compassionate. We all know that. Don't carry this burden of guilt. It's undeserved.'

Riva wiped her cheeks with her hands. 'That's what Jonathan the priest said. He told me that Sed forgives me and because of that I can be free of guilt, but I find that hard to believe.'

'It's true,' I said, 'and what's more you're here helping us make things right. That's the best way to prove you're not like the others.'

Asher called Riva and me over to the table. 'Tell Grimm what you know about Farkus,' he said. 'Is he going to be a problem?'

I shrugged. Riva said, 'He was always arguing with his brother and they often sounded a bit dim-witted. However, he's fiercely proud of being Midrashi and I know he idolises Blunt. I think we fooled him yesterday but I can't be sure.'

'He watched us for a long time after we parted,' I said. 'I think he was still suspicious of us.'

Grimm nodded. 'If he's worth his salt as a soldier, he'll still be thinking about you and he'd have noted where you were headed. I think we need to be on our guard. I'll still send some men out tonight to do some damage but I'll warn them to be even more vigilant than normal. I wish I'd known in time to warn the others who left a bit earlier.'

He called Felix over. 'There's a patrol lurking along the river near here. When you go out tonight be extra careful.'

'Do you want us to get rid of them?' Felix said.

Grimm thought about it, rubbing his chin. 'Best not,' he said. 'If they don't return, Blunt might send more out looking for them and it'd make him focus his attention on this area. So far, he's been looking for the saboteurs amongst the Xanthi. I'd like to keep it that way.'

Asher put his hand on Grimm's arm. 'Not all the locals are on our side. There's a particular family that would like to cause us a lot of trouble. Once they hear about the dam, they might put two and two together.'

Grimm nodded. 'We must stay vigilant. But, from what you've told us it's not long now before the dam collapses,' Grimm said. 'Get some rest while you can.'

I searched for Shadreer and Jondalee in case they were in calling distance. *Goodnight,* I called. *See you in the morning.*

*Sleep well, hatchling,* Shadreer said. *We will keep watch through the night.*

*Please keep an eye out for Joffre. He was very upset when he left.*

*Do not fear,* Jondalee said. *I will take care of the little fellow.*

# Twenty-Six

## Boyd Speaks

In the morning, we helped the Xanthi onto the backs of the three dragons. Zeb and his son, Artie, were on the red dragon and the others were on Hizaree and Silvana. Jaxon and his men climbed up behind them; one on each dragon.

'They understand what you're saying to them, Zeb,' Rog said, 'so just tell your dragon where you want to go.'

'His name is Fitzee,' Rimini said.

The Xanthi looked very uncomfortable perched up on the dragons' backs. The first fellow on Hizaree was shaking so hard I thought he'd fall off.

'Hang on tight,' I said. 'Press your knees into the dragon's flesh. Don't be afraid. They'll look after you.'

Artie turned around and grinned like a loon. 'This is awesome!' he said.

His elders didn't seem as excited as the young man. I didn't blame them. I remember how terrified I was the first time I flew on a dragon, and at the time I was strapped on with a harness!

Rog reached up and slapped Fitzee on his back leg. 'Off you go and good luck!'

The dragons jumped up, unfurled their wings and, as their passengers shouted in fright, they soared off towards the east. I saw Zeb lean forward and then the red dragon angled towards the south-east and the others followed suit.

'Right,' Rog said, 'let's get to work.'

Rimini and I helped the well-keepers dig the tunnel. First, we had to haul all the prepared timber posts down from the forest. We stacked them up in several piles, as close as possible to the wall face so that we didn't have to travel too far to collect them when they were needed. That took longer than I expected, but considering we had to carry them without the help of a wagon or cart, downhill from the forest area and then across to the middle of the huge dam, we did well to finish that by midday.

Rog let us rest for a short while, long enough to have a hot drink, while he examined the dam wall.

'Just as I thought,' he said, tapping his knuckles against it. 'They've coated the exterior with cement. It'll take us a little longer to break through but it won't stop us. The pickaxes will do the job.'

Rog told us he expected the wall to have an inner core of stone, or stone and cement, and he wanted to try to tunnel that far in, depending on how long it took. First, he told the three largest well-keepers to attack the wall face with their pickaxes. His shoulders relaxed and he breathed more easily once they'd broken through the hard shell, to the rocky soil behind it. My guess is he'd been worried that it would be concrete all the way through. He divided us up into two crews. One group would work, while the other rested and kept watch. We changed places every two hours. That way we kept our energy up, while the work proceeded unabated.

On our crew, the well-keepers did the digging, while Rimini and I carted baskets of dirt and rubble away from the cavity. We tipped it down the slope, just past the guards' hut. By nightfall, we'd made a good dent in the wall and the first of the timber props were in place. The dragons had returned and had settled back into the clearing we'd used when we camped up in the forest.

Rog seemed pleased with our efforts. Rimini and I were exhausted. I had blisters on the palms of my hands, along the fleshy mounds below my fingers. Rimini kept blowing on her hands so I guess she had the same problem. My head kept drooping while I was waiting for the evening meal to heat up. Shortly afterwards, both of us fell asleep to the sound of the well-keepers telling yarns around the campfire.

The next morning, there was more of the same. For all the effort we were expending, all the baskets of dirt we tipped out alongside the guards' hut, and the steady rhythm of the well-keepers digging and scooping, it seemed to take forever before the next timber props were up in the now large hole. They were put up against either wall with an extra beam stretched across the top, below the roof of the tunnel. We tied them in place with rope.

One of the well-keepers told me that if they were digging a tunnel for a mine, or for a new water-supply—a tunnel that would be used for a long time—then they'd bolt the timber together with iron brackets. However, as it would all soon go up in flames, the ropes would suffice.

By the end of the second day my hands were bleeding and so were Rimini's. Rog saw the condition we were in and told us we wouldn't be needed in the morning.

'I'm sorry to let you down, sir,' I said.

'I saw how hard you worked,' he said. 'You've done well.'

I tried to argue. 'But you need us and we—'

Rog held his hand up. 'We well-keepers do this all the time. Our hands are calloused from years of this sort of thing. I'm surprised you've lasted as long as you have.'

Rimini sighed and rubbed her eyes with the back of her hand. I could tell that she felt as miserable as I did.

'Cheer up,' Rog said. 'There's nothing to be ashamed of. I'm delighted with the progress we've made in such a short time. Tomorrow, you can go on watch and we professionals will finish the job at hand. No, don't argue.'

Then he called over one of the men who had wielded a pickaxe and pointed at our hands. 'Sort this out will you please, Red?'

The well-keeper nodded and, telling us to wait where we were—as if we had any intention of going anywhere—he went over to the pot of water that was heating on the fire. He took a bowl and scooped some water out. Then he poured some salt into it. He carried the bowl over to us and put it down on the ground.

He squatted down in front of us and told us to hold out our hands. He took a piece of cloth out of his pocket, saying, 'Don't worry. It's clean.' He dunked it in the salty water and then washed our hands. It stung like heck. Rimini sucked in her breath when he dabbed at her palms.

'Don't touch anything,' Red said, before wandering off towards his kitbag. He came back a short while later with a roll of white cloth and a pair of scissors. He unrolled the white cloth, cut some off and then bandaged our hands. He didn't show any emotion when he was doing my hands, but he smiled gently at Rimini when he got to her. She had saltwater running freely from her eyes.

'Never mind, little lady,' he said. He wiped the water off her cheeks with his thumbs. 'You'll be better in no time.'

I decided the implication was there that mine would also be better soon.

The next morning, when the work began again, Rimini and I stood around feeling like a saddle on a chicken: completely useless and irrelevant. We didn't know where to put ourselves. In the end, we sat leaning up against the wall of the guards' hut and watched the well-keepers work.

Around mid-morning we saw the dragons flying overhead.

'Where do you think they're going?' Rimini said.

I shrugged. 'Who knows? Maybe they've gone hunting. I just hope they come back in time to take us away from here.'

'They know what they're doing,' Rimini said. 'They've not let us down yet.'

At midday we helped the cook prepare and serve a light meal to the workers. Many of the well-keepers slumped as they sat and ate their food. They looked exhausted.

'Not long now, men,' Rog said. 'I think we can call a halt by late afternoon.' The well-keepers nodded and some even sat up a bit straighter. 'We've made excellent progress.'

'Will we fire it up then?' Red asked.

Rog shook his head. 'I gave them four days. We'll rest up and have an early night. We'll set it alight around mid-morning tomorrow and then we'll head back to the others.'

He turned to me and Rimini. 'Here's a job for you two. Search the guards' hut for any oil or alcohol. Anything that will burn. We'll need it to soak the timbers, or at least oil a good patch on each of them to get the blaze going. We brought some with us but not as much as I'd like. The more we can use, the quicker we'll get the job done.'

By late afternoon, Rimini and I had stock-piled our find from the hut. There was a large container of lamp oil, a ceramic jug of cooking oil and four flagons of brandy. Rog was delighted.

The men had finished the tunnel. They hadn't quite reached the core of the damn wall but Rog was satisfied with how far they'd gone.

'It'll do the job,' he said.

We went back up to our original campsite and Rimini, Rog and I searched the surrounding area for tubers and edible plants. It didn't take long to find some and soon there was a large soupy stew bubbling in the pot, ready for us to eat.

We had a happy time around the fire. Rog took one of the flagons we'd found and shared it around. He even let Rimini and me have a taste but I was disappointed. It burnt my throat. Some of the well-keepers told stories of other expeditions they'd been on in their youth. Then we settled in for an early night. Several of the older men competed for the loudest snorer in camp but eventually even that didn't stop me from sinking into a sound sleep.

When we woke in the morning, the dragons were back waiting at the far end of the campsite, where they'd previously slept.

As we broke our fast, Rog explained how the firing would be done. Someone wearing a face mask to help them breathe once the smoke began to build, would go into the tunnel and set fire to the deepest props. Then, he'd work his way back up along the tunnel, soaking the other props with oil and lighting them as he went.

'He must work quickly,' Rog said, 'or he'll be overcome with the smoke. The trick is to stay low and run between the props.'

'Wouldn't it be better to soak the timber on the way down the tunnel?' I said. 'Then all you have to do is set them alight on your way out.'

'Yes, of course.' Rog ran his hand over his hair and sighed. 'I guess I'm as tired as the rest of you. Of course, that's the way to do it but you'd still have to stay low and be quick.'

'I'll do it,' I said. 'I rested all yesterday, so I'm a lot fresher than any of your men. They look worn out.'

For a while I thought he was going to refuse me. He studied his men as they sat around the fire. Most of them had dark smudges under their eyes and several were yawning.

'Very well,' he said. 'We'll wait down at the wall face with the dragons. As soon as you're out of there, we'll fly away. I don't know how long it'll take to work but I don't want to wait around to find out.'

'Sounds good to me,' I said.

Rimini leant against my shoulder. 'Please stay safe,' she said.

'Don't worry,' I said. 'It'll be a doddle.'

I suppose I should have been afraid but my excitement drowned the fear. *Wait until I tell Seeger*, I thought.

'Very well,' Rog said. 'Everyone, pack up your gear and then use the opportunity to rest up.' Red sighed as he flung the dregs of his drink into the fire. 'Be patient, Red,' Rog said. 'All in good time. I'd like to see what Blunt and his crew are up to.' He turned to the dragons. 'Would one of you be willing to take me?'

Fitzee bugled and nodded his huge head. 'Thank you,' Rog said. 'I'll just pack my gear and then I'll be with you.'

Rog and Fitzee left soon after. The other two dragons lay down, resting their heads on each other's back. The rest of us packed our gear and then lay down or sat next to it and relaxed. Several of the older well-keepers fell asleep again.

Quite a while later, Rog and Fitzee returned. The well-keeper leapt down off the dragon's back and ran over to the campfire.

'Wake up, people!' he shouted. He waited until he had everyone's attention. 'There's a large contingent marching towards the eastern range. The fellow in the raven-feathered cloak is near the front of that group. I think they know where our crew are. Time to move, everybody. Down to the dam wall.'

Rog must have been thinking over the lighting process as we walked down to the tunnel. When we got there, he whispered something to Red who picked up three pitchers of oil.

'Red's going with you,' Rog said. 'He'll help you soak the timber so I can be sure it's done right.'

I frowned and pouted a little.

'I'm not saying I can't trust you, boy,' Rog said. 'It's just that you've never done this before whereas Red's had practice. All right?' I nodded. 'Here, you take the flint.'

He turned to address the rest of the troops. 'They won't be long. Get yourselves seated on the dragons, ready to take off. Off you go, Boyd.'

I smiled at Rimini and gave her a little wave. In return, she dipped her head in a quick nod. Red and I walked into the tunnel and headed towards the first set of timber beams. He slopped oil on both of the uprights and then carefully spread some along the connecting ropes. He did this all the way along the tunnel.

When we reached the end, he put the pitchers down and handed me a long piece of cloth.

'Right, son,' he said, 'tie this over your mouth and nose and breathe through it. Give me a few minutes before lighting it up. Spark the flint onto the rope. Then run like the blazes to the next prop and do the same. Don't dawdle. Don't stop to watch the flames. Just make sure it's caught alight and then run to the next one. You'll have plenty of time to get out before the fire is a threat to you but the smoke could kill you long before. Understand?' I nodded. 'Good. I'll see you outside.'

With that, he ran back along the tunnel towards the opening. I waited until he was nearly at the entrance, holding the flint and running my fingers over its surface. When he was far enough away, I turned and looked at the soaked ropes. I took a deep breath and thought, *Well, here we go.*

I held the flint over the nearest rope, god-spoke to Sed, *Help me do this right,* and then I struck the flint.

# Twenty-Seven

## Seeger Speaks

In the morning, Maraed unravelled Asher's handiwork and I was no longer disguised as a bundle of dirty laundry. We were all so tired when we reached the caves the night before that no one had thought of it then. Mid-morning, after the soldiers and archers had all been fed, we sat outside the cave eating some toasted bread. I could see her studying me.

'I think it's time we unwrapped you,' she said.

I put my hand up to my head and felt the gauze wrapped around it. 'Do you know, I'd almost forgotten it was there!'

The bandages were easily removed except for a few patches where blood had stuck them to my skin. She soaked a cloth and moistened the gauze with it. Before I knew it, the bandage was gone. She studied me for a while and then nodded approvingly.

'You'll keep,' she said. 'The bruises will soon fade and, except for the cut over your eyebrow, I don't think there'll be any scars. How does your head feel?'

'Not too bad,' I said. 'It aches a little, more so when I'm tired, but it's nothing to fret over. Thank you.'

She smiled. I smiled back. Then she gathered up the used bandages and took them into the cave to throw them on the fire. I saw Riva flick a cheeky grin at Riff. She seemed pleased about something. I was going to ask her what it was all about but Kieran shouted, 'Come have a look at the army camp.'

We all went to the escarpment and peered over the edge. Although we couldn't hear anything, being too far away for that, we could see there was a lot of running to and fro. It looked like someone had dug up an ants' nest. Little figures ran backwards and forwards and, although it seemed chaotic, you could see there was purpose in the mayhem. We watched the army scurrying about for a while.

'I wonder if any news about the dam has got through,' I said.

'I doubt it,' Kieran said. 'Jaxon would have kept a close eye on things.'

'I hope the farmers move their animals in time,' Riva said.

Riff put his arm around her shoulders. 'I'm sure they will.'

'I suppose Ranald, Marlo's dad, will know by now,' I said. 'Hopefully, he won't think it's anything to do with our little minstrel troupe.'

'Nah,' Kieran said. 'Zeb and his men would have just told them there's something wrong with the dam. There'd be no need to mention us.'

We were about to move away from the ledge when Riff said, 'Hey! There's the patrol we met the other day. Looks like they've got a prisoner.'

Over to the right, we could see the Xanthi soldiers walking back towards the camp. They weren't following the exact line of the river but were, instead, moving diagonally away from it heading towards the main part of the camp. In the middle of the patrol, we could see a bound figure, his head down and his shoulders slumped.

'I wonder who the poor beggar is,' Riff said. 'I hope it's not Dervin or one of his friends.'

We watched them make their way across the river flats. Farkus was in the lead and the men moved with precision. Their prisoner had trouble keeping up with them and occasionally stumbled or moved off-line. His captors reacted with impatience, shoving him back into place.

Then there was a commotion behind us. We hurried back down to the caves and saw Felix's patrol stumbling up the path towards us. They were calling out and others were shouting back at them, so I couldn't work out what was going on.

Then I heard Shadreer. He was somewhere up on the rocks above us. *They have caught Felix,* he said. *We saved the griven but we could not rescue Felix. We are so sorry.*

*What? Felix? I don't understand.*

*His men will explain. We are so sorry, hatchling.*

*I'm sure you did your best,* I said. *Thanks for saving the griven.*

'What is it, Seeger?' Kieran said, grabbing my arm and pulling me out of the way of someone going into the cave.

'Shadreer says the patrol has captured Felix,' I said.

Riff and the others all gasped. Maraed covered her mouth with her hand and looked as though she was about to weep.

'He said something about saving the griven,' I said, 'and he's very upset. He said the men would explain.'

'Well come on then,' Kieran said, pushing me in front of him. 'Let's go.'

We all filed into the cave behind the last of the returning patrol members. Most of the others had already flopped down onto the dirt. They all looked beaten and exhausted. Grimm stood over them, his arms folded across his chest.

'Someone tell me what happened,' he said, 'and it had better make sense or you're all in trouble.'

No one answered. Most of them sat with their hands hanging down between their knees and their heads slumped forward. Several of them had saltwater running down their cheeks. They all looked as though their mother had just died.

'Speak up!' Grimm said. 'You, Sam, what happened?'

One of the men wearily lifted his head and looked at Grimm. 'I'm sorry, sir,' he said. 'We messed up.'

'Obviously!' Grimm said. 'Details please.'

Asher put his hand on Grimm's shoulder. 'Go easy,' he said. 'They're all in shock.'

Grimm shook Asher's hand off and snapped at him, 'This is army business, Ash, so step back.'

Asher did as he was told but his lips were pursed and his brows swooped down over his long, pointy nose. He hurried over to the cook and whispered something to him. The man nodded and immediately began to stoke the fire. Asher collected some cups and laid them out in a row, in front of the cook.

'Sam,' Grimm said, 'start from the beginning.'

Sam slowly nodded. He took a deep breath and then let it out in a whoosh. 'Right,' he said. 'Well, we set out as usual last night. Felix told us there was an enemy patrol in the area so we were extra careful. We headed towards the army camp and hid in the trees on the southern side.'

Grimm nodded. 'Yes, yes.'

'We waited until most of the camp was asleep and then we snuck around to the quartermaster's tent. There was only one guard on duty, which we thought was a bit stupid. Especially as they'd lost some of their gear already, thanks to us. Anyway, we tiptoed around to the back. Jorge lifted up the bottom of the tent and then ... No, wait, it was Bill. Bill lifted the flap and—'

Grimm held his hand up. 'Perhaps you could skip all that and get to the part where you lost Felix.'

Sam scratched his nose. 'Right. Fair enough. Thanks,' he said as the cook handed him a drink. He cradled it between his hands and let the steam drift up past his nose.

The cook and Asher handed out drinks to all the others and all the while Asher murmured, 'Drink this up. It'll help you feel better. Drink up, lads.'

Grimm glared at them, his right foot tapping on the cave floor. 'Fellas, please,' he said. 'Don't interrupt. Go on, Sam.'

Sam sipped his drink, wiped his hand across his mouth and said, 'Where was I? Oh yes, that's right. We raided the tent and got some good stuff. Cooky, I think it's in Bill's backpack ... No, wait, I think it's in Jorge's. Or, perhaps not. Do you have it, Fred?'

'For pity's sake!' Grimm said. 'It doesn't matter! Tell me about Felix.'

Sam rubbed his eyes with his free hand. I could see it shaking, even in the dim cave light. 'Felix. Yes. Well, we took our time coming back up here, being extra careful because of the enemy patrols. There's more than one wandering about down there. We swung around the base of this range, thinking to come in from behind.'

He sipped his drink again. I thought Grimm was going to explode with impatience but he held himself together.

Surely he could see how distraught these men were?

'Anyway, that's when we heard the griven,' Sam said. 'They were bellowing like I'd never heard them before.' He looked up at Grimm who nodded at him. 'Felix said they sounded upset so we'd better go have a look. I'm surprised you didn't hear them up here, the way they were carrying on. No? I'm surprised. Oh, I said that, sorry. So, we crept back down the path through the rocks and onto the area where the griven had been grazing. And there they were!'

He looked at Grimm and nodded.

'Who were?' Grimm said through gritted teeth.

'The enemy. They were trying to round up the griven and take them with them. The griven weren't having any of it. I reckon they thought they'd end up as the army's dinner if they got taken. So, they were bellowing and squealing and swinging their big horny heads at the foreigners and kicking them with their hooves. The enemy had a rope around one of the beasts but that wasn't doing them much good. We crept a bit closer to watch and to intervene if necessary. Then we crept a bit closer again.

'So, we sat there and Felix had that stare he gets when he's making his mind up about something. You've all seen it, right? I guess he was deciding whether the griven needed help. Then the dragons came swooping down. The foreigners screamed and let go of the rope and the griven took off. The dragons roared and chased after the beasts. I guess they wanted the griven for their supper ... No, wait, it'd be their breakfast by then. Anyway, the dragons saved the griven from the enemy, even if it was for their own stomach's sake.'

'The dragons told me about it,' I said. 'They didn't eat them.' Everyone stared at me. I smiled and looked at Sam. 'Sorry to interrupt. Please go on.'

'Right. Good. Thanks. Where was I?' He rubbed his nose. 'Oh yes, that's right. Everything would've been all right but, you see, we was all tired. It'd been a long night and, well, we let our guard down.'

He stopped and stared into his mug.

'Go on, son,' Asher said.

'Well,' he said, 'the thing is ... A few of us cheered.' Some of the men dropped their heads even lower. 'I'm not naming names. It could have been any of us. Anyway, the soldiers heard us and rushed us. My flipping heck, they was fast! Took us completely by surprise.

'We turned and ran but Felix tripped over a rock or something. I heard him grunt as he fell. I turned back to help him up and saw the soldiers almost upon us. Felix yelled at me to run. Then he said it was an order. So, I ran. I thought he'd be right behind me. But, when we couldn't hear anyone chasing us no more and we stopped to catch our breath, Felix wasn't with us.

'Jorge and I climbed up onto a high boulder and tried to see if he was still coming behind. That's when we saw they'd caught him and they was tying him up. We didn't know what to do. Felix had ordered us to run. If we crept back down, we'd probably be too late anyway and he wouldn't want us to give ourselves up or give away our hiding place.'

He sighed and put his cup down. 'We came back here as fast as we could. We're sorry, sir. We failed Felix and we failed you and we all just want to die.'

No one said anything for a while as we processed what we'd just heard. Felix—strong, capable, brave Felix—had been captured. What would happen to him? Would they kill him? Would they torture him? Would he reveal our hideout? No, surely that wouldn't happen. He'd never do that. *Oh Sed, I god-spoke, please look after Felix. Please bring him back to us.*

Grimm just stood there, his arms still folded across his chest and his lips clamped so tightly together that they were just a thin line.

Asher bent down and patted Sam on the shoulder. 'You did what Felix told you to do,' he said. 'It's not your fault. Rest up and then, after you've had a sleep and something to eat, you can help us do something about it.'

Sam nodded and he leant back against the cave wall and closed his eyes.

'Come on, Grimm,' Asher said, 'let's talk about this somewhere else, so these fine men can recover from their long night and the shock of losing their leader.'

He took Grimm's elbow and led him away. Kieran, Riff and I went back out to the escarpment and peered over. We could see the patrol, with Felix in the middle, making their way to the army camp. They didn't have long to go now.

# Twenty-Eight

The men wanted to send a team out to rescue Felix straight away but Grimm wouldn't let them go, not in the daylight.

'We can't let emotion rule our actions,' he said.

For the rest of the day, Grimm, Asher and Marc, the leader of the swordsmen, huddled together making plans. Eventually, Marc went over to the archers who were still awake and brought one of them back to join the leaders' meeting. It didn't help that Jaxon, the second-in-command, wasn't with us.

That night, Marc led a contingent of swordsmen and archers to raid the enemy camp to rescue Felix. They came back in the early hours of the morning without him. Several were wounded and all were dispirited.

'He was heavily guarded,' Marc said, 'and those Xanthi know how to fight. We could have done it if we had more men.'

'Don't worry,' Grimm said. 'We'll try again. We just need to have another think about how we'll proceed. Have something to eat and rest up.'

# Twenty-Eight

A call came from above and we all raced up to find out what was happening. We saw a troop of men marching towards our stronghold. We could clearly see Lorik in his black cloak out in front, dragging a bound figure alongside him.

'What do you make of this, Grimm?' Asher said. 'Do you think Felix caved and told them where we were?'

Grimm leant his hands on the edge of the escarpment and studied the scene before him. 'I don't think so,' he said, 'and not just because it's Felix. The patrol would have reported on the other few men seen fleeing from them. I think they're sending a troop to intimidate what they think are a few resistance fighters. If they knew who we really were, they'd have brought the whole army.'

That made sense to me. I know I probably had Felix on a pedestal but the man had always impressed me with his calm manner in a crisis and his silent, strong presence. I couldn't see him being intimidated by Blunt or Lorik, even if they did physically hurt him.

'How many of them are there, do you think?' Asher said.

'Around two hundred, two-fifty,' Grimm said. 'Enough to be a problem but not enough to overwhelm us. We have the advantage. Once they're in the gully in front of us, they'll be boxed in.'

Marc came up behind Grimm. 'They'll be in big trouble if the flood comes while they're down there.'

'But Felix is with them!' Maraed said. 'You can't let that happen.'

The professional soldiers ignored Maraed's outburst but Riva stepped up and put her arm around her. Riff patted Maraed's arm with his good hand. I agreed with Maraed. So did Kieran; I could tell. Perhaps it was because we'd spent a lot more time with Felix. We thought of him as family. I reckon his archers would think the same as us. They idolised him.

While the troop were still out on the plain, the archers lined up along the edge of the escarpment and propped their bows along the rock-wall, ready to fire when needed. Shadreer and Jondalee positioned themselves either side of the gully, draping themselves along the top of each ridge. Once they'd settled into position, they faded into the background. If you didn't know they were there, or where to look, you would be hard-pressed to see them.

Finally, led by Blunt and Lorik, the enemy marched into the gully and up to the steep sloping front of the escarpment. They halted at the base. Lorik pushed Felix—still bound and bleeding from cuts on his head and arms—to stand in front of him.

'Good morning,' Blunt called. 'We have one of your people here. We'd like to discuss an exchange.'

'What would that be?' Grimm shouted down to them.

'We'll release this sorry specimen into your keeping,' Blunt said, 'and you take yourselves off back home. I'm sure you have some farm work to do.'

Asher stepped up behind Grimm and muttered, 'He thinks we're Xanthi. He's still got no idea who we are.'

Grimm stepped down from his vantage point and gathered us around him. 'Asher's right,' he said. 'We could play on his ignorance.'

'Don't forget the dam will collapse at any time,' Marc said. 'It's the fourth day.'

'Hello up there,' Blunt called. 'We don't have all day.'

I put my hand up. 'Let me speak to them. Please? I know something that will make the Xanthi question their loyalty to the Midrashi.'

Marc turned on me. 'Shut up. You're just a kid.'

# Twenty-Eight

I reeled back, unused to being spoken to like that. I shut my eyes and god-spoke. *Oh Sed, if I'm being arrogant then please forgive me, but if you can use me then please open a way.*

Asher poked Marc in the chest with his long, bony finger. 'Now listen here, you. This lad has probably seen and done more than you have in your entire lifetime. He's not just any kid. He's a dragon-master. He's a clever young man who knows things about the Xanthi's belief system that I doubt you know anything about. Well, do you know anything about them? No? I thought not. I say we let Seeger have a try. If it doesn't work, well then the archers can let their arrows fly and you and your swordsmen can run down the slope and start hacking away. All right?'

He folded his hands across his chest and glared at Marc. The swordsman looked for support from the others gathered around but no one backed him up.

Grimm said, 'That sounds as good a plan as any other. All right, Seeger, have at them.'

'Yes, sir,' I said.

I walked back up to the edge of the escarpment and looked down at the enemy. Lorik was smirking, clutching the lapels of his cloak in his left hand, while his right hand still held on to the rope that bound Felix. I wanted to wipe that smug smile off his face.

Maraed stood next to me. 'You can do it,' she said, 'and don't forget they don't know there are two dragons watching them, ready to pounce when you tell them to.'

'Ask them to,' I absent-mindedly corrected her as I stared at the men standing at ease at the bottom of the slope. I turned to smile at her and she smiled back. Then, she leant forward and kissed me on my cheek. Suddenly I felt as though I could do anything.

'Hey, Lorik,' I called. 'What's with the cloak?'

That caught him short. He didn't expect someone to know his name. He frowned and flicked a glance at Blunt, who shrugged in return.

'I, young man, am a priest of the raven god,' he said. 'Have some respect.'

The Xanthi standing behind him nodded in approval.

'If you respect the raven,' I said, 'why are you wearing a cloak covered with their feathers? The raven is sacred. How is that respectful?'

Some of the Xanthi looked thoughtful and all of them watched Lorik to see what his response would be. Again, Lorik looked at Blunt who shrugged back. The Xanthi closest to them frowned and exchanged glances with each other. I suppose they couldn't understand why their holy man had to look to the Midrashi leader for an answer.

'The ravens gave me their feathers,' Lorik said. 'Don't waste our time, boy.' He shoved Felix, who staggered briefly before regaining his feet.

'If you're a priest of the raven god,' I said, 'then what's his name?'

Again, the surrounding Xanthi studied Lorik intently. Lorik's eyes shifted from side to side. The Xanthi began to whisper among themselves. Lorik looked very uncomfortable.

'Don't be obtuse, boy,' he said. 'It's the raven god. The raven. That's his name.'

Now the Xanthi adjusted their weapons and the whispering grew louder; it sounded like the rustling of leaves.

'No, it's not,' I said. 'The god's name is, Rafnagud.'

One of the soldiers near Lorik exclaimed, 'That's right! Why didn't he know that? Some priest he is!'

'The god is Rafnagud and his servant is the raven,' I said. 'For too long you've lied using his name. God will not be mocked. Your punishment is coming!'

Now, I meant the flood that would soon be on its way. I had no idea how true I had spoken but I suddenly heard Joffre speaking to me.

*I have returned with some friends. We're going to be very unkind to the fellow who is wearing our kinfolk's feathers.*

An unkindness of ravens swooped over my head and down the slope of the escarpment. They headed straight for Lorik, who stood watching them with his mouth hanging open. He dropped Felix's rope. He flapped his hands, shouting, 'Shoo, birds! Shoo!'

Instead of helping Lorik, the Xanthi drew back. One of the men pulled Felix to the side and began to untie his ropes.

'Rafnagud has sent his judgement!' Asher shouted.

The birds dove in and began to ferociously attack Lorik, pecking at his head and hands and face and anywhere else they could shove their beaks. Lorik screamed, trying to bat them away with his hands. My stomach heaved. Riva turned and shoved her face into Riff's chest. Grimm swore under his breath. Several of our archers muttered and cursed but they didn't relax their grip on their weapons.

'Did you know?' Maraed said.

I shook my head. 'I was talking about the flood. Trust Joffre to have perfect timing.'

Blunt turned to the Xanthi and yelled, 'Someone help him!'

No one moved. Blunt pulled out his sword and raised it above his head. He was about to start flailing at the birds when down from the edge of the ridge plunged Jondalee. The Xanthi shrieked but they didn't rush to help Blunt.

Jondalee gripped him with his talons and lifted him up into the air. Blunt screamed and dropped his sword. Then, Jondalee flew away with the Midrashi.

By this time, Lorik was just a heap of bloodied clothing on the ground. The cloak had been torn to shreds. The ravens lifted it off him and flew away towards the southern forest. All, that is, except Joffre who landed on my shoulder.

The Xanthi stared in horror at what was left of Lorik. Some had dropped their weapons in shock. Those of us up on the escarpment were also stunned with disbelief. Who would have thought a little raven would save the day and in such a devastating manner?

Shadreer swooped down, picked up Felix and carried him gently up to us. The Xanthi ducked when the dragon flew past but they didn't attempt to attack him. Instead, they waited until he'd taken Felix and then they drew their swords and turned on some of the men with them. Grimm said they must have been Midrashi. It didn't take long.

While they were still milling about below us, several of the archers cried out and pointed to my left. Fitzee, Hizaree and Silvana were winging towards us, carrying the well-keepers.

Fitzee called to me, *Hatchling, tell the two-legs to move to higher ground. The water is coming. They must run!*

I shouted down to the Xanthi, 'Run! Run to higher ground. The dam has collapsed and the flood is coming.'

They stood and stared at me. I could see the oncoming wave. It had already surged through their camp, obliterating everything in its path.

'Run!' I shouted. 'You don't have much time.'

The Xanthi still milled about, unsure what to do without their leaders.

# Twenty-Eight

Fitzee and the others had landed and they waited at the bottom of the pass.

*Hizaree,* Shadreer said, *go warn the griven to move up into the hills. Fitzee and Silvana, come assist me as I herd these stupid two-legs out of the gully and up to safety.*

Having said that he swooped down towards the front of the assembled Xanthi, breathing short bursts of flame and screeching at them. The other two dragons joined him. Finally, the Xanthi turned and ran. The dragons skilfully directed them back down the gully and then up to the left where there was higher ground.

The great wall of water headed towards us at a tremendous rate. The last of the Xanthi made it up the slopes just as the flood arrived. I didn't know that water could travel at such speed. It was fast, even faster than a wagon being pulled along by racing camels. As it tumbled and churned its way along the river valley, everything was carried in its wake; tents, wagons, trees, boulders, men ... All we could do was watch in awe.

It was some time before the waters had slowed down and we could move about safely. The next day, early in the morning, Riff and I searched for the griven and found them huddled together on the narrow path that led from the grazing field up into the range. They were close to where we had parked the wagon on our return from Dirven's farm. We took them some water in a couple of buckets and gave them some turnips and tubers that we'd carried there in our pockets. They, of course, thought that they had suffered the most out of all of us.

*First, you abandoned us to the elements,* Trevor said. *Then those horrid soldiers came and tried to steal us. They wanted to eat us. They kept talking about roast beef. It was disgusting.*

*Then the dragons chased us,* Harvey said, *and they tried to eat us. I thought they were our friends.*

*They are,* I said. *They rescued you from the soldiers.*

Harvey snorted. *That's one version of the story.*

*Then the flood came and nearly washed us away,* Trevor said. *Poor Chops and Biff were delirious with fear.*

*No, we weren't,* Biff said.

*Don't interrupt,* Trevor said.

*Never mind,* I said. *You're all safe now. We're going to move across to Dervin's farm in a day or two. Shadreer says the waters only reached his bottom fields. The ones closest to the house and barns are all fine.*

*I suppose we'll have to pull you all there,* Harvey said. *It's all work, work, work with you.*

For the next day or so, the dragons helped rescue stranded Xanthi and returned them to safe ground on the other side of the river. Azree, Fiddha and half a dozen other dragons came down from the mountains to help with the evacuation and the after-flood clean up. Many of the Xanthi were reluctant to mount the beasts at first, but Zeb, Artie, Dirven and Gisela came along for the ride to reassure them. Having Joffre flying overhead, or sitting on one of the dragon's shoulders, helped reassure the Xanthi that their god approved.

Once the men were all safely delivered to the northern region, Azree, Fiddha and the new dragons flew back and forth, ferrying Rog, his men and most of Grimm's army to the dam to begin the repairs. Azree said it was the least they could do, seeing as they'd had a peaceful time up on the mountain while the rest of us had been busy.

At the same time, Shadreer, Jondalee, Fitzee and Hizaree left on a special mission. They circled overhead, calling their goodbyes to me, and then they wheeled around and headed back the way we had first come.

'Where are they going?' Kieran asked.

'They've got something they have to do,' I said. 'They'll be back in a few days.'

We were on our way to the farm. Riff turned to speak over his shoulder to me as he guided the griven through the now deeper ford. 'What about the negotiations with the Xanthi? Don't they need to be here for that?'

Asher lightly thumped Riff on his ruined shoulder and then immediately apologised. 'I'm so sorry, dear chap,' he said. 'I completely forgot. I feel such a dimwit.'

Riff laughed. 'That's the nicest thing anyone's said for a long time.'

'What?' Asher said. 'That I'm a dimwit?'

Riff laughed again. 'No, that you forgot my arm wasn't normal.'

Asher beamed at him. 'How lovely!' he said. 'But you don't have to worry. The dragons have entrusted the task to Seeger and me.'

We reached the farm early the next day and the children were keeping look-out, sitting on the front fence. They ran to the farmhouse, announcing our arrival at the top of their voices. When Dirven and Gisella stepped out of the front door, the children ran back so that they could watch the remaining soldiers and archers march in behind the wagons. Grimm had thought it wise to keep some of the fighting men with us, just in case.

Our little army set up camp in the field in which we'd held the concert. Dirven had invited us there, when he'd heard that our well-keepers were helping to restore the dam wall. Officials representing the Chief of Xantar arrived soon after, and Asher and I negotiated the peace treaty on behalf of The Flight. The Xanthi agreed to let the dragons live on or near Old Ylani in peace, provided they restricted their hunting away from settled areas. They also agreed to allow the dragons to soak in the river and to use the riverbanks for their courting rituals. It was a satisfactory arrangement for both sides.

In the evenings, some of Dirven's neighbours turned up bringing extra food and drink and after a serious discussion about how they would co-exist with the dragons, Nikluss and Angus would strike up a tune and the evening would turn to singing and dancing. Some of the Xanthi brought their instruments along and, in a couple of days, our two minstrels had become a band.

Sadly, other neighbours were more wary of us. Many had lost someone in the flood. Although some of the Xanthi had made it to higher ground, many were still in the camp when the water surged through.

Some of our soldiers and archers maintained their distance from me. They thought I'd magically called up the avenging ravens. It's not easy being different.

One day, I was standing in the field with Dirven, Asher and Maraed. We were checking on our griven and Dirven's goats. Then I saw them, coming from the direction of the river.

'Look, Asher,' I said, pointing to the dragons flying towards the farm. 'Here they come.'

Asher clapped his hands together. 'How lovely!' he said. 'What are they carrying? What's that between them? It's not, is it? It can't be.'

'It is,' I said.

'I'll get the others,' Asher said. He turned and ran back to the farmhouse, calling as he ran, 'Riff. Kieran. Riva. Felix. Come see the surprise! Boyd. Rimini. Maraed. You won't believe it!'

'He's an excitable chap.' Dirven grinned at me. 'Someone's been very clever.'

I nodded, my face already aching with the strain of my huge smile. Jarl had done a brilliant job. The dragons were flying in formation, with a huge tarpaulin stretched out between them and attached around their backs, just in front of their wings. Something very special lay on the tarp.

A small crowd had gathered in the field by the time the dragons had landed with their precious load. They settled onto the ground carefully, making sure their timing was perfect. Once they were down their cargo stood up, walked forward and tipped his head so that the enormous bag that hung round his neck, slipped off and fell in front of him. He reached in and pulled out a piece of parchment, which he held in front of him.

The parchment read, 'I am Myrmee, home at last.'

Everyone cheered. Felix, who'd recovered by then from the Midrashi's rough treatment, and Kieran, Boyd and Asher ran forward to untie the buckles and straps that attached the tarpaulin to the dragons. Riva and I headed straight for Myrmee and hugged the darling old fellow. He was weeping with joy.

*I am home,* he said. *I did not think I would live to see the day.*

*Welcome home, Myrmee,* I said. *It's so good to see you again. Are you still writing your memoirs?*

*Of course, dear hatchling,* he said.

Dirven asked, 'Why didn't he fly here?'

'He's an old dragon,' Riva said, 'and his wings are too weak to carry him all this way.'

'How's he going to manage living up on the mountain?' Dirven said. 'It gets mighty cold up there and there's not a lot of water. He'd have to be able to get back down here to the river.'

*I thought I would live down on the plains,* Myrmee said.

*We've already promised the Xanthi that you'd stay away from their farms.*

'We hadn't thought of that,' I said to Dirven. 'He's spent over a hundred years living in a stable. I don't know how he'd cope living on the mountain. He says he'd hoped to live closer to the river.'

For a while no one said anything; we were all lost in thought. Shadreer moved up next to Myrmee. The dragons looked at me as if I was going to magically provide an answer.

*Do not worry,* Myrmee said. *If I die up there well then—'*

'I've got an old barn he could use,' Dirven said. 'I just keep extra feed in it during the winter. He'd be quite cosy in there and he could easily stroll down to the river whenever he needed to.'

Riva hugged Dirven. 'That would be wonderful! He could keep doing his writing, as well.'

Dirven said to Myrmee, 'Would that be acceptable to you? Your friends would be welcome to visit here any time. I've always wanted to get to know some dragons.'

Myrmee dipped his head. *How very kind,* Myrmee said. *That would be delightful.*

Thus, the old dragon moved into one of Dirven's barns to live. The other dragons visit him often and bring him treats to eat. Once Caspar and Juno got over the shock of having the huge beast move in, they began to frequent the barn and now they often sleep perched on the old dragon's shoulders. The donkeys and goats prefer to keep a safer distance.

Joffre decided he didn't quite fit in with the wild ravens in the southern forest, so he chose to live with me but he visits Rimini almost every other day.

After Rog spoke on their behalf, Boyd and Rimini were given leave to join the well-keepers even though they don't have eighteen years. They prefer living in the barracks, and not just because they don't want to go home.

On our return, Riff made maps of each area we went to on our trip, as well as a large one that covered all the territory. Talia was very impressed and has reinstated Riff in the well-keepers. He's their official cartographer (a fancy word meaning, 'map-maker'). He and Riva are going to marry and Mother is busy fussing and planning. The other day she said something about Daisy being a bridal attendant! Father told her not to tease the piglet with false hope.

After a brief reunion with her parents, Maraed came to live with Kieran and Asher in Seddon, and I'm very happy about that. Asher is busy planning new adventures. He says there's still a whole world waiting to be explored.

We never saw or heard from Blunt again. Jondalee refused to talk about it. The only thing he said to me was, *Gravity was not his friend.*

Yesterday, a messenger bird brought me a letter from the old dragon.

> Greetings dear hatchling,
>
> Great news! Azree and Fiddha are sitting on a large clutch of eggs. It has been a long time since I have seen baby dragons. Everyone is very excited.
>
> Dirven and I often converse together. He speaks and I write my answers. He sometimes brings his little boy with him. He has so few years that I am surprised his mother allows him to leave the nest. Perhaps, one day, the youngster will also be a dragon-speaker?
>
> Asher has written to me about his plans to visit the city of Xantar and beyond. He says he

has always wanted to map the region north of Old Ylani. I was delighted to hear that you and some of the others will come with him. Shadreer is too busy to go on the trip but Fitzee and Hizaree are excited about it and I think some of the younger dragons are keen for an adventure.

Perhaps, after this trip, we will convince you to stay here with the Flight. A dragon-speaker, after all, should be with dragons.

Your old friend, Myrmee.

The End.

If you enjoyed this book
please consider adding a review.

Stay Updated with Staurolite Books

Be the first to know about our upcoming
releases and content from our authors.
Visit staurolitebooks.com.au
to subscribe to our newsletter.
We promise not to flood your inbox—
just the latest and greatest from
Staurolite Books!

Read on for the first chapter of the
soon to be published
*Beast-Speaker 4: Dead Man's Fingers*
the next exciting instalment in the
Beast-Speaker series.

# Beast-Speaker 4: Dead Man's Fingers

## Mac

They came riding in on dragons. It had been so long since I'd seen one of those creatures that I thought they'd become things of legend. But there they were, riding the thermals above the valley, skimming the air like giant birds from the beginning of time. I watched them from the mouth of my cave but they didn't see me.

Some of the dragon-riders were armed but they didn't seem as though they were looking for trouble. There's a certain set to the mouth, the angle of the shoulders, that tells if a person is looking for a fight. The riders were alert but relaxed. The last time people came looking for me they pretended to be peaceful, but they had weapons hidden under their cloaks. The wolves dealt with them.

One of the riders had a servant of Rafnagud, the raven god, sitting on his shoulder, uncaged and untethered. Dragons and ravens. These weren't ordinary folk.

There was an old grey-hair and some females as well. They were wise to be on guard in these hills. Most creatures protect their females. If they're gone, so is the species. That's why I think I might be the last of my kind. I haven't seen a female since before silver frosted my pelt. Long before the township down below was built. Long before there were wolves in the valley.

From my home in the hill, I watched the dragons swoop over my lake, then set their riders down on the path that leads into the town. Two of the younger ones lifted the grey-hair down and placed him in the arms of the tall, armed female. I thought the old man might have needed my help. He didn't seem well. Then they set off towards Wulverstane.

Their humans gone, the dragons circled back and plonked themselves down into the water on the edge of the lake. I wanted to shout, 'Be off with you! You'll scare the fish.' But I stayed hidden in the shadows and kept my peace. Eventually they took off and found a perch in the hills, closer to town. I hoped they wouldn't burn the place down. Dragons can do that, you know.

When I first moved into this place there was just me and the fish, but it was too good to last. People started to visit the valley and then, one day, a couple of families built houses. Then more came. Eventually, there was a whole town. For a long time, I hid in my cave and only went out in the moonlight to sit on my rock to fish but, as time passed, the people and I learned to get along. I left them alone and they didn't bother me. I've even taken fish to families that were struggling to feed their young. I can't bear to watch littluns go hungry.

Many turns of the sun ago, a werewolf passed through the valley. I knew what he was as soon as I smelled him. I'm always a little sad for the creatures. The poor things can't help themselves. Usually, they don't know what they're doing until it's done. The stranger was on his last legs and, if the moon hadn't been high and full, he probably would have died without causing any damage. But fate is fickle. A couple of the townspeople found him lying in a field. When they tried to give him aid, the wolf took over. He didn't kill them, he was too weak to do that, but his claws and teeth still did some damage.

There have been wolf-people in the town ever since. Some families even choose to keep the wolf strain in the family, initiating their child at the full moon once he or she has thirteen years.

When the changes first began, and people were killed, they came to me for help. I suppose they thought I'd found a way to master the wolf. They didn't understand what I am. I couldn't fix them – once a werewolf, forever a werewolf but I did my best to help them learn to live with it and to gain some control. I know something about healing. You don't live this long without learning a thing or three. So, I became their healer and when anyone tries to give me trouble, the wolves take care of it. They treat me with respect.

When the dragons came, carrying their riders, I hoped they'd be sensible. Most of the dragon-riders were quite young and deserved to live a full, long life. I didn't want anyone torn limb from limb.

# A Postscript on the Tragedy of Child Soldiers

*Most readers will find the story of Seeger and the other child soldiers in the Beast-Speaker books confronting. When we realise that the books are based upon research done by the author into the very real plight of child soldiers in our own world, inspired initially by watching a video on the work of World Vision with former child soldiers, we feel even more confronted. While we do not live in the world inhabited by Seeger and his companions, we do live in a world in which thousands of children are forced to be soldiers. The Beast-Speaker trilogy not only deals with the reality of child soldiers, but also with their struggles of coming home, and the challenge of rehabilitation. In our own world, we can choose to get involved and do something to help. We are thankful to Rev Tim Costello of World Vision Australia for agreeing to write a postscript sharing the work that World Vision does with former child soldiers.*

Mark Worthing, editor, *Stone Table Books*

# A postscript on the Tragedy of Child Soldiers

There is no image more haunting than that of a child soldier in a pseudo military uniform brandishing an automatic weapon that is almost too big for him.

Look into the pained eyes of the child soldier. Brainwashed, brutalised, and turned into a killer, he is crying for help that he doesn't expect to come. He is in need of rescue.

Like thousands of others, he has probably been stolen at gunpoint from his village and forced to fight in an adult war, under the threat of brutal torture. Every day for him is a living nightmare.

The use of child soldiers remains alarmingly common in conflicts across the world, including Syria, Iraq, Nigeria, South Sudan, Afghanistan, Sierra Leone, Uganda, and Liberia, Up to half of the child soldiers in the world are in Africa

There are now an estimated 250,000 child soldiers globally, most aged between 15 and 18, but some as young as 10.

They fight on front lines, participate in suicide missions and act as spies, messengers or lookouts. Their futures have been lost to violence, hatred and fear.

Between 20 and 30 per cent of child soldiers are girls. Some are forced into sexual slavery or "given" to military commanders as wives. Many are forced to bear children.

Most child soldiers are abducted or recruited by force, while others, who are orphaned, join out of desperation, believing that these armed groups offer their best chance for survival or are lured by the false promise of an escape from poverty. Most of these soldier children come from desperately poor communities.

The child soldiers' childhoods and human rights are

taken away once they are recruited. They are often brainwashed to think it is "normal" to be fighting in combat zones and develop psychological problems that may haunt them for the rest of their lives.

Those who are rescued, especially those with children they have given birth to in captivity, are often not easily accepted back into their communities. These young souls have missed out on crucial elements of childhood, and been exposed to the kind of abuse and violence no child should ever experience.

World Vision supports the UN's Children Not Soldiers campaign and advocates with governments to end child recruitment. We help to support local community members and groups who are working to keep children safe. And at rehabilitation centres we help former child soldiers to recover from their experiences, return to education, reunite with their families and rebuild their lives.

We are guided by Psalm 82 which states: "Rescue the weak and the needy; deliver them from the hand of the wicked."

We recognise the invaluable role that public campaigning—and books such as this—that bring the reality of child recruitment to public attention—have in keeping this important issue in the international media and in influencing change.

We work to ensure extreme poverty, inequality, lack of protection and fear cease to be everyday realities for children living in the midst of conflict zones.

Rev Tim Costello—Chief Advocate, World Vision Australia 2017

www.ingramcontent.com/pod-product-compliance
Lightning Source LLC
Chambersburg PA
CBHW070240140726
47909CB00017B/553